CW00468557

The Handy Nanny

K. Sterling

To Christina L., Criss W., and Sue D. for sharing their time and invaluable help. I am so blessed to have these goddesses as friends and cheerleaders.

Thank you to Mia Gardiner for her brilliant assistance.

I continue to grow and shine thanks to Roshni's support and friendship.

And to my Melissa. For her gentle heart and generosity. I'm so grateful for her friendship.

Finally, to my dream editor, Charles Griemsman, for his patience and kindness, and for being my NYC sensitivity reader.

The Handy Nanny

by K. Sterling

Art by @epsilynn

The Handy Nanny Playlist

What You Won't Do For Love	Bobby Caldwell
Heat Lightning	Mitski
CUFF IT-WETTER REMIX	Beyoncé
Love On The Brain	Rihanna
Cupid	112
Gravity	John Mayer
Snooze	SZA
PLASTIC OFF THE SOFA	Beyoncé
Slow Dancing In The Dark	Joji
Slide	Calvin Harris, Frank Ocean, Migos
Oil	Gorillaz, Stevie Nicks
Leave The Door Open	Bruno Mars, Anderson .Paak, Silk Sonic

Content Warnings

Grief

We're meeting two characters at opposite ends of their journey through grief. Morris's grief is fresh and raw and Penn is finally facing the loss of his mother and the impending loss of his father.

Loss of a sibling and a parent to a stroke.

This book was difficult to write *every day* because I fell in love with Michelle first and it hurt to see Morris and the Mosbys in so much pain. But it was important for me to highlight the fact that pregnancy-related mortality rates among Black and AI/AN women are over three and two times higher, respectively, compared to the rate for white women in the US. Families like the Mosbys are shattered when their mothers, sisters, and daughters are lost due to racial disparities in our healthcare system.

If you'd like to learn more, I found this to be a good starting point: https://www.kff.org/racial-equity-and-health-policy/

issue-brief/racial-disparities-in-maternal-and-infant-health-current-status-and-efforts-to-address-them/

Cancer

Both Morris's father and Penn's father are in recovery, but there are brief mentions of their treatment. Penn's father is in his mid-eighties and his condition is much more delicate than Morris Sr.'s, who is several years younger than Gus.

Suicide/Suicide Ideation

Mentioned briefly as Morris is grieving his twin sister's death.

May her memory be a blessing.

Chapter One

She was gone and she'd taken the magic with her.

Morris would claw his way through that six feet of dirt and die with her if he could. His brain couldn't comprehend *how* she could be there, beneath his feet and out of his reach. And forever? It just didn't seem right or fair to expect him to live like that. He felt like he was gone too, and Morris didn't know how he was supposed to go on without his twin sister. They had shared a soul. There was a sacred, unbreakable thread that had kept them tethered to each other from birth. Now Morris was unraveling and would never feel whole without her.

"What about the baby?" His mother's arm hooked around his as if she knew what he'd been thinking and was pulling him back. "Your father and I can try—"

Morris shook his head quickly, but he needed a moment and mopped at his eyes with his scarf. He'd run out of Kleenex before the service had started. "I'll take Cadence. You have your hands full with the bakery and Dad's just getting back on his feet." The family had celebrated his father's cancer-free diagnosis a month earlier, and Morris had hosted his sister's baby shower at the bakery two weeks ago. "Everything's already at our place," he said, and his mother sucked in a breath, reminding Morris that it was just his place now. "She's all I have left."

"Don't say that!" His mother hugged his arm tighter, pressing her face into his sleeve. Her body shuddered on a hard sob, but she smothered it and pulled herself together. Morris's jaw began to ache so he unclenched it. The pain behind his eyes was relentless, like an anvil being struck, his brain pounded flat from crying and pacing all night. "And you know what she'd want us to do."

"I know. I'm sorry."

He wiped his eyes again and pulled in a deep breath, marshaling his sister's memory and her strength. Michelle had stopped for no one and nothing got in her way. She was the mastermind behind the Mosby Music machine and had made Morris, but first and foremost, she was his big sister—by less than a minute—and nothing had mattered more to her than family.

Morris looked back at the row of limos waiting for them. His father was with Morris's aunts and Cadence. The baby had been a source of so much hope, as the family looked forward to putting the fear, stress, and pain of his father's illness behind them. Michelle had decided to have a child on her own because she didn't know when she'd find her perfect partner, and she wanted their father to see and hold the next generation of Mosbys before it was too late.

Morris Mosby Sr. had beaten colon cancer, but his daughter was taken by a stroke a day after giving birth to his first granddaughter. *Everyone* had warned Michelle that she was doing too much—she always did too much—and when she went into labor, she didn't stop working until Morris took her phone from her and handed her a hospital gown. She was back at it a few hours after her C-Section. Morris had begged her to take just a few days off, but Michelle's heart was in her work and she swore she'd have it all.

You're taking both of your girls with you when you get that next Grammy.

She'd babbled about matching gowns for her and Cadence and a designer stroller for the red carpet while nursing the baby and catching up with emails on her phone. Morris could feel that something wasn't right. Michelle had told the nurses she'd had headaches and was feeling numb, nauseous, dizzy, and off when they arrived at the hospital. But they hadn't listened and had insisted they were symptoms of early labor, and later that many of her complaints were common after a C-Section.

Michelle had fallen asleep with a smile on her face though. She had let Grandma change Cadence and Morris had then nodded off in the recliner with the baby on his chest. Michelle's smile was the last thing he'd seen as he drifted off and dreamt of being the world's best uncle. But Morris had woken up to his mother's screams; Michelle was gone and she'd taken all the magic in Morris's world with her.

Chapter Two

Rise and *shine.*

Pennsylvania Tucker's eyes snapped open just as the sun's first rays touched the city. He never needed an alarm clock because he could feel the sun creeping over the horizon and tapping on his shoulder, whispering that it was time to rise and bring as much shine to the world as he could before the sun went back down for the day.

He did his best to rest when the sun did because Penn wasn't a night person. He never knew what to do with himself so he filled the quiet hours with projects to keep his mind busy until he passed out. Last night's projects had been fixing his sister Penny's trusty roller skates and her fishing pole. Her skates now had fresh toe stops, wheels, and bearings. Penn had added rainbow laces as well, giving them a new lease on life.

Penny's fishing pole was a little bit more of a challenge. It had been their mother's and Penn had repaired and replaced just about every inch of the pole and reel. Their father had been on Penny's case for years to retire it to the mantle, but she stubbornly refused to even look at a new rod. Thankfully, Penn had found a similar model from the same manufacturer at a church tag sale and was able to replace the inside of the reel so it was almost as good as new. On the inside. The outside was still held together by duct tape and memories, but Penny would be tickled by Penn's handiwork when she turned up.

His sister had a way of drifting in and out with the breeze, so Penn left her stuff on the bench by the door. She was even more of a wild child than Penn and there was no telling where Penny might be. It had been a beautiful, but balmy evening, so she could have found a tall tree to climb and camp in for the night. Or she could be snuggled up and sleeping it off with a kindergarten teacher. Penny said she liked preschool and kindergarten teachers because they knew how to embrace chaos and were used to cleaning up messes.

Like most of the lesbians Penn knew, his sister lived for chaos and was a magnet for messes, but he never worried about Penny. He'd practically raised her himself and Penn had taught his little sister how to survive on her own in the city and the wilderness. And she was a Tucker. She could think her way out of any situation, but if her brain failed her, she could charm her way out.

Both Penn and Penny had inherited their mother's gentle, open heart, her love of nature, and her passion for yoga so he rolled out of bed and unrolled his mat in front of the window.

"A little Surya Namaskar," he murmured, pressing his hands together and pushing them toward the sky. He went through the sequence of movements, keeping his mind clear, but he always smiled when he planted his hands on the mat, straightened his arms, and arched his back in Urdhva Mukha Svanasana. Penn would remember his mother's face, her nose almost touching his as they mirrored each other's movements.

Look at my bright little son!

They'd kiss, then lower their heads and straighten their

legs, completing the rest of the sequence. She always did yoga in the sun—never in a gym or a studio—and started every morning with a sun salutation at sunrise with Penn until he went off to college.

This morning, he felt focused and refreshed after working through several poses, setting his intentions for the day and manifesting positive, healing energy. But maybe Penn should have manifested another project or an errand because he was out of ideas as he rolled a joint and waited for the coffee maker.

After a four-month gig as a nanny for an ambassador's infant twins, the quiet Lenox Hill rowhouse where he lived felt like a sensory deprivation tank. They'd inherited it from their late mother's parents and Penn and his father had lovingly restored every inch of the house while his sister had filled it with plants, crystals, vintage botanical prints, and their mother's pottery.

Penn sipped from one of the many coffee mugs his mother had made for him and contemplated the back garden as he drank and smoked. It was Penny's purview as the family's reigning plant nerd supreme, but he didn't think she'd mind if he built her a new potting bench.

He wasn't fanatically opposed to capitalism, but Penn liked to recycle, reuse, and repurpose everything he could and preferred to barter for things he needed instead of buying new. People were often happy to trade lumber scraps for his famous chocolate cake or a basket of muffins. So Penn kept an eye on the neighbors' weekend projects in case they needed a hand, and they were happy to call him if they had leftovers. Penn reckoned he had enough wood and could saw a fantastic potting space for Penny with the antique cast iron sink he'd rescued from a kitchen demo.

His mental calculations were put on hold when he heard his phone buzzing. Penn turned in circles as he hunted for it, scanning the counters and tabletops around the kitchen and the living room. He hadn't touched it after he came home from seeing off the last family he worked for at the airport the evening prior, so he went to check by the door. It was next to his keys and Penn frowned when he saw a text message from his best friend and boss, Reid Marshall. He knew better, but Reid had ordered Penn to sleep in and put his feet up.

> Reid: Sorry. I know I made you take a week off but I need you at Briarwood Terrace ASAP.

That got Penn moving. He put out his joint and was pouring coffee down his throat on the way to the bathroom before he got to the period at the end of "ASAP." Penn shot off a message to his sister to let her know that he wouldn't be swinging by their father's place in Hoboken today. He asked her to check on Gus for him, then jumped into a fresh T-shirt and a clean pair of overalls. His hair was a wild mess from falling asleep with it wet so Penn pulled it all into a loose bun and brushed his teeth.

"I can let this go for a few more days," he decided as he considered the stubble on his jaw and chin. Reid would have said something if he was sending Penn to work for royalty.

Reid did say as soon as possible so he put on a pair of Converse and grabbed his messenger bag and skateboard on his way out the door. It was only a few blocks and around the corner to 42 Briarwood Terrace. Penn enjoyed the sun on his face and the gentle spring breeze, high-fiving people as he zipped around clusters of pedestrians.

But Penn came to an abrupt stop and fumbled with his board when he found Gavin, Reid's housemate and best friend, sitting on the steps in front of Briarwood Terrace waiting for him. Gavin had his head in his hands and Penn could *feel* the grief rolling off him. Grief poured from the house, an invisible tide of sorrow that washed over his feet, making them heavier as Penn trudged forward.

"What happened?" His voice had cracked and Penn was terrified. "Is it Fin or Riley?" He asked, fearing the worst. Penn loved Reid's little brother and Riley Fitzgerald was Fin's best friend. Penn felt as responsible for them as he did Penny.

"No," Gavin rasped. He shook his head and pointed over

his shoulder. "I wanted to warn you. Reid's really broken up about this—" He paused and pushed out a slow, steadying breath. Penn could see from Gavin's red, puffy eyes and raw nose that he was pretty broken up too. But it was hard to know if he was grieving with Reid or grieving because his best friend was in so much pain. "He doesn't know what to do, but he thinks you can help."

"Of course," Penn said, nodding as he gave Gavin a hand up and pulled him into a hug. "You know I'll do anything for you guys."

Gavin held him tight for a moment, a rare admission of vulnerability from the notoriously stoic grump. "Thank you." He clapped Penn on the back before straightening and clearing his throat. "You've never let us down, but this is..." Gavin sniffed hard and gave his head a shake. "I don't have any words. He'll explain, as much as anyone can when something this brutal happens."

"Okay. I'll do whatever I can," Penn promised and left Gavin on the stoop. He still needed a little more fresh air, but Penn charged into the lobby to see what Reid needed.

"Mornin', Norm," Penn said. He reached over the desk to slap the elderly doorman's hand as he hurried past the desk.

"Is everything okay? The boys seem like they're really upset," Norman whispered to Penn.

Penn held onto Norman's hand and shushed softly. "They are, but I'm going to find out what happened and we'll take care of them," Penn promised.

"I'm glad they called you."

"Me too." Penn gave his hand a gentle squeeze but avoided Norman's aching knuckles.

He didn't know what he was facing when he hurried down the hall to the converted conservatory, but Penn raced in as if Reid was about to drown and was ready to pull him out.

Hell or high water.

That was Penn's motto when it came to his family and his friends. And the water was high, indeed, as Penn waded into the apartment. Reid was in what looked like the remnants of a suit, but he was haggard and crying as he stared out the kitchen window at the narrow patch of garden.

Penn gripped Reid's shoulder, offering strength and absorbing as much of his friend's pain as he could. "What happened and what can I do?"

"Penn!" Reid turned and pushed his face into Penn's shoulder.

"I've got you." Penn pulled Reid into a tight hug. He held on as Reid's body trembled and he sobbed hoarsely.

"It's not fair!" Reid gasped and had to take several breaths before he could continue. "You know my friend, Morris, and his sister, Michelle?"

"The twins? He's the big record producer, right?" Penn asked.

Reid nodded but his face crumpled and he had to hold onto the counter. "Michelle died a few days ago. The family kept it quiet because they didn't want any publicity but Morris called and told us yesterday. We just got back from the service and the repast."

"Oh, God. Wasn't she having a baby?" Penn's heart sank when Reid jammed his fist into his mouth.

"She—" Reid clenched his jaw and shook his head. "I don't want to do this to you, Penn, but I don't know who else—!"

"It's okay!" Penn soothed.

Reid made an agonized sound as he scrubbed his face. "It's not!" He cried behind his hands. "I'm so sorry, Penn. She had a stroke after delivering the baby—" He gave up and Penn gathered Reid in his arms. They cried together. Gavin and Reid were right. There were no words for the brutality of it and no way to make sense of such a loss. It was so unfair and made a person wonder if there was ever such a thing as justice. After losing his mother to a stroke, Penn had an acute understanding of the helpless fury that accompanied that kind of loss. He gave Reid a place to pour out his grief and shared his pain as they cried together.

Penn had met the Mosby twins a handful of times and had liked Michelle. Gavin had first met Morris at Brooklyn's prestigious Saint Ann's School when they were children. Both were gifted young musicians and it was Morris who had introduced Gavin to his best friend, Reid Marshall.

The three had remained close friends despite the Mosbys' hectic lives in the music business. The twins, particularly Morris, didn't always enjoy all the attention from social media, tabloids, and the paparazzi so they kept a low profile. He had a reputation for being reclusive. But they had been at Gavin's birthday party last month and Michelle and Penn had talked about how the last trimester of her pregnancy was going.

"I am so sorry." That was all Penn could say. Michelle had only been a passing acquaintance and Penn had only spoken to her a few times, but he'd been drawn to her bright, fizzing aura and her amazing smile. She was a beautiful woman on the outside and her soul was just as stunning, from the few glimpses he'd been afforded. It was such a tremendous loss. "Tell me how I can help."

Reid held on for another moment, gathering his strength, then leaned back in Penn's arms. He wiped his face and his cheeks puffed out as he looked around and refocused. "I had a talk with their mom and Evelyn said they're all handling it as well as you'd expect, except Morris. He's devastated, but he has the baby. He doesn't know anything about kids, let alone newborns. I'm so worried for him and Cadence."

"I'll go," Penn stated. He felt an immediate pull and

certainty that it was exactly where he was meant to be. *They need me.* "I'll take care of them."

"Thank you," Reid said, loading the words with heartfelt gratitude. "I can't fix this—" His voice crumbled and he had to take a few breaths. "I can't bring her back or take away Morris's pain, but you're the closest thing I have to an angel. And that's what Morris and Cadence need right now. I know you'll handle Cadence with care and keep a close eye on Morris. He isn't good at letting new people in, but he'll trust you because I sent you. Eventually," he added with a wince.

Penn waved it off. "I know where he's coming from and I'd be over it too if I'd had cameras shoved in my face like that since I was a kid."

That got a soft chuckle from Reid. "I always told him that was the price of being a genius. People will call you Mozart if you start a record label at sixteen and release hits like that. Morris just wants to be 'normal' and I always want to know *how* when there's nothing normal about being that talented."

"I never understood why anyone thought being famous would be fun," Penn mused.

"It's never been fun for Morris. That's why he let Michelle handle all PR and she was the brains behind the brand. She was so good at everything. They loved her on the radio shows and on the red carpet. And she had everyone lining up to work with Morris. She kept the world out of his studio so he was free to make whatever his heart desired."

"I could always tell that they were a team and had each other's backs," Penn said and Reid nodded.

People usually looked at Penn funny whenever he explained that he could just *feel* things. For him, it was like hearing and seeing. Penn's emotions shifted when he was around other people, picking up their feelings as though he had an internal mood ring. His little sister, Penny, was the same and they had definitely inherited their empathic abilities from their mother. Most people mocked Penn and Penny, calling them hippies and weirdos, but Reid, Gavin, Fin, and Riley had always appreciated their gentle, sensitive natures.

"Listen," Reid said, taking out his phone and opening their messages. Penn could see that he was typing an address. "Evelyn reached out to Gavin because Morris has never been involved in the business side of Mosby Music. He was the music and it's going to take three people to replace Michelle."

"He has to be overwhelmed, but Gavin's a good start and he'll help Morris find the right people," Penn predicted. Gavin was an accountant and understood money and investing the way Penn understood babies and toddlers. He checked his phone when it buzzed and nodded at Reid's text.

"Morris Sr. had already asked about hiring a nanny so Michelle would have an extra set of hands. It was supposed to be a surprise, and because Morris doesn't know *anything* about babies. He needs a lot of help, but Gavin and I don't want Morris or his parents to worry about Cadence right now. I told them I'm sending someone to help with the baby. But if Morris asks about paying you, tell him we're taking care of it for now and we can see what he wants to do in three or four months."

"Good idea. He might get the hang of it and from the sound of things, Morris might not be comfortable with having a nanny there around the clock."

"Are you going to be cool with that?" Reid raised a brow at Penn. "I'll be paying you for live-in care because a newborn *is* around-the-clock. And the next few weeks could be really rough."

Penn shrugged. "This feels like something I'm supposed to do and I'm not worried. I've been to that dark place and I know there's light on the other side. I can help him find his way through," he said, then groaned when Reid pulled him into another hug.

"You don't know what this means to me, Penn."

"Hey!" Penn hugged him tight and rocked them. "We're brothers and you've always been there for me. I know how much you love Morris. We'll help him get through this."

Reid nodded as he dried his face. "Everything hurts so much right now, but Morris will be in good hands."

"He's got his family and he's got you and Gavin. And now he's got me," Penn vowed, then went to make sure Morris knew he wasn't alone.

Chapter Three

She had to know.

Morris wondered if Cadence was being the sweetest little pea because she knew her mother was gone and that everyone was in pain. She'd fuss if her diaper was full, but that was about it. She had set her own schedule and took her bottle every three hours during the day and woke up exactly once in the middle of the night to get topped off. And Cadence did not want to be bothered when she was ready to sleep.

At the moment, she was resting resplendently in a sage-colored Babybjörn bouncer. The sleek, soft ergonomic chair was designed to be moved from surface to surface and keep her safely harnessed and reclined. Cadence's chair responded to her every move, soothing and comforting her so she was calmer and nodded off more easily. Morris wished he had an adult-sized version.

"She looks just like Michelle, doesn't she?" He asked. His mother reached over the back of the sofa and shushed him as she patted his chest.

"More and more each minute."

"I already asked you that, didn't I?" Morris said, giving his head a quick shake.

"Twice in the last half hour, but it's alright."

"You don't have to stay. The nanny will be here soon."

His mother hummed as she came around the sofa and gently tugged Cadence's blanket back up to her chin. She bent and pressed the lightest kiss to the baby's cheek. "I want to stay and make sure you're all settled."

"You're staying because you want to see who Reid's sending and you're not sure if you can trust them."

"I trust Reid," she stated and nodded firmly. "I'd trust that boy with my life and I don't know why the two of you—"

"Don't start." Morris got up and went to pace by the stairs. It was too easy to check out when he stopped moving. He couldn't sleep when he laid down and shut his eyes, but he could lose a whole hour just staring at the baby. Or a wall.

"Michelle even said you two should give it a shot."

"And I told her it would be weird. We've always been like brothers, and aside from the fact that Reid's gay, he isn't my type."

"He's always been handsome. Reminds me of a young Cary Grant."

Morris squinted at her, wondering why it was so hard for his mother and sister to understand that while he might love Reid, he was looking for more from a future partner, aside from them being queer and attractive.

Not that Reid wasn't one of the best human beings on the whole planet. And he was a very attractive man. But the two of them had never felt *that* kind of attraction toward each other. Maybe it was because they had met and bonded at the peak of their awkward teenage years. Reid had been tall with sharp angles and big feet. Morris hadn't had his growth spurt yet and was at his stockiest. They shared a love of *Magic: The Gathering* and computers; there wasn't a lot of interest or awareness of *anything* remotely sexual.

By the time they were both old enough and secure enough as young gay men, there was just too much history. Morris couldn't pretend to be cool and put the moves on Reid. Not when he knew Reid remembered what Morris was like when he was short, wheezing, and sucking on an inhaler. And Morris had seen Reid through too many allergy-induced bloody noses.

It was one thing to fall for someone and still love them after all of life's ups and downs, but there had never been much of a veil between him and Reid to begin with. And you couldn't unsee one of your best friends projectile vomiting nachos and popcorn at you in the back of a minivan. There was no way to transition to romance from there and Reid had agreed that it was better if there was *some* mystery at the beginning of a relationship.

"Reid's not interested in dating anyone, Mom," Morris said simply. He wasn't going to explain Reid's sex life to her. She wouldn't like knowing that Reid never dated and preferred to scratch the itch by meeting older businessmen in hotel bars. Everyone loved and depended on Reid for various reasons, and he thrived on that trust and love. He had no interest in being in a romantic relationship and found enough emotional fulfillment in caring for his brother and their friends. "He would have made a great monk if he wasn't an atheist," he added, causing her to recoil. That usually worked because as much as his mother adored Reid Marshall, she couldn't think anything worse than her son marrying an atheist.

"People change, Morris." She shrugged, then turned when they heard a soft knock. "That'll be Reid's nanny!" She hurried to get the door and peeked through the hole. "Oh, thank goodness!" She pulled it open and gasped in relief. "I'm so glad it's you, Penn!" She said as she reached to give the tall, smiling man in overalls and a faded Mr. Rogers T-shirt a hug.

Not this hillbilly-looking motherfucker.

But Morris held up a hand and waved as his mother towed Penn into the house. Morris would never own up to it, but he had always been a little jealous of Penn. He'd moved in with Reid just as Morris's career took off and had replaced him. Penn hadn't done it intentionally, and Reid had done his part to keep their friendship strong. It was just hard not to resent the new guy. Especially when he was so damn easy to like.

"I'm so sorry for your loss and I'm here to help in any way I can, ma'am." Penn had scooped Morris's mother into a tight hug. Everyone knew Evelyn Mosby and she knew just about everyone.

"Thank you, sweetheart. You know better than to 'ma'am' me. Call me Evelyn. Or Evie." She actually allowed him to hug her, shocking Morris. His mom was *not* a hugger except with close friends and family, but she sighed and held onto Penn for a moment. "She would want us to laugh and to get back to work. Especially Morris," she said and pointed around Penn at him. "Taking care of Morris and making him smile was Michelle's first priority."

"She's gonna have to give me a little more time with this one and I don't know if I can work without her. Or if I even want to," Morris said with a shrug. It was about all he could muster at the moment. He was so tired and he felt like he was miles away from Penn and his mother even though they were standing just a few feet in front of him.

"You take as much time as you need." Penn held out his hand. Morris had half a second to admire Penn's hot pink fingernails as he accepted it, then grunted when he was gathered into a warm embrace. He wished there were miles between them again, but Morris gave him a stiff pat on the back, refusing to acknowledge how soothing it was being wrapped in Penn's arms or how...*nice* he smelled. Morris wasn't expecting someone who looked like he lived in a van and sold art on the street to smell so peppery, green, and *clean.*

"Thanks." He tried to disengage but Penn's arm remained draped around Morris's shoulders.

"I'll be hanging out here around the clock for a while so my sister, Penny Lane, will be by to drop off some of my things if that's okay," Penn said, looking from Morris to Evelyn.

She pushed out another relieved breath and nodded. "Whatever you need, sweetheart. I already feel so much better now that you're here."

Not that he'd admit it out loud or that he was particularly happy about *who* Reid had sent, but Morris did feel better having a highly qualified caregiver in the house for Cadence. And there was something soothing about Penn's presence, even if it was a little too close for Morris's comfort at the moment.

"It's cool," Morris said as he wiggled his shoulders and side-stepped out of Penn's reach. His mother cut her eyes at Morris, silently scolding him, but they were saved when Cadence sniffled and squirmed in her chair.

"There's our princess!" Penn said, hurrying around the sofa for a closer look. Cadence rubbed her eye with a fist and began to fuss. "Shhh! Shhh! Shhh!" He gently kneaded her foot and glanced over his shoulder at Morris and Evelyn. "Is it okay if I pick her up?"

"You go right ahead!" Evelyn insisted and Morris looked at her like she'd sprouted horns.

"Who are you and what have you done with my mother?" He asked her and shook his head. "You ran the nurses off every time they tried to hold her."

Evelyn swatted at him dismissively. "We didn't know them. We *know* Penn. And Reid wouldn't have sent him if he didn't trust him and that's good enough for me. Should be good enough for you too, seeing as you don't know the first thing about babies. Are you sure you're ready for this? Your father and I—"

"I've got this," Morris said, cutting her off before she could start again. He held his breath as Penn unbuckled the harness and lifted Cadence. His large hands cradled the baby's head and body and he hummed softly as he swayed from side to side. She seemed content so Morris turned his attention back to Evelyn. "The plan was for you to work *less* and spend more time with Dad. You were going to travel once his doctor gave him the all-clear and you can't do that with a baby. I have nothing else going on in my life and she's all that matters."

"For now," Evelyn conceded. "But I won't let you lock yourself away forever." She gave his cheek a tender pat and her eyes shimmered as they searched Morris's. "I miss her so much and my heart hurts so bad, but I'm worried about you."

"I know and I'm sorry. I'm trying," Morris swallowed the sob that had rolled up his throat and swiped a tear from the corner of his eye. "I'll be alright," he lied. He was just hanging on by his fingertips, but he'd find a way because Cadence needed him and he couldn't let Michelle down.

There was a soft cough from across the room. "Her diaper's full. Where's the changing station?" Penn whispered and looked around, but Evelyn sprang into action.

"Why don't you let me take care of it while Morris gives you a tour and shows you the guest room? I need to go in a few. I want to check in at the bakery and get back to the house. You know people will be coming and going all day and your daddy is going to kill me if I leave him with my sisters for too long."

Most of their out-of-town relatives had flown out after the repast with the exception of Morris's aunts. But word had spread of Michelle's death and friends and neighbors were turning up with food and to offer their condolences. It was too much for Morris. He had gone home and everyone was warned that he wasn't answering the door or the phone.

"Sure. Let me give you a tour," Morris said flatly. He didn't have the energy to be warm and welcoming and there was no point in pretending if Penn was moving into the guest room. The *last* thing in the world Morris wanted at the moment was a new roommate. But his mom was right: he didn't know anything about babies, and he didn't like changing diapers. He was already a little scared of what had come out of his niece, frankly.

"That would be great," Penn said as he passed the baby to Evelyn. He flashed Morris one of his I'm-your-buddy-and-we-can-do-anything-if-we-put-our-heads-together smiles.

"My room's over there on the other side of the kitchen." Morris waved at his door and Penn joined him as he headed up the stairs.

"It's a gorgeous place and we're not too far from Reid and Gavin's," Penn noted.

"It's about a ten-minute walk. The nursery's over here." Morris gestured at the first room on the left. He ignored the closed door at the end of the hall.

"This is absolutely perfect!" Penn said excitedly and went to explore Cadence's room. Michelle had chosen a nighttime forest theme in soft grays and pastel colors with sleepy foxes and rabbits. Around the room, owls perched on painted branches and hovered from the mobile, keeping watch over the crib.

"Thanks." Morris avoided looking at the rocker. He had turned it toward the window but he could still see Michelle, rocking and humming as she rubbed her giant belly. It had been Morris's job to guide her from the rocker to her bed after she fell asleep reading to Cadence.

"Hey," Penn murmured and Morris jumped when his arm was squeezed. "Are you okay?"

"Yeah." Morris nodded. "I must have drifted off for a moment."

Penn hummed sympathetically. "When was the last time you slept?"

"I don't know. It's been hard." That was an understatement because Morris couldn't explain the restlessness and the gnawing ache he experienced whenever he was alone. But there was a piercing omniscience in Penn's gaze as it held Morris's, as if he understood.

Penn was silent for a moment, then said, "I lost my mom to a stroke right after college and it was like half of me was gone. It hurt, how alone I felt. Especially when I tried to sleep. My mind couldn't cope with her being gone and I couldn't rest with this...giant emptiness. You and Michelle shared a special bond because you're twins so I can't imagine what this is like for you."

"It's a lot like that," Morris said weakly. He couldn't pull his eyes from Penn's and was tempted to ask if he could read minds. There were rumors that he was psychic and Morris had scoffed before, but he could almost believe them now that they were alone.

"Cancer sun and Leo moon," Penn stated, pointing at himself.

"What?"

A grin tugged at the corner of Penn's lips. "You can tell me to butt out if I make you uncomfortable. Sometimes, I can be a little too intuitive and too direct."

"No. It's fine," Morris said and raised a shoulder. "I think this is the first time I've talked to someone and felt like they actually get it."

"That's why Reid sent me."

Morris envied how easy it was for Penn to be so open and free with his feelings. And it was confounding that Penn would choose to return to a situation involving loss like this, something this deep and dark, given his own experience with his mother. Morris felt like he'd been stuck here for weeks and he couldn't imagine coming back once he'd found his way out.

"Are you sure you want to do this? I'd understand if it's too hard," Morris said, but Penn made a dismissive sound as he turned them.

"This is exactly where I need to be. Show me where the guest room is and let's talk about dinner. I bet you haven't eaten a decent meal in days either."

He really was a psychic. Morris grimaced and gripped his stomach as they stepped into the hallway. "I'm kind of afraid I'll go down like a load of bricks if I do. I'm so tired and I haven't been able to sleep, but I feel like I'll sleep for a week if I eat and stop moving."

"Go for it, if that's what you need," Penn said and Morris snorted.

"I can't do that."

"Why not? I'm here to take care of Cadence and keep an eye on you. *Rest* and do whatever gives you the most peace. I'll help in any way I can and I won't judge you or be offended if you need to set boundaries."

"Thanks," Morris said, then gave him a sheepish wince. "I kind of like to keep my feelings to myself and I'm not much of a hugger."

"I hear you!" Penn put up his hands and took a step back. "But just remember that you don't have to ask if you ever feel like you do need a hug," he said and raised both of his thumbs.

"I'll keep that in mind," Morris replied. He recalled that he was giving Penn a tour and glanced at the door at the end of the hall. "That's her room. I had to close the door because I kept seeing her in there. I don't know what to do with her things."

"You don't have to decide until you're ready and we'll help you," Penn said, giving Morris another turn and a push to get him going. "Is that the guest room?" He asked and pointed at the room at the other end of the hall.

"Yeah. Office/guest room. We turned Michelle's old office into the nursery and moved her desk and all her books down the hall. We didn't get a lot of guests."

"I'm sure it'll be great," Penn assured him.

But Morris was embarrassed when Penn pushed the door open and peeked inside. The guest room had been an afterthought and became their overflow room. Both Morris and Michelle had put off decorating the nursery until the last minute because they had been too busy. He'd hastily crammed Michelle's books into boxes and pushed them down the hall the day before the decorator arrived, just eight weeks before Cadence came. Boxes lined the walls, along with all the extra packages of diapers and baby gifts they hadn't had a chance to unpack.

"It needs some work," Morris conceded as he looked around Penn.

"You weren't expecting guests," Penn reminded him while he tapped out a message on his phone. "I've got nothing but time, man. And now I've got a plan," he added.

They finished the tour with a quick pass through the recording studio in the basement and a viewing of the back garden. That had been Michelle's passion project and Morris was a bit ashamed at how neglected the area looked after just a few weeks. Morris explained that Michelle hadn't been able to do more than waddle out and aim a hose toward the end of her pregnancy.

"No worries! Penny and Riley will get this sorted out in no time!" Penn promised while shooting off another text.

"Okay..." Morris said, but Penn halted him and waited until their gazes had locked.

"I mean it, Morris. There is *nothing* for you to worry about. I'm here to help with Cadence for as long as you need and you have a whole team of friends who love you to take care of everything else. All you have to do is rest and heal and tell us if there's anything else we can do to help."

Morris's relief was immediate. He didn't have a choice but to step up and take Cadence and she was all he was living for at the moment. But the weight of the responsibility and the sense of duty he felt to be strong and carry on for his family and friends was crushing.

The change in his mother was immediate as well. "Thank you, Penn," she said when they rejoined her and Cadence in the living room. She kissed Penn's cheek and accepted another one of his big bear hugs. "I haven't been able to take a moment and process this on my own, I've been so worried about Cadence and Morris—"

"Mom!" Morris protested, but she shushed him and pointed.

"You know this is exactly what she'd tell us to do if she was here. She put too much work into making your dreams come true and that baby was *her* dream."

Morris's cheeks puffed out as he breathed through the pain and waited until he could speak or see past the tears muddling his vision. "Alright. You know I always do what she tells me to do," he said. "I'll call and check in with you later," he said and kissed her goodbye. He left her and Penn and went to make himself a cup of tea.

He reached for his box of Earl Grey and a mug, listening as his mother shared a few more notes with Penn before she left.

Morris opened the lid and screamed when a fake snake sprang out of the box.

"Damn it, Michelle!" Morris yelled. She loved her pranks and there was no telling how many she'd left stashed around the house.

"You good in there or do you need me to catch it for you?" Penn offered, then held onto Evelyn as they giggled and wheezed.

Morris pulled a face and acted disgruntled while he prepared his tea, but his lips twitched at the corners as he worked. It felt good, like his sister had left him a small gift.

"I told you," Evelyn said with a watery laugh. "All she ever wanted was for him to smile and to make him laugh. See what you can do about that, Penn."

"I'm on it, ma'am."

That made his mother feel better, but as much as he appreciated it, Morris didn't want Penn there, making him laugh and taking care of Cadence. He wanted his sister and his old life back.

Chapter Four

O nce Morris went down, he went down hard and slept for two solid days, much to Penn's relief.

Penn had found everything he needed to make his famous butternut squash mac and cheese and turned the browned bananas on the counter into banana bread. Morris had eaten two bowls and half the loaf before stumbling into his room and falling face-first into bed.

"Sleep for as long as you need, brother," Penn had told him as he eased Morris's door shut.

With Morris settled, Penn was free to get to work. He wasn't sure if they'd all fit, but Penn unpacked and organized all of Michelle's books. She had to have close to five hundred. Luckily, Penn was able to barter with the neighbor for some leftover wood and molding to build and install bookshelves. Penn and Cadence enjoyed the afternoon in the tiny yet tranquil backyard with Penny and Riley. The light construction and gardening hadn't disturbed Morris and Penn was able to rearrange the guest room and get ahead on some baking.

Penn was completely taken with Cadence and the two had

become inseparable. She snuggled right up to him and was happiest when Penn put her in the pea pod sling and carried her against his chest. He read out the title of each book and told her what he knew about it while he decided where it went. She cooed and gurgled happily in the sling as he kneaded dough, and reclined in her bouncer in the shade like a princess while he and Penny worked out back.

On his third day there, Penn was waiting to take a hearty vegetable lasagna out of the oven when Morris emerged from his bedroom. Penn had laid out a comforter and a play mat on the floor so Cadence could get in a little tummy time while they read a picture book.

"Hey! I bet you're starving," Penn said, rolling and scooping Cadence into the sling as he got up. "I thought about waking you but I figured you needed to sleep more."

Morris rubbed an eye groggily. He was wearing a white terry cloth robe over a pair of gray sweatpants with one of the legs hiked up over his calf. His white socks slouched and slid off his feet as he shuffled into the kitchen. "Yeah... I didn't realize I was out for so long."

"No worries! We got along fine and dinner's just about ready," Penn said cheerfully, avoiding the peek of bare chest beneath Morris's robe. While he preferred to wear as little as possible in any given situation and wasn't the least bit bothered by nudity, Penn's attention had been snagged by that perfectly modest V-shaped strip of bare skin. He struggled to remember what he was saying as the room grew warmer. "Um... Evie said you don't eat a lot of meat, which is perfect because I'm a vegetarian."

"Michelle got me into eating mostly plant-based but we'll eat whatever when we're over at Mom and Dad's," Morris explained. His expression tightened and he coughed into his fist. "I'll eat whatever they're having," he amended.

"It's okay!" Penn said as he reached for Morris and put an arm around him loosely. "It hurts like hell right now because you miss her so damn much. Just breathe and take it one moment at a time," he gave Morris a light, reassuring squeeze. Penn applied just enough pressure for Morris to feel safe and supported.

"That's..." Morris rasped and nodded jerkily. His shoulders pulled inward, but he allowed it. "I know everyone's worried and they all mean well. I'm just not ready to laugh again and move on."

"You don't have to worry about that here with us," Penn stated. He handed Morris the potholders. "You take all the time you need. Grab the lasagna for me, I've got my hands full," he said, gesturing at the baby.

"You two seem to be getting along."

"Yup. She's my new best friend. We got the rest of her toys and gear unpacked and all of her new clothes are in the laundry," Penn said while Morris took the lasagna out to cool.

Penn had also found a box of prank snakes, fake bugs of all types, unrippable rolls of toilet paper, gag gum... Michelle had even kept a journal full of ideas and notes on how to improve upon past pranks. Her shenanigans were just as well-planned and smoothly executed as every other facet of her life and Penn couldn't help but admire her for it.

He'd learned a lot about her as he arranged her books and sorted through the other artifacts she'd packed away while preparing for Cadence's arrival. He wasn't at all surprised when he found the books on IVF, nursing, and infant care. She had her whole life planned out with Morris, and Michelle wasn't going to wait for love to find her once she was ready to have a baby.

Penn decided he'd give Morris a little more time, then he'd pick up where Michelle had left off with her journal and her box full of pranks. He hoped she'd left a few more hidden around the house and wondered how long he could get away with it before Morris realized Penn had taken over for her.

Make him laugh again, Penn.

That had been Evelyn's most fervent wish and Penn's instincts told him that was what Michelle would want as well. She'd even left what Penn took as a directive, written in Sharpie on the front of the prank journal:

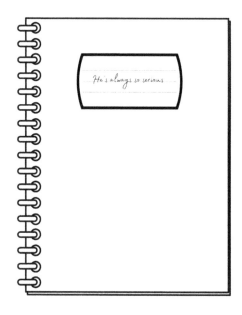

Penn had accepted the challenge because he was a firm believer that a smile *never* hurt and laughter was always the best medicine.

"Cadie's a big fan of my dancing," Penn said as he raised his arm. He let it swing at the elbow like a loose hinge, then did the robot, making Cadence squeal as the two of them lurched and swayed. Penn caught Morris's smirk before he bit down on his lips.

"She clearly doesn't know better because that was terrible.

Watch this!" Morris told her and did the wave wearing the oven mitts. "Give it a little pop and lock," he said, tensing and popping while he beatboxed.

"Nice!" Penn declared and pumped Cadence's tiny fists with the beat as he bounced along with Morris. She was too young to actually understand what was going on but babies responded well to rhythmic movement.

"We might be onto something," Morris said. He held out his hand and Penn grasped it as they locked ankles and jumped together in a circle.

"How do I still remember how to Kid 'n Play?" Penn laughed. They danced toward each other and kicked, tapping ankles before moving apart.

"You never forget the classics." Morris held his hand up for Penn so he could slap it when they were done. They high-fived and Morris gave Cadence's fist a gentle shake. "Maybe I am ready to laugh a little. Thanks for keeping an eye on her while I crashed."

"That's my job, Morris," Penn said, tipping toward him conspiratorially. "Taking care of people makes me happy. It's what I do."

"Right..." Morris nodded slowly but his brow furrowed. "Why, though?"

"Why?" Penn parroted.

"Yeah. Why do you get off on making other people happy? Don't you have better things to do with your time? No offense!" Morris said hastily. "You seem really smart, talented, and competent. Couldn't you do something a little more...worthwhile?"

"You don't think this is worthwhile?" Penn asked and Morris winced.

"Sure, but I doubt most people appreciate all the things you do."

"True..." Penn said, then shrugged. "Money helps balance out the disappointment. Reid makes sure I'm well compensated and I use that money to do cool things for the people I love. Which is *awesome.*"

"Fair enough... I guess. I don't know how you haven't burnt out."

Penn made a thoughtful sound as he looked down at Cadence and ran a finger along the curve of her cheek, cherishing its fullness and her petal-soft skin. "I spend my days with magical beings and it just feels good to be kind and help people. I get a lot of satisfaction out of solving problems and I'm happiest when I feel useful," he explained simply.

"That's weird," Morris replied, but Penn could tell that he was kidding.

"It's okay. You can admit you like me."

"What are you talking about? When did I say I didn't like you?" Morris asked.

Penn raised a brow back at him. "Cancer sun and Leo moon. I could always *feel* that I was rubbing you the wrong way, I just didn't know how."

"It wasn't *you* or anything specific that you did," Morris conceded and Penn gasped.

"Now we're getting somewhere!"

Morris pulled a face. "I just didn't want everyone to like you more than me or think you were a better friend after I left."

"After you left?" Penn asked cluelessly.

"Reid and Gavin were mine first, but I had to mess everything up by going off and getting famous," Morris explained.

Penn groaned as he reached for Morris and stopped when he remembered to go easy on the hugs. "I'm so sorry and I should have been more sensitive about that."

"I can't believe you're apologizing to me when it was all in my head."

"I know, but it makes sense and I should have seen it," Penn argued, tapping on his temple.

"That's silly. We ran into each other a handful of times and it's water under the bridge. How about dinner? This smells incredible and I'm starving," Morris said, pointing at the lasagna and sweeping the past aside.

It felt like they were starting with a clean slate in that sense. Morris no longer seemed skeptical or wary of Penn. And instead of returning to the solitude of his bedroom, Morris snuggled with Cadence on the sofa while Penn made a salad and set the table. Penn was proud, for sure, but he was oddly distracted too as Morris reclined on the sofa with the baby on his chest. Penn had an unusually difficult time assembling a basic green salad and spilled a jar of capers while making the dressing.

"You're right," Morris said between bites once they sat down to eat. "This hurts like hell and I didn't know it was possible to be this tired. But it's been nice to escape for a while with you and Cadence."

"That's why I'm here," Penn said, which gave his conscience a nudge. His eyes still strayed to Morris's lips as they talked. He had to have the softest-looking lips Penn had ever seen and he smelled soft too—like an expensive shave and clothes right out of the dryer, despite the fact that Morris hadn't shaved in days and had been wearing his robe for hours. Penn knew that he was asking for trouble and immediately shoved the observations to the darkest recesses of his mind.

"I think I could use a glass of wine. How about you?"

K. Sterling

Penn's Vegan Butternut Squash Mac & Cheese

12 ounces of pasta

1/2 cup of reserved pasta water

1 1/2 cups pf peeled, cubed butternut squash

1/2 large sweet onion, chopped

1/2 cup raw cashews

1 Tablespoon fresh lemon juice

1 teaspoon sea salt

1/2 teaspoon dijon mustard

1/4 teaspoon garlic powder

1/4 teaspoon white pepper

1/4 teaspoon smoked paprika

1/8 teaspoon turmeric

1/8 teaspoon nutmeg

1 Tablespoon of nutritional yeast

1/2 Tablespoon white miso

Cook pasta of choice, reserving 1/2 cup of water before draining. Add squash, onions, and cashews to a pot and cover with water. Bring to a boil, then simmer until vegetables are tender. Drain vegetables and cashews and add to a blender with lemon juice, salt, dijon, garlic powder, pepper, paprika, turmeric, nutmeg, yeast, miso, and reserved pasta water. Blend until smooth and add sauce to pasta or pour over anything that needs a blanket of creamy, cheesy smoothness.

Chapter Five

Morris's coma after Penn's arrival had been mercifully deep and dreamless. He'd always had trouble sleeping and Michelle's death had made it impossible until Penn arrived. Morris owed it all to Penn's reassuring presence. There was no reason to worry about Cadence because she was in the most capable hands possible. And for the first time since Michelle's death, Morris didn't feel alone. Penn understood how empty and lost Morris felt and there was no pressure or expectations. He didn't have to keep his chin up, be brave, or carry on. All Morris had to do was hang on and keep breathing, which suited him just fine.

It wasn't as easy when Morris crawled back into bed for a second attempt at sleep. He nodded off eventually, but Morris dreamt about Michelle. He searched the house for her, going from room to room, calling her name. He woke up crying and drenched in sweat as if he'd spent hours racing up and down the stairs and through the hallway.

Penn had left a glass of water by the bed but it wasn't enough. Morris needed a little physical and mental space between himself and his pillow. He threw back the covers and got out of bed to get a fresh glass of water. Everything was turned off and the lights were low when Morris wandered into the kitchen.

He felt like it had been weeks since he had opened the refrigerator. It had only been three or four days, but Morris was surprised when he peeked inside while he was drinking. The shelves were neatly stocked with brightly colored produce and jars of homemade sauces and cooked beans. When he closed the door, Morris's brows jumped at the sound of a soft mechanical hum upstairs.

He left his glass and followed the noise up the steps and down the hall to the guest room. He peeked around the opened door and was pleasantly shocked to find Penn murmuring softly to himself as he worked at a sewing machine. His back was turned to Morris so it was hard to see what he was working on, but that wasn't much of a shame. Morris was enjoying what he could see.

And what Morris could see...

Very little consideration or sewing prowess had been wasted on Penn's pajama shorts. They appeared to be the remains of a tattered pair of pajama pants and they were all that Penn was wearing. His long, lean back, toned arms, and legs were covered in tattoos. Penn's bare feet tapped and bounced while he worked and his hair was twisted into a lopsided knot on top of his head.

Morris forgot his bad dream and was enjoying the moment as he cataloged Penn's many tattoos. They were all line drawings and Morris recognized several from his favorite Shel Silverstein books, including *The Giving Tree* and *Where the Sidewalk Ends*. But a faint cry snapped Morris out of his reverie.

Penn grabbed his phone and turned from the sewing

machine. "Did I wake you?" He asked as he rose. The baby monitor's app was open on Penn's phone and Morris could see Cadence stirring in her crib on the screen.

"No. I had a dream, but I came up to see what that sound was," Morris said, gesturing at the sewing machine on the desk. His eyes caught on the light blue fabric.

"I hope it's okay. I asked your mom if I could make something for the nursery with one of Michelle's quilts and she told me to help myself."

"It's fine," Morris murmured distantly. Penn had probably picked it because the colors would coordinate well in the nursery, but Morris was a little sad because it was Michelle's favorite comforter. "I was probably going to donate it with the rest of her clothes and bedding."

"There's always Warm Things and Fin can work that out with you when you're ready," Penn said and Morris nodded. Fin's company had expanded and was donating quilts, scarves, hats, and mittens made from recycled textiles to nursing homes and shelters all over the East Coast.

"I'd like that," Morris said. "She had a lot of nice pantsuits and dresses. I think Michelle would want her clothes to go to one of those organizations that help women get back on their feet."

"We can totally make that happen once you're feeling up to it. I need to take Cadie her midnight snack," Penn said, reaching for the dresser. A bottle was prepared and waiting and Morris stepped aside so Penn could pass. "Unless you want to." Penn offered Morris the bottle.

He considered it, then shook his head. "I'm already having a rough night and I don't think *Cadie* wants me blubbering all over her." Morris liked the new nickname. It sounded like something Michelle would pick.

"Fair enough. Hang out for as long as you want. I'll be up for hours."

"Thanks. I could use a little company," Morris said.

He watched Penn go, then took a few cautious steps over the threshold. It was Morris's house and Penn was just borrowing the room for a while, but it still felt...improper. Morris's cheeks were warm when he glanced at the bed. It had been moved under the window and Morris blinked in confusion at the new book-lined shelves on the other wall. The desk was at the foot of the bed, under the chandelier. To give Penn more light while he worked, Morris assumed.

The plants from Michelle's room were scattered around the room and arranged on the windowsill. They looked healthy and Morris was glad Penn had thought of them. Morris would have forgotten and felt terrible for killing her beloved succulents, lilies, and orchids.

A smirk tugged at Morris's lips at the overalls hanging in the opened closet. Penn had several, along with four pairs of Converse and two sets of leather flip-flops lined up in a row beneath them. There were two neat stacks of T-shirts and two hoodies on the top shelf. An old Army duffle bag was folded and wedged in the corner. Morris was able to make out a name despite the faded letters.

TUCKER, A.

Morris assumed that was Penn's father and wondered if he was why the long-haired nanny was so organized and efficient. Despite his unkempt appearance and unpretentious attitude, Penn's space radiated the same cozy, yet well-organized warmth he did. He'd only inhabited the guest room for a few days, but it already smelled like Penn—clean and softly peppery, with just a hint of something green.

There was also the faintest whiff of marijuana whenever Penn was in the room, but Morris already knew about that. You just assumed that Penn smoked a lot of pot as soon as you laid eyes on him. Penn had asked if it was okay if he smoked in the garden a few times a day and before bed at night. Morris didn't have a problem with responsible pot use and Penn was considered to be an extraordinarily competent person. He didn't have a driver's license so he was of no danger to the public unless he crashed into someone with his skateboard.

Morris finally faced the newly installed bookshelves, focusing first on the craftsmanship and the crisp white molding before appreciating the way the books were arranged. Penn hadn't just unboxed and shelved them, they were organized by subject with all of Michelle's business books in the middle and at eye level and special areas dedicated to art, music history, and Black history. There was also a whole pink and green column devoted to her sorority albums, pictures, and mementos.

"I hope that's okay," Penn said when he returned. He sounded wary and was chewing on the end of his thumb as he watched Morris from the door.

"This is great," Morris replied, but his eyes drifted to a framed picture of Michelle and him in Paris.

Penn cleared his throat and rushed into the room. "I put the more basic business books where you could find them if you needed them. And I tried to make it easy to find the ones that had the most wear and tear in case they were her favorites and you wanted them for Cadence later," he said, pointing at various shelves.

He'd knocked the wind out of Morris with that one and he needed a moment. Morris blinked back tears and sniffed hard.

"Thank you. This is exactly what I was going to do. It just would have taken me four years to do it because I'm a big baby."

"Knock that off!" Penn wagged a finger at him. "This is *hard* and it'll take some getting used to. Ease into the memories and talk about her when you can. And don't beat yourself up. It already feels like ripping open a wound, without finding reasons to feel guilty."

A weak chuckle wafted from Morris as he drifted closer to the picture. They were both posed and pointing and the camera angle suggested they were the same size as the Eiffel Tower. Morris didn't want to be a typical nerdy tourist, but Michelle made him do it. The picture had been on her bedside table because she said it was her favorite memory from the trip.

The ache in his heart became a roar and Morris longed for her. He opened his mouth to swear at God or call his sister's name, but gathered the feeling up and sucked it down.

"Don't do that," Penn said and kneaded Morris's shoulder. "Pain and grief like to grow roots in the dark and they'll twist and spread until they choke you and block out the light. It hurts and it'll be hard to talk about her at first. But let yourself feel that pain so those wounds can heal. You'll start to feel her warmth again, like the sun shining through the cracks. And you'll find that the more you talk about her, the easier it gets and you'll take comfort in those moments with her."

"Okay. I can handle baby steps," Morris said, wiping his eyes and pushing out a cleansing breath. Penn was right. The pain had been excruciating before it passed, yet Morris could still hear her laughter as they took the picture and when she had teased him about it over breakfast the next morning.

"That's exactly what I'm talking about." Penn held up a hand but it took a moment for Morris to clasp it. "When you're ready, just take it one step at a time."

"Maybe half a step," Morris said, rubbing his temple. "I'm still tired, but it's hard to sleep and I can't stop thinking about her."

"Hold on!" Penn gestured for Morris to wait while he darted around the bed and into the guest bathroom. He returned a moment later with a large joint. "Want to hang out in the garden and finish this with me? You shouldn't have any trouble falling asleep, but we can hang out for as long as you need."

Morris hesitated the way he always did when someone offered him drugs.

What if my mom finds out?

But Evelyn had changed her mind about marijuana after Michelle talked Morris Sr. into trying it to help with his pain, nausea, and loss of appetite during chemo.

"Sure," Morris said, the way he often did when it was pot or the occasional mushroom. He didn't trust powders or pills. He had a feeling his mother would give him a pass this time or possibly approve.

The night was clear and all was calm in Lenox Hill as they reclined on the patio steps and passed the joint back and forth. Morris was soothed by the distant honks and muffled music from passing cars. His city never slept, but she'd whisper and tiptoe through neighborhoods like Lenox Hill and shout at you in the East Village, Greenwich Village, and the Lower East Side. He found comfort in knowing he wasn't the only one who couldn't sleep and needed distraction.

Penn gave Morris chills when he leaned close and said exactly what he had been thinking about the city.

"Nights can be tough for me," Penn confided after taking his fourth or fifth drag off the joint. "My thoughts get real heavy and I worry a lot about my dad. He had prostate cancer and he barely made it through chemo. He's getting up there in years and I know he won't be around for much longer. And then I start to miss my mom because I didn't get enough time with her."

That surprised Morris. Penn was so open and emotionally fluent, yet he packed away his own cares and sadness until he was alone, like he was ashamed of having bad days or feeling down.

Weed made Morris quiet and he grew entranced with the low rumble of Penn's voice. It was deep and velvety—a drowsy lullaby set to the muted backbeat of the city.

"I used to *hate* how I couldn't get away from Mom after she died. I swear, I'd see her and I'd hear her like a dozen times a day. It was hell until I got used to it and realized that all those little moments meant that she was still here and that I didn't *have* to let her go. I can still hear her voice and see her smile when I'm teasing Penny. And, Jesus, she's always staring back at me when I look in the mirror," he said with a soft, wavering laugh. "Now, I'm grateful because I'd be empty without all those memories if I had let myself forget. I'd be lonely without her."

"That's beautiful. She sounds like she was amazing," Morris said.

Penn whistled and shook his head. "There will never be anyone like Laurel Tucker," he declared, then smirked at Morris deviously. "Except maybe Penny Lane. I was really indulgent with my sister when she was growing up because she was so much like Mom and I wanted to let Penny grow wild."

"That might come back and bite you in the ass," Morris joked, even though he couldn't believe that Penn could get something like that wrong.

"Maybe," Penn agreed, but he looked pleased with the idea. "Mom studied journalism and photography in school, but she was an environmentalist and an activist first. She met my dad at a protest in Central Park. Mom passed him a sign and ordered him to follow her and that was it for him. But they realized they were both passionate about preserving nature and the planet and loved being outdoors. They became inseparable and I was born roughly nine months after their first camping trip," he added with a lewd wink, making Morris laugh.

"So, that's how a city boy becomes a hippie," Morris murmured. He gave Penn a gentle nudge with his elbow so it was clear that he'd meant it as a compliment.

"Yeah. We're a little weird, us Tuckers," Penn confirmed and explained that they had spent as much time as they could in the Catskills—camping, hiking, and fishing—because that's when Laurel was happiest. She never caught anything and didn't eat fish because she was a vegetarian, but Gus had taught her how to cast like a pro. Penn said that being on the water with his dad was like meditating for Laurel. And Penn and his sister often went fishing with Gus to keep him company and feel closer to their mother.

But it was more than the sexy timbre of Penn's voice or the joy those memories and his family gave him. It was the realization that one day Morris would be able to look at Michelle's things or think about her without flinching and swallowing a shuddering breath before it could grow and swallow *him* up. One day, Morris would laugh as he told Cadence about her mother and he'd be able to reminisce with his parents about family trips and holidays without it feeling like a punch in the gut.

He was lighter when they came back into the house, and Morris was already drifting off when his head flopped onto his pillow. Instead of dreaming about Michelle, he dreamt about a fishing boat and Penn's capable hands holding Morris's, teaching him how to cast and reel on a quiet lake at sunrise.

Chapter Six

A week later, Morris was still sleeping a lot throughout the day, but he was more alert when he came out of his room, and he doted on Cadence if he caught her while she was awake. Penn encouraged Morris to nap with her when the timing worked and would move Cadence to her bouncer or her crib after they were both asleep.

Nurturing the bond between Morris and Cadence while giving him room and time to grieve was a challenge, but Penn believed it was vital. Morris smiled more around the baby and she lit up and her eyes followed him every time he walked into the room. He wasn't ready to hear it yet, but one day Morris would see how much of Michelle radiated from Cadence. In the meantime, Penn would let Cadence work her magic and help heal her uncle's wounds.

Penn had the perfect opportunity one morning when Morris appeared bright and early, just as Cadence released a loud, lusty post-bottle burp.

"Brava," Morris said to her, clapping softly on his way to the coffee maker.

"I was just about to deliver your coffee. Just had to get our little lady settled," Penn said cheerfully, but Morris shook his head.

"You don't have to keep doing that. I'm trying to get back on a regular schedule, but it's been tough. I'm tired all day, even though I have been sleeping better at night." He winked at Penn as he stirred in a spoonful of sugar.

"Hey. I'm always happy to have company and weed just hits better when you've got someone to share it with."

It had become their new routine after Cadence went down for the night. Penn would shower and roll a joint and Morris would be waiting on the back porch. They'd chat—with Penn doing 90% of the talking—until Cadence rang for her midnight snack. Morris would be face-down in his bed and softly snoring when Penn returned to check the locks and wash the bottle.

"You need to let me buy next time," Morris said, but Penn gave him an impatient look.

"Please. I have a hook-up so I get it super cheap, and it's not like you're putting much of a dent in my supply."

"If you're sure..." Morris appeared distracted and Penn caught him staring at his chest.

Penn looked down at himself, remembering that he wasn't wearing a shirt. He usually hung out in his pajamas until Cadence went down for her morning nap. "Does this bother you?"

"What? No." Morris shook his head quickly, but he was blushing as he studied his coffee.

"I don't wear a lot of clothes at home and I'm a big believer in kangaroo care for babies. And adults," Penn added cheekily.

"Kangaroo care?" Morris asked with a befuddled frown.

He's always so serious.

"Skin-to-skin contact helps with digestion and regulation of body temperature. Babies gain more weight and have more stable heartbeats and they sleep better and cry less. They also have stronger immune systems. You should put on the sling and try it with her. It's an instant hit of oxytocin, dopamine, and serotonin for you. And aromatherapy because she smells like heaven," Penn explained.

"I'll think about it," Morris said hesitantly. "I'm not as comfortable being undressed around people unless I'm on the beach or at a pool party. Or you know…"

Penn laughed and nodded. "I get it. I promise I'm not a nudist and it's cool if you'd prefer I wore a shirt when I'm down here."

"No!" Morris waved dismissively. "I'm a little old-fashioned and I have hang-ups about my own body, but I don't mind. I think it's cool and I wish I had your confidence."

"Seriously?" Penn couldn't believe it as he leaned back and gave Morris a once-over. He carried himself with cool, quiet swagger, even in a Roots T-shirt, joggers, and white cotton socks. "I don't follow social media or…the entertainment industry in general, but I remember that magazine article about you that came out a few months ago. Those pictures were everywhere because you looked *hot*."

Morris's nose wrinkled dubiously. "There was a whole team of stylists and the photographer had like four assistants. Michelle made sure I—" He explained, but Penn cut him off.

"I'm looking right at you," he said, gesturing at Morris. "You were off-limits because you're one of Reid's best friends, but if you weren't and we'd met at a music festival or a record store…" Penn nodded, widening his eyes at Morris in approval. "I'd wanna see where you were headed and if you wanted to get to know each other a little better."

"No!" Morris laughed, loud and light. His blush deepened and they smiled at each other as Cadence burbled in delight on the table. He was really cute when he blushed. "That's…"

Morris rolled his eyes. "Generous, and I wish you could tell that to the chubby twelve-year-old in me who still feels a little weird taking his shirt off at the beach. And I envy you. It's always a tense moment when I undress around a guy for the first time. The first three or four times, actually," he amended.

"Why, though?" Penn asked. "The amazing thing about our bodies is that they're all different in infinite, beautiful ways, but also all the same! That's the alchemy that creates a spark between two—or more—people. You won't get a reaction if you mix two of the same things."

"That's one way of looking at it," Morris conceded.

The moment stretched and got a little awkward. Especially for Penn because once he noticed he had chemistry with someone it was hard for him to *un*notice it.

He's always so serious.

Penn had a feeling they could have a lot of fun together.

"Have you met Reid's new recruit?" He asked, quickly changing the subject before he got carried away. And Penn was prone to getting carried away when the chemistry was right. Things progressed pretty quickly from the music festival or the record shop and Penn always warned that he'd be out the door before the sun came up. Penn was there for a good time, not a long time.

"No... I haven't had the pleasure yet," Morris said slowly.

"Dash. He's one of Penny Lane's best friends in the whole world."

"Great?"

"He's quiet like you, but he's a little more..." Penn struggled to find a kind way to put it. "He's a little naive and *pure*." He nodded. "He's sweet and likes to blend into the background because he doesn't realize how hot he is. Everyone thinks he's a flake and I think he knows it, poor thing."

"Is Dash his real name?" Morris asked, sounding intrigued.

"Yup! Dash Griffin. His dad played pro football and Dash played in high school and college, but he said it was too intense and physical for him."

"That's too bad."

Penn shrugged. "He graduated with a degree in nursing, but Dash said he was too squeamish so he went back to school and got a degree in early childhood education. He was teaching second grade until Penny talked him into sending Reid his resume."

"Poor guy, indeed. I hope it works out," Morris said.

"Of course, it'll work out! I've been helping him with his confidence because Reid wants him to get out of his shell. Sounds like you could use a little help too once you're ready to get out and about more."

"We'll see." Morris sighed into his coffee. "My parents have been on my case and I'm at the point where I'm sick of sleeping, but I still don't want to do much more than this," he said and raised his cup at Penn. "In fact, I'll probably head back to bed after I finish my coffee and eat something."

"But you got up early, cleaned up, and you came out for a chat! That's real progress!" Penn offered his hand. He didn't want to do it, but Morris eventually slapped it. "There you go! I made some pumpkin and blueberry muffins. Eat one of those and it'll be a total win."

"Thank you for keeping the bar really low," Morris said with a snort, but he was smiling, and ate two muffins before he kissed Cadence and headed back to his room.

"Definitely calling that a win," Penn told the baby once it was just the two of them again. He'd only been with Morris and Cadence for a week and a half, but they had already come a long way.

Chapter Seven

O *kay. No more sleeping.*

His body protested as he stood, aching in places Morris had forgotten existed and pinching and spasming when he stretched and straightened his back. He felt a hell of a lot older than thirty-eight and Morris thought he looked like a haggard version of his father as he stared at his reflection and brushed his teeth.

Morris had promised Morris Sr. he'd get out of bed at a decent hour and do something when they talked the night before. But Morris hadn't picked up any momentum by the time he trudged out of his room to get his coffee.

"Way to keep the streak going. Let's start easy!" Penn suggested as he placed a bowl of oatmeal in Morris's hands. It was loaded with fresh blueberries and the warm orange and cinnamon-scented fumes made his mouth water. "It's going to be a rainy day so I thought I'd make us some lentil soup and lots of naan. You have to try my naan with tahini and honey. It's my favorite snack, plus it's packed with antioxidants, calcium, fiber, and lots of immune system boosters!"

"Sure... I'll try it," Morris said, but he had a feeling he wouldn't be as excited about Penn's ancient variation of a PB&J.

"How about this?" Penn said, clapping his hands together excitedly. "We're also getting low on diapers. You keep an eye on Cadie while I run around the corner to the market and I'll make you one of my famous chocolate cakes."

Morris felt another flash of irrational fear. But this time, his mother might truly kill him if she found out he was eating someone else's chocolate cake. "I wouldn't want to hurt your feelings, but I'm a pretty tough critic when it comes to cake. Especially chocolate cake. You know who my mom is."

"I'm sorry." Penn shook his head as if he had misunderstood. "Did you just challenge me? Because that's my Nana Tucker's chocolate cake recipe and it's won numerous blue ribbons."

"You go on." Morris flicked his fingers at the front door. "Go on and run to the market. Make sure you pick up some tissues because you're probably gonna cry when I tell you it's not as good as Evie's chocolate cake."

"I'd accept that, but I have a feeling you're going to be eating those words. And two big pieces of cake!" Penn boasted prematurely and held up two fingers. One nail was painted blue and the other was orange, probably for the Knicks game later in the evening.

"We'll see."

"It's on," Penn declared, pointing at Morris and then at Cadence. "Once she's down for her morning nap."

They made small talk while Penn puttered around the kitchen until it was time for him to rock Cadence to sleep. She went down easily in her bassinet and he was off with his list, leaving Morris alone with the baby for the first time. Penn was just going a few blocks to Morton Williams for less than a dozen items, but he left Morris with his own list of tips and tricks in case Cadence woke up while he was away.

"No sweat." Morris said, leaning so he could see into the bassinet. Penn had left it by the open back doors so Cadence could enjoy the cool breeze and the sound and the smell of the rain if it started sprinkling. But Penn also wanted her to get used to the sounds of the city. Morris thought that was a good idea because New York was no place for light sleepers.

There was a tap at the door and Morris wondered if it was Penn; maybe he'd left his keys. Morris opened it and found himself face-to-face with a punk sprite. While he'd never believed in fairies or fairy tales, there wasn't a better word for the beaming, pig-tailed, tattooed wisp waiting on Morris's stoop. Her big green eyes sparkled and her lips twitched as if she was ready to let Morris in on a secret. Oddly enough, Morris was dying to hear it and he felt an overwhelming urge to tug on one of her strawberry blond braids.

"Hi! I'm Penn's little sister, Penny!" She declared before she rose on her toes and flung her arms around Morris's middle. She was as light as a butterfly, but her embrace was warm and her effervescent giddiness was contagious. Freckles dusted her nose and her shoulders, her limbs and collarbone were decorated with flowers, bees, and constellations. Crystals dangled from her earlobes and twinkled from the many charms and pendants around her neck. Morris would have guessed she was Penn's sister if she hadn't told him.

"It's great to finally meet you," Morris said sincerely, and was truly delighted as he hugged her.

"I've been back and forth a few times to drop off deliveries for Penn, but we didn't want to disturb you," she explained. She leaned and craned her neck. "Is Cadie around?" Her nose twitched adorably as she slid Morris a sly grin. "I need to sniff your baby. That little girl smells like heaven and it's been almost twenty-four hours since my last fix."

"She just went down for a nap," Morris said, waving at the bassinet.

"I promise I won't disturb her!" Penny skipped across the room in a giant pair of cut-off overalls. There were colorful patches on the pockets and Morris suspected that they were hand-me-downs from Penn. They looked cute on her, though. She'd paired them with a rainbow-striped tank top and tall pink socks and black Converse. Penny held onto her pigtails as she bent over the bassinet and inhaled deeply. "Someone would make a fortune if they could put *that* in a bottle," she said quietly, then looked around. "My brother's not here."

"He ran out for some groceries and diapers."

"You're out of diapers already?" She asked and Morris chuckled. Just about everyone who turned up for the baby shower had brought diapers.

"We have hundreds but they're mostly twos or threes and we're running low on the N's."

"Ah." Penny nodded knowingly. "Shouldn't need them for too much longer. She's turning into a little ham. And look at these rolls!" She whispered, pointing into the bassinet.

Morris stretched his neck so he could get a better look. The baby was indeed turning into a little ham and Morris was sad at how quickly she was growing and changing. He was still nervous about being alone with her when she was awake and Morris hadn't gotten past his squeamishness with the diapers, but he wanted her to stay just the way she was.

He didn't want Michelle to miss Cadence's first words and her first steps. He wanted Michelle to be there for Cadence's first birthday cake and to teach her how to use the chunky forks and spoons in the kitchen.

"Hey!" Penny whispered and her arms were stretched wide

as she rushed across the room. She hugged Morris's middle again and squeezed him tight. "She's still here! I promise."

"Not you too," Morris said with a weary sigh, but he was smiling as he kissed Penny's hair. She was soothing and radiated the same warmth and indomitable kindness as her brother.

"I'm much worse than Penn, I'm afraid."

"Eh. I'm getting used to it."

"Good. Penn really likes you and he's infatuated with Cadence. You're both perfect for him," she stated. Her temple rested on Morris's shoulder and she was still squeezing him, but he didn't mind being hugged for once.

He knew what Penny meant. Penn didn't *like him* like him, and it was a great long-term position for him as a nanny. Yet Morris's mind wandered. He didn't really have a type, but hacky sack guys would probably be at the bottom of Morris's list. He had enjoyed what was under Penn's overalls, though...

"Thanks. The last two weeks have been a blur and I don't know how I would have survived without him." He could have been overwhelmed with Cadence and the reality of living without Michelle. Instead, Morris had been given space and time to wallow and muddle through his grief. And a lifeline when the loneliness was too much. Penn was there and just knew when Morris needed a hug and a sympathetic ear. "I've never been this tired in my life, no matter how much I sleep. But Penn doesn't judge me for hiding from the world and he's pretty adamant that I take all the time I need."

Penny made a sad, knowing sound. "That's because he's been there. I was a lot younger when our mom died. I missed her but Penn did everything he could to keep life as normal for me as possible. Dad was crushed and he just shut down for a few years. Penn was so strong and carried both of us because he said he hurt worse when he stayed still. He'd cry at night, though," she added softly. Her vision grew distant and blurred.

"He's always moodier at night. He doesn't want to bring anyone down or make us worry so he waits until he's alone to stew or cry. I know something's bothering him if he's sewing or sanding into the wee hours."

That caught Morris's attention. "He's been sewing a lot at night. Should I be worried?" He asked.

Penny jumped and gave herself a shake, refocusing. "Has he?"

"Yeah... He made a slipcover for the rocker and some other odds and ends for the nursery." The slipcover had touched Morris far more than a slipcover should. But he had cried *happy,* relieved tears when he walked into the nursery and found the rocker covered. Michelle's ghost wasn't there to sucker punch him. The rocker was still there and it somehow felt more like her in a more comforting way. And Penn had made Cadence a smaller quilt for tummy time, a large floor pillow, and a diaper holder from what was left of Michelle's favorite quilt.

Penny's lips pursed before they spread into a lopsided grin. "I have a feeling he's dealing with some deep, deep emotions because this reminds him of Mom."

"That's not good," Morris said but Penny tilted her head. "It's not?"

Morris's brow furrowed as he became confused. "It is?"

"You can't fix something if you're afraid to look at it and touch it. He's always been good at mending other people's wounds, but he'll sand every inch of wood in this house before he'll let someone in and heal his. He'll never tell you he's hurt or ask for help."

"Why?" But Morris shook his head because he already knew the answer. He'd already solved that riddle during their bedtime blunt-smoking sessions. "He's the problem solver, never the problem."

"Exactly." She said, smiling conspiratorially at Morris. "I can see that he's opened up to you, though. It makes all the sense in the world."

"Does it?" It didn't make sense to Morris that a hillbilly from Hoboken could see into his soul the way Penn did.

"I don't think he knows many people who've been where he's been, thank goodness. And I think he feels like he's helping himself when he's helping you." Her clear green eyes glittered as she studied Morris, but he didn't detect any sadness.

"I hope you're not expecting me to save him while he's saving me because I'm just keeping my chin above water at the moment."

"You're doing awesome!" She pumped her little fists encouragingly. "And this is exactly what he needs. He's finally found someone he can open up to because he doesn't feel like he's being a burden."

There was never a sense that Penn was dumping his troubles or fishing for sympathy. If anything, Penn was showing Morris a way through the pain, anger, and crushing sadness and offering glimpses of what life was like on the other side.

"I really haven't done much more than listen because that's about all I'm good for lately."

"That's about all anyone can do when the unthinkable happens," Penny said sagely, sounding like her big brother. She took Morris's hand in both of hers. "It might seem like she's gone, but I can feel her here!" She whispered. "She's still looking out for you and there's so much of her in you and that little angel over there."

Morris couldn't speak; he just nodded at the bassinet. He could see more and more of Michelle in Cadence every day.

Penny gasped excitedly and gestured around them. "She's feeling extra vibrant now because your heart and your thoughts are so full of her! I have to go, but keep that up!"

"Go? You just got here," Morris said, causing Penny to gasp again.

"I stopped by to drop off Penn's mail but have a date with Dash for lunch." She reached into one of the big patch pockets to retrieve a stack of envelopes. "It's mostly junk, but there's something from Uncle Silas about the cabin," she said as she passed them to Morris.

"Nothing urgent, I hope," Morris mused.

"Not urgent, but Penn will want to put it off," she predicted. "Uncle Silas is our mother's cousin. He wants Penn to have the family cabin up in the Catskills because he's getting older."

Morris hissed and nodded. "I don't blame Penn. That's pretty rough."

"It is," she agreed solemnly. "But Penn will call and they'll get to talking about all the fun we had there when we were kids. Penn's gonna promise Silas that the cabin's in good hands and that we'll take our families and friends there. That's going to mean everything to Silas and he'll feel better because those memories will get passed on. No one wants to be forgotten and Uncle Silas just wants to know that we'll remember him and Mom the way they were when we were all together and happy."

"Aren't you like...thirty?" Morris asked her in disbelief. "How did you get to be so wise?"

"Ha!" She let out a loud, inelegant snort. "I'm twenty-nine. My dad is a retired Army Ranger from New Jersey and my mom went to Sarah Lawrence. So did I," she added out of the side of her mouth.

"That explains a lot, but your parents sound like an odd pair."

"Boy, were they! Dad's more conservative and old-school, but he believed in a lot of the same things Mom believed in and he still had her back when he didn't. And they really loved each other and being out in nature together."

"Right. But a soldier and a tree hugger?" Morris argued and Penny shrugged.

"Dad did his twenty years with the Army and I think Mom and Penn gave him a new purpose after he got out. He was almost Penn's age when they met and Mom was still in college. Dad stayed home with Penn while she finished school. He said being a stay-at-home dad changed his life and was better than anything he did before he met Mom."

"It sounds like your parents lived for each other and for the two of you. I'm so sorry for your loss," Morris hugged her and sniffed curiously, but carefully. She smelled almost exactly like Penn.

"They did, but it's a lot easier for me to talk about Mom because I had Penn for support. Everyone worried about me because I was a child, but I had Penn, Reid, Gavin, and a legion of therapists. Penn was on his own, looking after me and Dad."

"I didn't realize…"

"He always looked out for me, though. Mom was gone a lot, trying to save the world, and Dad had his own business for a while. He did carpentry, plumbing, landscaping, some electrical work… But Penn never minded. He liked braiding my hair and making me breakfast and he'd let me ride on his back to school. He was always there when I got out of school or practice, and we'd do my homework on the train or at the table while we were cooking dinner. Dad made sure he was home in time for dinner and so did Mom when she wasn't off protesting or giving a speech somewhere."

None of that surprised Morris. It was clear that Penn adored his sister. He talked about her often and Morris suspected that she was one of the few reasons Penn bothered with a smartphone. Penny, Gus, Reid, and the baby monitor:

Penn had no other use for his phone and barely knew how to use it.

"Sounds like he was an awesome big brother."

"The best!" She said with a firm nod.

"What about Nana Tucker's chocolate cake?" Morris asked. "I'm going to have to move and change my name if this cake is as good as he says it is."

"Oh, he's baking you Nana's chocolate cake?" A devious grin spread across her face. "When's the wedding?"

"Stop," he said, but she squealed as she grabbed his face and kissed him.

"I'm getting a new big brother!" She sang, then stopped and held up a finger. "I already had the very best big brother in the whole world. Now I get *dos!*" She said and a second finger popped up before her fists shot into the air. "And Penny wins again!" She announced victoriously, keeping her celebratory cheers to a low roar so she wouldn't disturb the baby.

"That's really flattering and you're the most adorable little sister ever, but we haven't had that kind of vibe. I could easily see Penn becoming one of my best friends, though."

"You haven't had that kind of vibe *yet.*" Penny said and leaned in. "But you will. *You will,*" she rasped at him dramatically.

Morris squeezed an eye shut. "Was that a Yoda impression?" He guessed and Penny lit up.

"It was! Was it good?"

"Are *you* single?" Morris teased with a flirty wink.

Penny's tongue pushed out. "Boys are so gross and the only one I'll ever love is my brother," she stated firmly, then checked the antique watch around her wrist. It was an ancient time-piece and Morris wondered which of her grandfathers or great-grandfathers she'd inherited it from. "I had better get going or

Dash might get confused and think he's picking me up and head over to our place."

She kissed Morris again and departed, leaving him a touch disoriented and tickled at the encounter. Penn had warned that his sister could be a hellion and headache, but Morris thought she was enchanting. And he really wouldn't mind having her as a little sister, he decided. It was just too bad that Morris wasn't into her big brother.

He wasn't as sure about that as he should have been, though, as he thought back to Penn's remark about hitting on Morris if they had met under different circumstances.

You were off-limits because you're one of Reid's best friends...

You were.

Was Morris still off-limits? Did he want to be? What if the cake was as good as Penn said it was?

There were too many questions and Morris didn't have the energy to pursue the answers in his current state. He did have the energy for another one of Penn's muffins and went to see if there were any in the basket of assorted baked goods on the counter.

Chapter Eight

The list of ingredients for Nana Tucker's chocolate cake was short and simple. Flour, sugar, vanilla, cocoa, the usual leavening agents for a butter cake...

"You're using *actual* butter and eggs?" Morris verified as he paced on the other side of the counter like he was officiating a baking competition.

"Yup! And sour cream!" Penn whispered as if he was breaking the rules.

Morris crossed his arms over his chest and beat a knuckle against his lip, looking concerned. "Huh."

"What?"

"Nothing!" Morris raised his hands and stepped back.

"I know better," Penn said as he pointed at him. "That face means you're worried."

"I was expecting you to use vegan butter or cashews."

"Oh, I could make you an epic vegan chocolate cake!" Penn said. He cracked an egg on the counter and added it to the bowl with one hand while stirring with the other. "I came up with a

Penny-safe version of Nana's cake for her birthday, but I'd be a fool to feed that to Evelyn Mosby's son."

"Huh," Morris grunted again. "We might be in trouble," he conceded, making Penn laugh.

"*You* might be in trouble. I'm aware of the power this cake wields and as Keeper of the Recipe, I use it sparingly."

"Calm down, Betty Crocker. It's still just a cake."

"We'll see." Penn had every right to feel smug and whistled happily to himself as he creamed the butter with brown sugar. His chocolate cake *never* failed and could make even the toughest cake critic weep.

Morris was certainly a tough critic and gasped when Penn added a cup of steaming-hot coffee to the batter at the end. "That's smart!" He whispered and nodded.

"Mmmhmm," Penn hummed. He poured the batter into three parchment-lined pans. "Coffee's hygroscopic so it holds onto water molecules. That was my only addition to Nana's recipe. It brings out the chocolate flavor and it makes the cake extra moist."

"Shit!" Morris scrubbed his face with his hands. He looked a little shiny like he was feeling the heat. "That's it?" He asked when Penn finished whipping the frosting.

"Deceptively simple, isn't it?"

The best things in life often were and you just couldn't go wrong with butter, sugar, a splash of vanilla, cocoa, and a pinch of salt.

Morris had drifted into the kitchen so he could peek over Penn's shoulder. "That's almost the same as Mom's frosting, but she melts chocolate and she uses something else with the butter," he said, not at liberty to divulge the "something else."

"It doesn't need the extra fat because I already have all that butter and I want to control the sweetness. The cocoa lightens like powdered sugar, so I don't need as much, thus creating a rich, chocolatey frosting without the overpowering sweetness," Penn explained once he was finished.

Morris clearly didn't like what he was hearing and whispered another curse. "Smart. I think you've got Mom against the ropes."

"Ha!" Penn removed one of the beaters and offered it to Morris. "Go ahead. It's perfectly sweet and only a little bit naughty."

Morris's gaze flicked from the beater to Penn's lips. For a moment, Penn imagined he was offering something far more dangerous than a taste of frosting. He had a feeling Morris was too.

"I should probably wait," Morris said weakly, his eyes still stuck on Penn's lips.

"Why? A little taste won't hurt."

They both knew that was a lie, but Penn wished he was tempting Morris with something a lot more illicit. Which was impossible and reckless.

Or was it?

Penn's teeth dug into his lip as he weighed all the pros and cons.

The pros were pretty obvious because Penn hadn't been kidding when he said that Morris would have been on his radar if it wasn't for Reid. He'd felt a definite spark the few times they hung out. But Penn had kept his distance despite the urge to get to know him better and find out how he was rubbing Morris the wrong way.

It was far more than basic attraction. Morris was incredibly sexy, but Penn could tell when the chemistry was there. And it was *there*.

They had always limited their exchanges to greetings and pleasantries, gravitating to opposite corners of the room or the table. Every now and then, their gazes would collide.

Were you staring at me?

Why would I be staring at you?

There would be blushing and possibly some eye-rolling, then it was a game and the only rule was don't get caught staring again. That was often followed by a few solitary rounds of "What if he was staring?" If there was time, Penn might play a little "Should I talk to him and clear it up?" But he generally resolved that with an easy favorite: "That would be weird and it was probably just me." He always assumed Morris was playing similar games or just didn't like him.

And if that was the case, Penn believed it was best to leave it alone. For Reid's sake, and because Penn didn't want to make it worse.

"One taste can get you into a lot of trouble," Morris said, reminding Penn of the many cons. Reid would never forgive Penn if he hurt Morris. And it would be the *worst* time to change his policy and give a man a chance because Morris was still up to his neck in grief.

But Penn wasn't looking at the dollop of frosting on the beater. His lips tingled as he swayed closer. "You're probably right. It's hard to stop with one taste."

"I don't have that kind of willpower." Morris licked his lips, making them glisten. They looked like they'd be sweeter than the frosting and Penn ached to find out.

Morris was right, though. One kiss wouldn't be enough and it was a slippery slope. "You should probably go over there and wait until it's done, then," Penn said, swinging his head at the living room.

An hour and fifteen minutes later, Morris was climbing the walls. "You're stalling," he accused testily.

"I am not. It needs *at least* an hour in the fridge. It'll be better tomorrow, you just have to remember to cut yourself a slice about an hour before you want to eat it or the frosting will be more like fudge," Penn said.

That earned a pained whimper from the sofa. "Who has that kind of self-control? And that sounds like a good thing." Morris popped to his feet. "Just give me a piece!"

"Okay!" Penn laughed as he went to the fridge and took out the cake. It was on a covered cake stand and Penn waited for Morris to hurry around the counter before lifting the glass dome with a dramatic "Ta-dah!"

"Oh, damn," Morris whispered as he leaned in for a closer look. "That's sexy," he said, admiring the classic dips and swoops in the frosting.

"I know." Penn leaned back against the sink and huffed against his knuckles confidently. "I don't miss or crave bacon and I could easily go the rest of my life without eating another burger. But I'll hop off the wagon for this cake," he said, nodding at the stand.

"Would you cut the damn thing?" Morris asked and waved impatiently.

Penn smirked as he brandished the cake knife. "If you're sure you're ready."

"Are we still talking about the cake? Get on with it." Morris threw him a hostile glare, but Penn wasn't sure if he was talking about the cake. He loved those serious frowns and turning them into smiles.

"Of course, I'm talking about the cake."

Penn cut Morris a large slice and slid it across the counter to him. A tall, frosted glass of cow's milk was waiting and Morris had his fork ready.

He swiped at the frosting with the tines of the fork first. Morris tasted it and shook his head at Penn pensively. "That is fucking perfect," he muttered. Morris held up the plate and turned it, subjecting the slice to a thorough examination "It looks light, but not dry..."

"My cake is never dry, sir. Just eat it."

Morris set the plate down and his tongue pressed against the inside of his cheek as he nodded. "I'll be the judge." He forked a generous bite and hummed in approval at the proper proportion of cake and frosting. In it went.

Penn was supposed to be watching Morris's lips for his reaction. But he grew warm and restless as Morris's tongue swept across them to catch a smear of frosting.

They both groaned and Penn covered his with a chuckle. "Well?" He asked expectantly.

"This..." Morris pointed at the plate with his fork. "This is *blasphemous.*" He shook his head as he took another bite. "Penny predicted I'd propose, but I didn't believe her. No one breathes a word about this to my mother. You understand?"

Penn's hand shot up. "Gay Scouts honor," he said and they high-fived.

"I'm glad you understand. So, are you cool with getting married in a Methodist church?" Morris asked, earning a pained grimace from Penn.

"I'm more of a commitment ceremony kind of guy if I'm being honest. I'd consider it for Evelyn, though."

"Already earning brownie points with Mom. You're her ideal son-in-law," Morris said with a wiggle of his brows.

"Think again, pal." Penn turned the cake stand and served himself a thick wedge. "I'm gonna be her favorite son."

"You wouldn't last a week."

There were more swears and groans from Morris as they ate. Penn did his best to ignore them, but his brain turned them into sex sounds. Which only confused Penn and made him feel conflicted because there had been a pleasant tickle in his tummy when he imagined being Evelyn Mosby's son. It had been a long time since he had a mom and Penn absolutely adored Evelyn. He cast a covetous glance at Morris and recalled the many pros he'd pondered earlier.

Penn had plenty of reasons to feel guilty because the things he wanted to do to Evelyn Mosby's son were not suitable for a good Christian woman's ears. He wouldn't be her favorite *anything* if she ever found out.

"I probably wouldn't," Penn agreed.

"I think it's safer if we keep this between us. Even though I already told Penny. You'd better swear her to secrecy," Morris mused while he scraped the last crumbs and traces of frosting off his plate with the side of his fork. He licked it clean, and Penn forced his eyes back on his plate.

"Yeah. That's safer," Penn said, but he wasn't thinking about the cake and he was doing his best not to think about Evelyn.

Nana Tucker's Chocolate Cake

3 cups packed brown sugar
1 cup softened butter
4 eggs
2 teaspoons vanilla extract
2 ⅔ cups all-purpose flour
¾ cup baking cocoa
1 tablespoon baking soda
½ teaspoon salt
1 ⅓ cups sour cream
1 ⅓ cups hot coffee

Cream brown sugar and butter in a mixing bowl. Add eggs, one at a time, beating after each addition until light and fluffy. Blend in vanilla. Combine flour, cocoa, baking soda and salt. Add alternately with sour cream to creamed mixture. Mix until combined. Stir in hot coffee until blended. Pour into three greased and floured 9-in. round baking pans. Bake at 350 degrees F for 35 minutes. Cool completely before frosting.

Chocolate Frosting:
2 cups softened butter
6 cups confectioners' sugar
2 ½ cups baking cocoa
1 teaspoon vanilla extract
1 cup milk

Cream butter and gradually beat in 4 cups of confectioners' sugar, cocoa and vanilla. Add enough milk and sugar to taste and until frosting reaches spreading consistency.

Chapter Nine

She struck again when Morris was least expecting.

Her magnum opus and Morris's worst nightmare began with a single roll of toilet paper.

That wasn't true. It started with an article in the *New York Post* about the Knicks. Morris liked the writer's assessment even if he was a little skeptical about some of the predictions. He wasn't paying attention as he rolled out of bed, kicked his boxers at the hamper, and strolled to the toilet to do his business. The Knicks *might* have a chance in the playoffs.

Morris was intrigued and growing more optimistic by the minute as he reached for the toilet paper and noticed the roll was finished. He tossed it in the wastebasket and twisted to get a new roll from the basket behind him. It took a little juggling, but Morris was able to get it installed with one hand while reading the article. He attempted to tear off a section and glanced away from his phone's screen when the paper wouldn't rip.

A closer inspection revealed that it wasn't real toilet paper and Morris scowled at the ceiling. "Nice. Really, really nice,

Michelle," he grumbled while reaching behind him for another roll. All of the remaining rolls were unrippable and Morris couldn't help but giggle. He felt ridiculous—naked, stranded on the toilet, and with his phone in one hand. He imagined yelling for her to bring him a real roll and knew she had a joke ready that would have left her in tears in the hall while he fumed. She loved corny puns and Morris suspected that she'd tell him she was on a roll when he told her to stop.

That made him laugh out loud, but Morris still had a problem. He swallowed his pride, flushed, gave the room a courtesy spray from the air freshener, then sent Penn a text message asking if he could deliver some toilet paper. Morris pulled a hand towel off the bar and was waiting with it draped across his lap when Penn knocked on the hall door.

"Hey, buddy. You get caught unprepared?" He asked sweetly, then cracked the door and reached around it to toss Morris a roll.

Morris caught it and gave the door a flat look. "I was not unprepared."

"You know, I always check and make sure there's paper before I sit down," Penn advised sagely from behind the door. "Learned the hard way after living with Reid. You're just a sitting duck and asking for trouble."

"I had toilet paper," Morris said tightly. "Michelle replaced all my toilet paper with gag rolls and I finally found them."

"I see... I still would have checked," Penn replied. "Kind of a rookie mistake."

"A rookie—? Can you save the lecture for later? I prefer a little more privacy," Morris added.

"Come on!" Penn said with a laugh. "It's been weeks. We're past all that."

Morris snorted at the door. "No. No, we're not. I'm not past having dignity and prefer to keep some things to myself."

"Really?" Penn made a thoughtful sound. "We all have bodies and they pretty much do the same things."

"I like boundaries. And reading the news and doing my business in peace."

"Hmmm...Are you sure that's good for you?"

"What?" Morris's eyelids fluttered. He wasn't sure what Penn was talking about or why he was making the moment as awkward as possible.

"Reading the news while you're handling your morning business. I think I saw something that said that raising stress levels while you're having a bowel mov—"

"Hey! Thanks for the tip. If you could just carry on with whatever it was you were doing, that would be great." Morris gave the mirror a loaded look, wondering *why* this was happening to him.

"What's wrong? Get a little squeamish when someone mentions poo—"

"No!" Morris objected, then cleared his throat. "I don't enjoy talking about *anything* when I'm using the restroom," he explained slowly.

"My bad!" Penn said and gave the door a jaunty tap. "I just thought that we had bonded and were cool now." The door opened and he tossed Morris another roll.

"We are cool," Morris said, lunging and swiping it from the air as the door swung shut. "But I'll never be that kind of cool with another human being. I wasn't even cool with using the bathroom around Michelle."

"Fair enough, I guess. Hope everything comes out alright," Penn said before it became quiet in the hallway.

Morris listened until he was sure Penn had gone. "I don't know what kind of commune he thinks we're starting here but some things will remain sacred," he said with a firm nod. He quickly placed a roll on the holder, ready to put the episode with Penn behind him. He gave it a yank to remove a long strip and Morris let out a yelp when it wouldn't rip. "Damn it, Penn!" There was a hysterical cackle from the hall. "This isn't funny," Morris called, but Penn's laughter just grew louder.

"Pretty sure it is!" Penn called back before the door opened again. This time, Penn lobbed a whole new, unopened pack of Charmin in Morris's direction.

"Thank you!" Morris snapped despite the laughter building in his chest.

"Someone sounds like a grumpy pants," Penn baby-talked through the door. "There's no reason to be in a crappy mood."

"Ha ha." Morris had to bite down on his lips because Michelle would have definitely appreciated the pun. Although, she would have told Morris to knock off his crap or would have said he was being shitty. Penn never cussed, though, so she'd have to settle for his G-rated version. "Well done, you two," he declared as he washed and dried his hands. "How did you know?" Morris asked when he pulled on his robe and opened the door.

Penn was leaning with his shoulder propped against the wall. "Found a few rolls myself and figured she'd left some in here too."

"You could have warned me," Morris suggested, and Penn shook his head.

"I ain't a snitch and I can recognize a master at work when I see one," he said as he tossed Morris the fake roll. "Plus, you're really cute when you're flustered. I've never seen anyone get so uncomfortable talking about *that*."

"I don't like talking about anything when I'm on the toilet. It's weird."

"Why?" Penn challenged. "Everyone poops. There's even a book about it in the nursery if you don't believe me."

"It is too early to be having this conversation."

"Hang onto at least one of those," Penn said as he gestured at the unrippable roll. "Wait until Cadence is old enough to laugh at bathroom jokes, then tell her about how her mommy was a prank sniper and use it to get Evie or your dad."

"Or you. It would serve you right," Morris said without thinking, then paused. Would Penn still be around? It had only been a little more than two weeks, but Morris didn't like the idea of Penn *not* being there.

"It certainly would," Penn replied. "But you got another thing coming if you think I won't be ready," he said with a salute and was whistling as he turned on his heel and jogged down the stairs. "Coffee's ready and I'm making waffles."

"Awesome. That almost makes up for the shit he just put me through," Morris muttered under his breath. A sharp laugh slipped from him and he clapped a hand over his mouth. Morris listened to see if Penn had heard him or if he'd woken Cadence.

All was calm and quiet so he ducked back into the bathroom and shut the door behind him. He began to whistle the fragments of a new melody and Morris took a moment to appreciate how *normal* he felt. The empty ache was already returning, but for just a few moments he had felt like his old self. And Morris had felt closer to Michelle and it had felt good, instead of feeling like something that could push him over the edge again.

"Maybe I'll get through the day without breaking down," he said and went to gather the unrippable rolls of toilet paper and put them away for Cadence. One day, she'd help Morris get his revenge.

Chapter Ten

If all else fails, talk to him while he's on the toilet.

He HATES that!

M ichelle was right and Penn thought she would have been pleased with how well the prank had gone. He hoped she enjoyed how much Morris had squirmed because it had cost Penn dearly.

The result had been hilarious and Penn couldn't wait to recount every moment in detail later to Reid and Gavin. But now he had to live with the sight of Morris's nearly naked body trapped in his brain. Penn hadn't meant to catch a glimpse of Morris when he opened the door to toss him the toilet paper, but there were *a lot* of big mirrors in that bathroom. Morris had held a towel over his groin, but what Penn had seen had been... perfect. And that quick glimpse wasn't going away and Penn was enjoying it far more than he should in very inappropriate ways.

That hand towel hadn't covered enough to stop Penn's imagination. Penn loved men of all shapes and sizes, but he had a thing for shorter, stockier men. Luckily for Penn, most men were shorter than him. And it hadn't been that long since Penn had gotten laid—just a few days before he was sent to care for Morris and Cadence, actually. So Penn was a little confused as to why the sight of Morris's naked body had *him* squirming.

It had been really *good*, though, what Penn had seen. And now Penn was imagining Morris naked as he sat at the dinner table. Morris was wearing a T-shirt and joggers and murmuring to himself as he assessed Penn's laptop. But he was gloriously naked from Penn's vantage point in the kitchen.

Morris was deliciously solid in the middle with wide, hard pecs. And those thick thighs and all that smooth dark brown skin... He had a lot of ass too and it was so firm and round. Penn had caught himself checking it out every time Morris's back was turned.

"I think I know what the problem is," Morris said, glancing up from the table. He bit into his lip and Penn held his breath.

His lips!

They were so perfect. Penn wanted to suck on them. And other things. Morris took good care of his feet and he had nice toes.

"Would you like to know?" Morris asked, frowning at Penn over the top of the screen.

"Hmmm?" Penn gave his head a shake and blamed it on their evening joint. He'd been in an odd mood after the toilet paper prank, both elated at how successful he and Michelle had been as a team and profoundly *sad* at how much he could miss someone he barely knew. Which made him miss his mother too.

He'd tucked all those turbulent emotions away until he could work them out over the sewing machine. Penn was making Cadence a pink and green quilt from some of Michelle's college and sorority sweatshirts. He'd saved the nicest ones for Cadence to wear later, but Penn picked several that matched the many photos of Michelle around her room and the rest of the house. He'd make copies of the photos and put them in an album so Cadence could see where her quilt had come from and hopefully feel more connected to Michelle when she used it.

But Penn couldn't immerse himself in memories of Michelle—see dozens of pictures of her incredible smile, smell her perfume, and touch all the things she cherished without some of her spirit imprinting on him. He'd done his best to be bright and upbeat for Morris and Cadence throughout the day, but it caught up with Penn after he put the baby to bed.

He meditated while they smoked, hoping for his usual clarity and calm. Instead, he got a text from Gavin about his expenses. Both Gavin and Reid were adamant that Penn be reimbursed for all expenses, including train and cab fare and any groceries he had purchased while taking care of Morris and Cadence. Even Penny was getting reimbursed for her deliveries to Morris's.

Penn didn't keep those kinds of records and he didn't really care about money. He had enough to pay his bills, get where he needed to go, and a nice cushion in case he, his friends, or his family had an emergency. That was all he needed, and Reid made sure all of his nannies were well-compensated and were paid on time so Penn didn't worry about his finances. Except when Gavin got on his case about his taxes or filing his expenses.

If there was anything Penn cared about less than money, it was technology. He loved his phone because he could take pictures and keep in touch with his dad, Penny, and his friends. And Penn loved the apps on his phone that helped him keep tabs on his dad and monitor the baby. But he didn't have a Twitter, a Tinder, or a TikTok, and Penn had no idea what people did with them.

He was even more clueless when it came to his laptop and had brought it down to ask Morris for help when it kept freezing after he turned it on. All Penn wanted to do was get into his bank account and look through the last few weeks of purchases so he had *something* to give Gavin.

"Would you like my professional opinion?" Morris asked, shutting Penn's laptop.

"I should have tried restarting it?" Penn guessed, and Morris's lips pulled tight as he stared at him. "I love that I can always tell what you're thinking," Penn said with a wave at Morris. His eyes and his face gave everything away and Morris *always* wore his heart on his sleeve. Penn didn't need his extra empathic abilities to know what mood Morris was in.

"And what am I thinking right now?" Morris asked as he sat back and crossed his arms over his chest. His T-shirt tightened around his shoulders and biceps rather nicely, but Penn still pictured Morris naked.

"Um..." Penn squinted, sifting through Morris's usual aura of grumpiness and sensing that he was deeply confused. "How did I mess up a perfectly decent laptop?" Penn attempted.

That got a severely exasperated snort from Morris as he pushed back his chair and stood. He picked up the laptop and held it out to Penn. "It *was* a perfectly decent laptop. Ten years ago, Penn. I can't believe it even turned on, but I wanted to get past the home screen just so I could go back in time to 2013."

"It still worked."

"When?" Morris countered, looking bewildered as Penn took it from him.

"I don't know..." Penn's lips twisted as he studied it. "Three weeks ago. Maybe..." His eyes flicked to the ceiling and he tried to remember the last time he'd checked his email or his bank account.

"How do you go *three weeks* without touching a computer?"

"Want to see me go for three months? Gavin would have a nervous breakdown, but I think I can do it." Penn flashed Morris a cocky grin and wiggled his brows.

"Do you need someone to teach you how to use a computer, because I've got time," Morris offered. "We could get you a decent laptop. I've got a few downstairs that I don't use. It wouldn't take long to set one up and put everything you need right where it's easy to find. I can teach you how to do anything you want to do."

"Do I get to teach you something in return?" Penn asked silkily, then paused.

What did you just do there?

But it was too late. Morris stared back at him with wide, unblinking eyes, his confusion growing like a pit between them. "Did you have something particular in mind?" He asked slowly and licked his lips again, snagging Penn's focus.

His eyes lingered on Morris's mouth. "A few things, actually," Penn admitted quietly. "But I'm sure you don't need a teacher," he added as he swung his head, flipping his hair over his shoulder. Penn hugged the laptop as he came around the table, pausing by Morris's chair. "Gavin can send me a new computer if it's that serious. You know where I'll be if you're still in the mood to teach me a lesson," he drawled, then tapped his brow in salute as he left Morris.

Penn didn't look back. He headed up the stairs before Morris could ask if he was joking or if he'd hit his head.

The truth was, Penn didn't know why he did it or what he would have done if Morris had flirted back. It was a terrible idea and Penn knew better. He never hooked up with anyone he could hurt. Penn couldn't risk either party developing feelings, so friends were off-limits. And Morris was in an extra special tier of untouchable friends because he was also one of Reid's best friends and Penn didn't want to lose either of them.

He couldn't help himself, though. Penn had tried to numb the loneliness with pot and it hadn't worked. He was still restless and aching after a day of being haunted by Morris's thighs and Michelle's smile. His sewing machine and memories of his mother were waiting in his room, but Penn didn't want to be alone, and he didn't want to cry on Cadence's quilt.

Penn's conscience caught up with him by the time he reached the top of the stairs. He had no business confusing Morris, no matter how muddled and lonely he felt. They were both in a vulnerable state, but Penn had been trusted to help Morris. Penn had learned enough about Morris to know that he wasn't built for flings. He was more traditional and a romantic who'd always wear his heart on his sleeve.

"If things were different," he told himself as he turned on the light and considered the sewing machine and the long hours ahead of him. "But they're not, so let it go," he said and mentally rolled up his sleeves and went to work.

Chapter Eleven

Morris was still pondering Penn's offer when they met at the coffee maker the next morning. Try as he might, Morris couldn't get it out of his head and he couldn't come up with a non-sexual way to interpret it.

Not that he minded.

It was just...

With Penn?

The idea wasn't nearly as ridiculous as it should have been and Morris hadn't dismissed it as quickly as he would have liked. In fact, it gnawed at him as he lay in bed and stared at the ceiling, listening for the faint hum of the sewing machine. He thought about getting out of bed and going upstairs and asking, but it was what would happen next that kept Morris safely under the covers.

Morris imagined accepting Penn's invitation and was enthralled and aroused. His hands had even wandered under the duvet and Morris was really into it until his heart and his common sense chimed in and asked what it all meant and what Penn wanted.

Then, Morris imagined Penn laughing and saying it was just a joke. That made a lot more sense and Morris was far more comfortable believing that. Penn might have left a door cracked, but Morris would have kicked it off its hinges if he turned up in the middle of the night to ask if he was serious. How did they come back from that? What if they couldn't?

Penn nudged Morris. "You okay?"

"Me? Yeah."

"Are you sure? You're extra quiet, but you're busy in there," Penn said as he pointed at Morris's forehead.

"I had a weird night," Morris said dismissively, ready to change the subject. "Mom messaged and said she's stopping by after she checks in at the bakery."

It was nice, the way Penn's face lit up and he pumped his fist. "Excellent! Evie's the best," he declared.

"I'm glad you think so. Most people are scared of Mom."

"Evie? What's there to be scared of?" Penn asked while preparing a bottle for Cadence. She was due to be up soon.

Morris snorted as he began hunting for something to eat with his coffee. "You've never been on her bad side and you're a hard worker so she doesn't get in your business."

Penn just laughed and waved it off. "You have to be a shark to run a successful business in this city. There's a fruit salad in the fridge and I made an English muffin loaf," he said as he pointed at a rustic-looking loaf on the counter. "There are some sliced tomatoes and mashed-up avocados in the fridge too for the toast if you're feeling decadent," he added with a wink. They heard Cadence cry from both of their phones. "My lady awaits," Penn said, giving the bottle an excited shake. He encouraged Morris to eat as he climbed the stairs.

"Thank God that was normal," Morris whispered to himself and whistled in relief as he went to prepare himself some avocado toast. The bread was glorious, toasted and slathered with buttery avocado, a thick slice of tomato, and a generous pinch of sea salt. He was happily munching on a piece at the counter when Penn returned with the baby. "Look at my girl!" Morris said, wiping his mouth so he could give her a kiss when Penn danced up to him and presented her cheek.

Morris finally understood why people got so silly about babies. Cadence smelled intoxicating and the sound of her laughter gave Morris goosebumps. And she was beginning to develop little rolls on her legs and arms! Morris made a loud growling sound as he chomped on her cheek. It was plump and soft like a ripe tomato and Cadence cooed back at him.

"Magic, right?" Penn said.

"Yes, she is!" Morris baby-talked. He gave her nose a nip.

Penn laughed softly. "But you might want to wait until the little lady has had a good burp."

"I'm good!" Morris held up his hands and leaned away.

"Any minute now," Penn sang as he went back to bouncing and patting her on the back. "I don't want to put you down until you've burped good and proper because I know you'll turn into a milk volcano if I don't," he told Cadence, but Morris sighed dramatically.

"It was just the one time and how many times do I have to tell you I'm sorry?"

They laughed, then glanced at the oven when the timer went off.

"That's a sourdough for our lunch."

"Want me to get it?" Morris asked, but Penn shook his head.

"I've got it!" He hurried to the table and snapped Cadence into the bouncer's harness. Penn gave Cadence a stern look as he backed away from her. "Do not erupt while my back is turned." He pointed before he spun and dashed to the oven, swiping a mitt off the counter as he passed. Penn had the loaf out and on a trivet in seconds and dashed back around the counter. "Alright, Madame Vesuvius!" He said as he unbuckled the harness, but they both heard the hiccup and knew it was too late. "Noooooo!" Penn cried, shielding his face and Morris dove to protect his plate as a tidal wave of milk spewed from Cadence.

Morris hissed sympathetically "You were so close!"

"I..." Penn laughed as he looked down at himself in dismay. Milk dripped from his beard, down his neck, and the front of his T-shirt was drenched. "I guess I was too close. I got some in my mouth," he said, shivering as he gagged.

Morris covered his mouth and tried not to laugh, but his chest shook and his eyes began to water. Milk dripped from Cadence's chair and the table and her onesie was completely saturated.

"To be fair, you did tell her not to erupt *while* your back was turned," Morris pointed out with a sheepish smile.

Penn didn't miss a beat. "I should have been more specific," he agreed and looked out the back doors at the garden. "It's already hot out," he said distantly.

"It's supposed to be in the mid-nineties..." Morris said, shrugging in confusion. He didn't see what the temperature outside had to do with the likelihood of volcanic eruptions inside the house.

"Beach party!" Penn declared as he scooped Cadence out of her seat. "I'll set up the lily pad pool from your parents and we can have a beach day while I clean the bouncer. I planned to do it this weekend anyways," he said with a shrug.

Penn was fully invested in his beach party plan and had transformed the backyard in less than half an hour. The French doors were thrown open, the floors had received a quick mopping, and an inflatable pond with an adjustable lily shade and sprinklers now took up most of the garden.

Cadence had been slathered with sunscreen and looked too precious in her shimmery pink bikini. It had a tutu and Penn had found a matching pink hat and sunglasses for extra protection from the sun. Not that the sun had a chance of finding Cadence with the pool under the oak tree and the shade guarding her.

Morris was more concerned for his own safety at the moment. He was in the kitchen, leaning against the counter and well away from the back porch and the sun, but felt like he was suffering heat stroke over the sight of Penn splashing in the pool with Cadence.

The chair's frame and cover were drying outside and Penn had left the wider, unshaded half of the pool in the sun so he could work on his tan. Penn didn't have any swim trunks so he'd borrowed a pair from Morris.

Unfortunately for Morris, he only had a few pairs packed away in his closet. Michelle had picked them for their trip to Greece and they were all on the short and tight side. She had been on a mission to find Morris a rich husband, but her plan had backfired. The husband hunters had swarmed Morris, calling him "Daddy" and "Sir." While Morris may have been too shy and old-fashioned to accept any of their offers, he did enjoy seeing Michelle's grand matchmaking plans go up in smoke. Even if it was at his own expense.

Morris watched Penn breach the surface of the shallow pool and screech as he dove toward Cadence, making her shriek and kick in delight. The swim trunks slid down Penn's waist, revealing the hard, round swells of his ass and a peek of the cleft before he yanked them up and dove again. The view was even "worse" from the front whenever they slid down Penn's narrower hips. Every now and then, there would be a flash of Penn's Adonis belt and the thin trail of hair beneath his navel and Morris's mouth would go dry.

There was a knock at the door before it opened and Morris turned and waved when his mother let herself in.

"Knock knock!" She called excitedly. "Thought I'd check in and see if you're free tomorrow." Evelyn dropped her tote bag on the table as she ran to give Morris a hug.

"That depends on what's going on tomorrow," he said, bending so she could kiss his cheek.

"Brunch?" She suggested. But her eyes lit up when she spotted Cadence and Penn.

Morris hoped she was distracted enough to let him out of brunch. "I might be busy..."

"Doing what?" She challenged, her focus sharpening as she cocked a brow at Morris. "Your father's starting to get out again but it's still too much for him to come all the way from Park Slope. He almost came over on the train while I was at the bakery the other day," she said, clicking her teeth and shaking her head.

"What?" Morris groaned and rubbed his temple. "His immune system's not ready for that."

"He knows better but he misses you and the baby."

"I'm sorry! I'll bring her tomorrow for brunch," Morris

conceded quickly. He knew that phone calls and videos of the baby weren't enough. They talked a couple of times a day and texted almost hourly, but his father was a hugger and he'd always been hands-on when they were little.

"He understands!" Evelyn said. She gathered Morris's face in her hands and hummed as she looked him over. "He's been worried sick about you, but you look better."

"I'm okay. I told Dad that I've been sleeping and Penn makes sure I eat."

"Telling us doesn't make it true, does it? I can see that you're feeling better and I'll tell him. But he'll need to see it for himself."

"Okay. I'll bring Cadie tomorrow."

"And Penn," she added, and Morris's nose wrinkled.

"I don't think—" He started, but she cut him off.

"We want to thank him for all he's done for you and Cadence."

Morris shook his head. "It would be weird to ask Penn to spend his day off with us."

"He's family now. Why on Earth would it be weird?"

"I'll ask him but I'm not going to push it if he has plans." Morris would ask but make sure that Penn knew it was totally cool if he had other things to do.

"Why don't I ask him right now?" She unhooked her sunglasses from the opened collar of her polo shirt.

"No! Let me ask him later!" Morris attempted but she shushed and swatted at him.

"What's going on out here?" Evelyn asked, putting on her sunglasses as she charged out onto the back patio and obliterated Morris's plan.

"Um... She threw up all over her bouncer and Penn decided to make it a 'beach day' since it's so hot," Morris explained as he intercepted her. "He's busy. I'll talk to him about it when Cadie's down for a nap."

"I'm sure you will," she said and rolled her eyes. "I don't blame you for wanting to keep him all to yourself." Her arm curled around Morris's and he didn't like the calculating smirk on his mother's face as she checked Penn out.

"Stop it."

"Make me," she dared him. "And you're either blind or a fool. Just look at him," she said and purred. "I like all that long and lean. Especially his legs. Looks like he could wrap them around you twice," she said, adding an appreciative groan.

"Mom!" Morris's face twisted.

"Are you blind or do you think I am?" She asked, turning and raising a brow.

"We're just friends. And I think I'm *technically* his boss."

"So?" She challenged. "I was friendly with your father before we started going steady. And Reid and Gavin still sign Penn's paychecks, if I'm not mistaken."

He gave her a dubious look. "You're reaching, and Dad said it was love at first sight."

"Not for me," his mother replied, then leaned toward Morris. "I thought he was too sweet," she confided in a loud whisper, making him laugh. His father was not sweet, but he had always worshiped Evelyn. "Thought he'd let me walk all over him, but he knows when a firm hand is needed," she added suggestively.

"*Mom.*"

She laughed as she skipped down the back steps. "I didn't know we were going to the beach! I would have brought a swimsuit!"

Morris didn't want to think about Penn's legs or the rest of him. Not like that. He recalled Reid saying that Penn didn't date. But not in the way that Reid didn't date. Morris had a feeling Penn's easiness with affection and nudity extended to sex. He was just generally more comfortable with his body and Morris sensed that Penn operated more on instinct and chemistry than tradition and societal norms.

Free love might work for Penn's city hippie lifestyle, but Morris was too much like his father. He was too romantic for hook-ups and Morris *wanted* someone to worship. One of his fondest childhood memories was of his father dropping *everything* whenever Percy Sledge came on so he could say "They're playing our song, Evie!" and pull her into his arms. It didn't matter if they were on a train or in a department store. Morris Sr. would insist and she'd pretend he was silly and making a scene, but Morris saw the twinkle in his mother's eyes and he saw his parents go back in time.

Their love was built to last and it kept them young, even when times were tough or the unspeakable happened. Morris saw how his parents turned to each other for support and strength and the way they fought for each other. *That's* what Morris wanted and he wasn't going to settle for less.

He felt a pang of sadness as he watched Penn splashing in the little pool with Cadence. Morris couldn't help but wonder how life with Penn would be different if they were more than friends. He was surprised by how happy the idea made him and how easy it was to imagine the two of them dancing the way his parents did.

Penn was so far from the type of men Morris usually lusted after. Morris admittedly shallow and his tastes tended toward football, soccer, and basketball players. And he had a weakness for men in good tailoring. Especially that flash of bare ankle when a fine man wore a fine suit with a sexy Italian Oxford...

Just the thought had Morris's body tightening, but he grew even warmer when Penn rose on his knees to adjust the sunshade for Cadence. Water spilled down Penn's tight, tattooed stomach and thighs, completely wiping all thoughts of bare ankles and Oxfords from Morris's mind.

"They're playing our song, Penn," he murmured softly and Morris chuckled to himself as he turned from the back garden. They'd probably be safe because you rarely heard Kid 'n Play at the dentist or a department store.

Chapter Twelve

"I'm telling you, this isn't a big deal! It's just brunch," Penn insisted. Morris was still disgruntled as he got out of the car and went to free Cadence from her car seat. Penn waited, resting his arms on the hood. "I'm looking forward to this. Who doesn't love brunch?" Penn added, earning a flat look from Morris.

"You practically live with us now and you're using your day off to hang out with my parents."

"I still don't see the problem. Sounds like a good time and I would have said I had other plans if I didn't want to go."

Everyone knew Morris's parents because his mom owned Slice of Evelyn, and that was the bakery their friend group patronized if they needed the perfect cake or cupcakes for an important occasion. Evelyn had become a social media star for her baking tutorials.

But Penn *loved* Morris's dad. He was recovering from chemo like Penn's father and only ventured out a few times a week. Morris had visited his parents a handful of times with Cadence so Penn could have a morning or an afternoon off.

Penn hadn't tagged along because it was good for Morris to stretch his legs and practice his parenting skills on his own. He was getting more confident and a beautiful bond was developing between him and Cadence.

"I want you to remember you said that and we're going to circle back and see if your feelings have changed after spending an afternoon with them." Morris had Cadence and the diaper bag as he came around the car and tossed his chin at his parents' brownstone.

Penn waved dismissively. "You put up with Penny Lane and her shenanigans. I can't see how this could be more exhausting than an afternoon with her."

They climbed the steps together and Morris juggled Cadence so he could press the buzzer. "I love Penny and you better watch what you say about her or we're gonna fight," Morris said, giving Penn a teasing nudge with his elbow.

Penn was glad Morris and Penny had clicked so well and was happy to share his little sister. She was his pride and joy. He might pretend she was a pest now and then, because it was obligatory as a big brother, but he had adored his carrot-haired sister from the moment he first laid eyes on her.

Gus often said she was just like their mother and Penn could see it more and more each day. Penn had never minded looking after her and liked to let Penny tag along, especially after their mother died. It had made it easier, having a piece of his mother to hold onto. Reid and Gavin had helped, of course, and Penn credited the whole gang at Briarwood Terrace with helping raise Penny. Now she had Morris as well. He'd be an awesome big brother and she'd make him laugh and enchant him the way she had delighted Penn since she was an infant.

"She's pretty great," Penn conceded just as the door opened.

Evelyn answered, looking stunning in a soft blue maxi dress

and sandals. Penn was used to seeing her in a crisp pair of jeans, bright white sneakers, and a polo shirt with the bakery's logo on it. She looked like a breath of fresh air and utterly relaxed as she welcomed them and took possession of the baby.

"Oh! Gramma's missed her little dumplin'." She cooed at Cadence while offering Morris and Penn her cheek.

"Hey, Mom," Morris mumbled as he kissed her and went to hang up his coat.

"You don't look old enough to be anyone's grandmother, Evie," Penn said with a kiss to her other cheek. "You're even lovelier when you're off the clock, ma'am."

"You better not be hitting on my wife, son," an older Black man rumbled as he ambled into the foyer and leaned on a cane.

Penn's eyes lit up and he was grinning as he turned. "You picking a fight with me on a Sunday, Morrie?" He asked and spread his arms wide, rushing over to get a hug.

The older man reached for Penn with his free arm and laughed as they clasped each other tight. "I was wondering when you'd show your face around here," Morris Sr. said with an affectionate pat to Penn's cheek.

"I can't smother Morris and it's good for him to get out with Cadie," Penn explained.

"Wait. You know each other?" Morris the younger asked.

Penn put an arm around Morris Sr. and they both laughed. "I thought you knew. Our dads have the same oncologist and did their chemo at the same clinic. I recognized Morrie from the bakery and he remembered me so I introduced him to my dad," Penn explained.

Morris Sr. gave Penn's chest a poke. "This is Gus's boy! The one I've been telling you about for months. He always had the good lollipops and extra Chapstick and beanies," he said and Penn waved it off.

He'd learned that patients often suffered from dry mouth

and that their lips chapped easily during chemo. And Fin was happy to send binfuls of blankets and scarves from Warm Things whenever Penn took Gus to his appointments because chemotherapy often caused cold sensitivity as well.

"They kicked us out of the clinic and said we can't come back," Penn joked. "Now we hang out at the diner every other Sunday afternoon to complain about the Knicks."

Morris Sr.'s grin grew wider as he looked at Penn. "I knew they'd be in good hands if Reid sent you," he said sincerely, catching Penn off guard.

He enjoyed accompanying Gus to lunch with Morris Sr. They had started out as "chemo buddies" and Penn believed "Morrie" had been crucial to Gus's recovery. Penn got a kick out of their gruff, persnickety banter and was grateful for their flourishing friendship. Their bond had strengthened Gus and often motivated him to get out of the house when his spirits were low. But Penn wasn't expecting those kind words from Morris Sr. He always said he saved all his sweetness for "the missus."

"Thanks, but that little girl over there has me in the palm of her tiny hand," Penn said and pointed at Cadence. She was squealing as Evelyn chewed loudly on her cheeks and the sound brought a loopy grin to Penn's face and gave him goose-bumps. "Tell me that's not the best thing you've ever heard."

"Makes your soul feel ten times lighter, doesn't it?" Morris Sr. agreed. "I've got the game on," he said, beckoning for Penn to follow as he turned for the living room.

"Oh no, you don't!" Evelyn said and wagged a finger at them. "We invited Penn to brunch so we could get to know each other better, not to yell obscenities at the TV."

"But we already know each other and they were trash last night," Morris Sr. argued. "And this guy never swears!"

He pointed at Penn but Evelyn wasn't having it. She

narrowed her eyes and her head tilted threateningly. "Those potatoes aren't going to fry themselves."

"Yes, ma'am!" Morris Sr. gave her a snappy salute and headed for the kitchen.

She rolled her eyes and was shaking her head as she turned to Morris. "You show Penn around and fix yourselves some mimosas. I have a new dress for Cadie and we need to get ready for brunch," she declared, then left in an elegant, imperious huff.

"Told you," Morris muttered under his breath and gestured at the dining room on their right.

"What are you talking about? We haven't been here for ten minutes and this is already the best brunch ever."

"Don't you go to Reid's for brunch just about every weekend?" Morris asked and Penn shrugged.

"It's a standing thing and it's always a good time. But you know how Reid and Gavin are. They're all about order and dependability. Your mom, on the other hand, embraces spontaneity and she has comedic flair and an eye for drama. Is she expecting more people?"

"It's just us. She always goes overboard. And why would you want any of that at brunch?" Morris asked as he reached for one of the bottles of champagne. There were four chilling in a punch bowl along with carafes of orange, peach, and pineapple juices.

"Because it beats listening to Gavin grumble about the stock market. You should come, though. They'd be so stoked to have Cadie there and I know they miss you," Penn suggested and watched Morris closely. It was obvious that Morris missed the gang and Penn sensed that he might be a little jealous.

"Maybe. Mom's started taking every other weekend off and wants to keep Cadie for us so we're free," he said quietly and looked over his shoulder.

"That's cool, right?" Penn asked and thanked Morris when he passed him a glass.

"It's great that she's taking a break from work and I'm glad they're getting more time with the baby. I just don't like what's behind it and there's too much expectation attached," Morris explained. Sort of.

"What are you talking about? I think it's great," Penn said, keeping his voice down.

Morris snorted into his glass. "Why is it great?" He challenged.

"Well... Aside from some much-needed rest for Evie and all the time Cadie gets with her grandparents, that's more time for you!" Penn looked at him like it was super obvious and a great thing, but Morris's face twisted into a sneer.

"Exactly. And Mom's already got a long list of ways that I can use that time. She thinks that I should get back into the studio or into skating or join a book club or *hang out with Reid more*." His brows rose pointedly. "She's giving me all this extra time and she isn't going to be happy if I play *Fortnight* in my underwear and eat nothing but cereal all weekend, is she?"

"I see your point..." Penn said. He could also see Morris stretched out on the sofa in his underwear and Penn really wanted to join him. He gave his head a quick shake to clear it. "Couldn't you meet her halfway? Because it isn't a terrible idea." Penn flashed him a sheepish look. "They're still skating in the park on the weekends. You could get in some skating and check in with Reid, then spend the rest of the weekend in your underwear. I won't tell your mom how much cereal you eat." He winked and took a sip from his glass.

"Did she put you up to this?" Morris looked at Penn like he was a traitor.

"She did not."

The conversation was dropped and immediately forgotten

when Evelyn returned with Cadence. Morris and Penn pushed and slapped at each other as they hurried around the table to get their hands on the baby. She was dressed in a blue sundress, bloomers, and sandals and looked like a perfect little clone of her grandmother.

"Look at my princess!" Morris pushed his glass at Penn, then reached for Cadence.

Penn accepted defeat gracefully and took a long drink from Morris's glass. "Might as well since you're driving."

"Let's go out back and take some pictures!" Morris said to the baby, dancing her from the room.

"Nice! We can add them to the collage," Penn said and Evelyn laughed softly as she watched them go.

"I'm glad we've got a moment to ourselves." She wound her arm around Penn's. "Mind if we talk in the hall? I want to keep an eye on the kitchen. The sink's acting up and I don't want Morris Sr. messing with it. I've got a plumber coming on Monday, but I wouldn't put it past my husband to poke his head under there the moment my back is turned."

"I can take a look at it," Penn offered, but she shushed him.

"I wanted to talk to you about Morris while we've got a minute. You've done wonders for him already and I can't thank you enough."

"That's what I'm here for and there's nothing I wouldn't do for Morris and Cadence," Penn said sincerely. "They're mine now too."

A happy sigh wafted from Evelyn as she hugged Penn's arm. "That's why I know I can trust you. Morris needs a gentle nudge—from someone other than me—to get out more and...do something," she whispered up at him.

Penn hummed in amusement, but he was more interested in the sink. His neck swiveled as he tried to look into the kitchen and troubleshoot from the hallway. Morris Sr. was currently grating potatoes at the sink but the water wasn't running. "He's on to you."

"Who?" Evelyn turned Penn's chin so he'd focus on her.

"Morris Jr., he knows this is a ploy to get him out more."

"Don't think of it as a ploy. Think of it as a mother looking after her son *and* a grandmother enjoying more time with her beloved grandchild."

"Is there a different definition for ploy? Because it sounds like you're plotting," Penn said, clicking his teeth at Evelyn.

"What's your point and are you in or are you out?" She cut her eyes at him and he laughed.

"Like you have to ask. I'm in and I have an excellent solution," he said, then smirked wickedly at her over his glass. "But it's gonna cost you."

"What do you mean?" She asked suspiciously.

"I'll tell you if you'll let me take care of that sink."

"Oh, you—!" She swatted his shoulder. "You can look at it after we eat. Tell me."

"I was already on your side. Morris should get out and do something that makes him happy. When he's ready," Penn stipulated.

"I don't want to rush him, Penn, but I can't lose both of my children," she said, her voice cracking into a shredded whisper.

"Shhh!" Penn was careful not to spill either of his glasses as he put an arm around her and kissed her temple. "I won't let that happen. I promise I'll keep an eye on him and I've got the whole team backing me up. My sister Penny's already adopted him and she won't leave him alone once she finds out he can skate. And you know Reid and Gavin are looking out for Morris."

She nodded and let out a shaky laugh. "I'm so glad he has all of you to get him *into* trouble."

"We do our best," Penn said and passed her Morris's mimosa. She tapped her glass against his and raised it.

"You know, I wouldn't mind if Morris wasn't getting out because he was spending more time with you," she said, winking at him before taking a drink.

Penn coughed into his glass and shook his head. "I'm gonna stop you right there. I love Morris and I won't deny that he's a *beautiful* man. But I love him as a friend and I don't do relationships."

"We'll see," Evelyn replied enigmatically and left Penn to check on the quiches and a French toast casserole in the oven.

He felt like he'd been outplayed as he topped off his drink before heading out back to join Morris and Cadence. Morris was lying on his back on a patch of plush green grass with the baby in the crook of his arm. He was holding his phone above their heads and might have been recording so Penn stayed on the patio, observing and enjoying his mimosa.

Penn blamed it on Evelyn, but told himself it couldn't hurt, as he imagined lying on the grass with Morris and the baby and the three of them taking family pictures. Penn allowed himself to become enthralled with the vision for a moment. He'd never taken anything that far, even in his head, with any of the men he'd been with. He never imagined anything more than a night or two because anything else was asking for trouble.

But he could see the three of them so vividly as Penn watched Morris and the baby. They were a family and they were *happy*. They were the center of Penn's universe and that scared him. That was a lot to lose and how would that change Penn? Too many people relied on him and Penn *liked* being the person people came to first when they needed help. That exchange of trust and love fed Penn's soul. Loving *everyone* was the core of his identity. Could he still do that if he gave his heart to Morris and Cadence? They'd deserve no less.

Morris smirked dreamily at the phone's camera, snapping Penn back to reality. The pictures from that sexy photo shoot had been all over the city, including on billboards in Times Square. Penn had been with men from all walks of life, but none of them had appeared in a sexy magazine spread and been proclaimed a musical savant. Penn chuckled into his glass as he imagined how ridiculous they'd look together.

It was a vivid vision and Penn didn't like how embarrassed it made him feel. He frowned down at his plaid shirt and brown corduroys, his preppiest ensemble. Penn raided Gavin's closet if he needed something for a formal event. Meanwhile, Morris carried himself like a model, even in a T-shirt and joggers. And his sneaker collection was insured because Morris owned pairs of Nikes that were worth more than cars. Everything Penn owned either came from a thrift shop or was a hand-me-down from Gavin. Penn found a way to recycle everything three or four times while Morris always had that "new clothes" smell.

He'd seen the inside of Morris's linen closet while putting away the towels. If anything proved how absurdly mismatched they were, it was Morris's bathroom. Penn would take another peek at it whenever he needed reminding. Morris was on the opposite end of the spectrum from Penn with his serums and sugar scrubs. And there were dozens of colognes. Penn thought that was great and appreciated Morris's efforts because he smelled as beautiful as he looked. But people would laugh if they saw them together and Morris would probably scream if he looked in Penn's bathroom.

Deodorants used scary chemicals to block pores and coat the skin so Penn didn't use them. He relied on good hygiene and a clean diet to maintain a pleasant personal aroma. He washed his hair and body with a bar soap he cured himself. It was made from nettles, goat milk, and shea butter. Penn added rosemary, eucalyptus, and lemon oils because they were great for his scalp and smelled fresh and bright.

They couldn't be more different, and Penn didn't want to change, so he waved and smiled at Morris and the baby, then went inside to see if he could get a peek at the sink.

Chapter Thirteen

His mother had said something to Penn. Morris could tell by how quiet Penn had become and he would redirect the conversation every time someone asked him a personal question. He'd find an excuse to compliment Morris's mother, get his dad on one of his tangents, or brag about how perfect Cadence was.

Morris tried to engage Penn as they were clearing the table, but couldn't compete with the sink for his attention. Biding his time was Morris's best option and it was nearly time to go, from the looks of things.

"He should be done soon," Morris said to Evelyn while hunting for Cadence's travel wipes.

Evelyn smiled softly and shook her head at the kitchen. "You'd better snatch him up! He's handy and can cook *and* he changes diapers."

"You said something, didn't you? Don't start with that again," he begged, looking around to make sure no one had heard her.

"Something's changed between the two of you," she

accused and pointed at Morris.

"They have not," he said firmly, but she hummed like she could see right through him.

"You know, I taught you to look people in the eye when you're talking to them and to give them your undivided attention if you want them to respect you."

"Yes, ma'am…" He didn't know where this was going, but she had taught him to always carry himself with confidence and demand respect.

"But you don't look like you're thinking respectable thoughts when you're talking to Penn."

Morris shook his head. "You're imagining things."

"Ha!" She wagged a finger at him. "You're hanging on every word and you're looking for signs and signals."

"No." He continued to shake his head. "Neither of us wants this to get weird."

"Why not? You've always been a little weird and it's always worked for you. Weird made you famous," she reminded him sharply.

She'd always encouraged Morris to be as weird and creative as he wanted, even when his peers teased him for being a nerd. Eventually, everyone came around when Morris used his love of computers, music, and poetry to release his first album when he was in high school. *Shout* magazine had called Morris a "modern Mozart" and his brand of weird suddenly cool.

"Not weird in a good way. We're friends—really close friends now—and neither of us wants to make this complicated. And things are getting easier at home. I can get through most of the day feeling *normal*. Why would I want to blow that by messing things up with Penn?"

"He says you're working again!" She patted his chest excitedly and her eyes sparkled as they searched Morris's. He was *tinkering* to pass the time whenever he was in a good head-space, but he didn't want to get her hopes up.

"I am not working," he said firmly. "I've just been goofing around and seeing how it feels to be down in the studio."

"And?" Her voice rose hopefully.

"It felt good scratching that itch in here," he said as he pointed at his head. "I needed to see the notes and words on a screen and hear it played back. It was amazing, changing the beat and blending and cutting. But then I wondered what happened next, after I was done. Who would I give it to? I've never made music without her."

In theory. The song was about Penn and it would never see the light of day. But Morris wanted to call Michelle down so she could hear it. And for a moment, he missed the process. His favorite part of creating an album was collaborating with his sister. She was his sounding board and could harness his weird-ness so it turned into something cohesive. And she always had a marketing plan ready before the first song on an album was finished.

"I'm proud of you for taking that first step. Have you called that therapist? She's helped me and your father and she does video calls if you don't want to deal with the train or traffic," Evelyn said.

Morris nodded. "Penn reminded me. I have an appoint-ment next week."

"You actually listen to him," she observed and humphed at Morris, making him laugh.

"He doesn't push, and he listens too."

She raised her brows at him, looking impressed. "I'm just glad you're talking to someone. He's good for you. I have your father and my friends at the church and in the choir. But you've cut yourself off from everyone except Reid and you'd be all alone if he hadn't sent Penn. And thank God, because Penn's an angel."

"He is," Morris agreed. "That's why I don't want to make things weird between us. In a bad way," he said pointedly. "I'm not ready to talk to anyone about recording or collaborating. I don't know if I'll ever be able to and it scares me. What if I never get the magic back?"

"That's just the grief and fear talking, baby. Give it time. Something will move you and you'll find the magic again," she promised. Morris grimaced and clutched his stomach because something—or someone—had moved him, but it was beginning to feel like a curse or an obsession. He only thought about writing and heard bits of melodies when he was with Penn or thinking about him, and Morris couldn't see how that wasn't a bad thing.

"Maybe. But I don't *need* to work and I'm focusing whatever energy I have on Cadence and rebuilding the other parts of my life."

His mother's expression softened and she blinked back tears as she nodded. "I'm sorry. I shouldn't push you. It's just that Michelle wouldn't let you give up."

"I know." Morris dabbed at his eyes with his sleeve. It had been the first time he'd cried in three days. He gave himself a mental pat on the back, congratulating himself on the streak.

"Is it just me or did it seem like your father was particularly pleased to see Penn?" She said, dismissing Morris's argument and changing the subject.

"I didn't realize Penn was Gus's boy. No wonder Dad's been after me to meet him," he said, glaring at the living room suspiciously. Morris had assumed his dad was setting him up and had refused on principle alone. He would have run like he was on fire if he'd known his dad was trying to set him up with

Penn. That bit of "omission" might have been intentional as well.

"I thought you knew. Everyone knows your father, and Penn's been coming to the bakery for years," she said, gesturing airily.

Morris suspected the surprise was part of the plan and wouldn't put it past Morris Sr. to play matchmaker. He wanted Morris to find his soulmate and settle down like he did. Morris wanted that too but hadn't had the same luck his father had. His first kiss wasn't perfect and it wasn't with Morris's soulmate. His dad had swung for the fences and hit a home run the first time. He had no idea what it was like out there.

Dating was wild and messy these days. And it only got wilder and messier because Morris was just famous enough for people to take pictures if he held a man's hand or kissed him in public. That worked for some people. But Morris wasn't interested in dating someone like that, unfortunately.

He had a feeling Penn wouldn't care for the extra attention. Or he just wouldn't care. He certainly wouldn't seek it out; he was too committed to keeping their lives as stress-free as possible.

"Don't encourage Dad," Morris said, pressing his hands together. "I'm going to check on Penn and see if he needs help. This was supposed to be his day off and he still found something to fix," he complained.

He almost ran right into Penn at the kitchen door. "All done!" He said cheerfully. "Morrie's in the recliner with Cadie and she's out cold. He told us to take off for a few hours. I was thinking we could do a grocery run since you brought the car. If you're in the mood. I can handle it on my own."

"No! Go to the co-op! Morris is a member and can take you," Evelyn said, snatching Morris by the elbow and dragging him to the door. "Make sure you grab one of the freezer bags and I'll get the cooler out of the basement."

"What did I *just* say?" Morris hissed at her, but she ignored him as she hunted in the coat closet for the bag.

"A walk and some fresh air will do you some good." She smiled at Morris, daring him to argue.

"Stop meddling."

Penn leaned around Evelyn. "What are we meddling with?" He whispered.

"Nothing! Nobody's meddling. I'm ready," Morris said, glaring at his mother as he got the door for Penn.

"Okie doke," Penn said and kissed her on the cheek on his way out.

He was relaxed and whistled happily to himself while Morris drove and they chatted comfortably as they parked and headed into the co-op together.

"Look at all the tofu!" Penn exclaimed, throwing his arms open as he went to fondle the selection.

"You might be a little too excited," Morris commented out of the side of his mouth.

He had fun, though, watching Penn become rhapsodic over the selection of seeds and the wide variety of kombucha.

"Come on. You know how expensive produce is by our place," Penn said absently while gathering mushrooms. He was clearly in his element and Morris was absurdly tickled by how nice "our place" sounded when Penn said it. "I want to check out the cookbooks and see if there are any we can add to our collection."

"Cool. Great," Morris said. A nervous laugh slipped out, but Penn didn't notice and was already scanning the back of a book. Morris had always imagined that it would be strange when the time came for him to live with someone other than Michelle. He had hoped he'd eventually find a man he wanted to cohabitate with, but Morris had pictured the transition as rocky because he could be picky. It had been easy with Penn, though. He was even more organized than Morris and enjoyed cleaning because he liked to keep himself busy.

Everywhere Morris looked, he saw signs. The universe and the people around them seemed to think they were a good fit.

"I still can't get over the fact that you and my dad have been friends for almost two years," Morris said. His curiosity got the better of him while they were loading bags into the trunk of his car.

Penn chuckled and gave his head a little shake. "I honestly thought you knew. Everyone knows your parents and Dr. Wilson's the best."

"It really is a small city," Morris remarked. But he suspected there was more to it than chance. He didn't want to steer the conversation into awkward territory so he kept his suspicions to himself. His instincts told him he should talk to Reid, then talk to Penn if he was still confused. "So, you're Gus's boy."

"Yup!" Penn grinned. "And I'm sure everything your dad's ever said about my dad is true. He can be a grouchy bastard and they love to give each other a hard time."

"They're a riot," Morris said, laughing as he recalled their father's many escapades. They liked to bicker about sports and old movies, but they also liked to tell jokes and raise a little hell at the clinic. Gus and Morris Sr. had been reprimanded for attempting to loosen the wheel on another gentleman's wheel-chair over a grudge. He was a Bulls fan and had hit on their favorite nurse, according to Morris's father. "But they've been good for each other."

Penn nodded slowly. "They have. I owe Morrie because he's kept my dad going. He wanted to give up when the chemo made him really sick, but he couldn't leave your dad hanging.

And Gus had something else to think about instead of how scared he was when he was at the clinic."

"Gus means the world to Dad. He talks about him all the time and I'm glad they're still hanging out," Morris said, then snorted. "We might be singing a different tune when we have to bail them out," he predicted.

"I say we let them stew and think about what they've done when the time comes."

"I see you've accepted that it's inevitable as well," Morris said seriously, but they both laughed as they got into the car. There was a lull so Morris did a little more fishing. "Is everything okay?" He asked.

Penn pursed his lips and squinted at Morris. "What do you mean?"

"Remember how it used to be weird when we'd look at each other? Before we were friends."

"Maybe..." Penn fussed with his shirt and gave the front a tug. "I can't wait to get home and put on something with less—"

"Fabric?" Morris guessed, earning a sarcastic laugh.

"I was going to say buttons, but it would serve you right if I came down in less clothes," Penn said, then hissed and shook his head. "I should have thought that one through."

"Don't threaten me with a good time." Morris murmured, keeping his eyes on the road. "I'd catch you staring and it would be awkward because I never knew if you were trying to make eye contact with me or if you were looking because you thought I was trying to get your attention. It felt like that again while we were eating and cleaning up today."

"I think I know what you mean. I was pretty distracted with the sink," Penn said and gestured vaguely. "Evelyn did pull me aside and ask me to give you a nudge out the door. I told her I would see what I could do when you were ready."

"She's predictable, at least," Morris said.

"She also hinted that we could spend more time together."

Morris glanced at Penn just as he looked at Morris and they both jumped and stared back at the windshield and the stoplight with burning red faces. "That's weird, right?" Morris attempted. "We already spend all our time together. You can't even get a day off without getting sucked into brunch with us."

"I had a great time and I didn't have anything else going on. I probably would have seen if Dad and Morrie wanted to go fishing."

"Too bad *Morrie* had other plans," Morris said with a chuckle.

"My dad's met Cadie. Penny brought him by twice, but you were sleeping and we didn't want to bother you. Want to come out to Hoboken with me one of these days?" Penn asked.

"Really?" Morris risked a quick look at Penn and he shrugged.

"Why not? We're friends, and you and Cadie are important to me. And he's asked a few times. I just didn't want to suggest it until you were ready to meet weird new people."

"Your dad's not weird." Morris smiled, but he might have been hoping for something a little more...

Romantic?

Attraction and chemistry didn't necessarily equate to romance, in Morris's experience. Penn had teased and hinted, but he had never signaled that his intentions were romantic. Which meant they were on opposite wavelengths because Morris was already composing lyrics and had picked out their song. It wasn't the best song for a couple's song, but they wouldn't be a traditional couple.

Not by any means. And Evelyn was right, that had always worked for Morris. The question was: what worked for Penn?

Chapter Fourteen

It was just supposed to be brunch, and Penn was expecting to have a wonderful time with the Mosbys. Instead, he'd been invited into a day in the life of a man who had it all. Laughing with Evelyn and Morris Sr. over mimosas and helping with the kitchen sink had nourished Penn's soul, along with all the excellent food they'd heaped onto his plate.

They'd passed the baby around, complaining about how fast she was growing while simultaneously bragging about how brilliant their little angel was. And Morris had been fully out of his shell and smiled more around his parents, making him even more alluring and drawing even more of Penn's attention. If such a thing was possible.

Morris was even more beautiful at home, with his family, and Penn practically ached to be part of that happiness. And he was struck by how easy it was to laugh with Evelyn and Morris Sr. and how much Penn already cared about them. He already loved them and thought of them as family, but to actually *be* a member of the family?

Penn had had to excuse himself for a moment, pretending he needed to peek under the sink. He'd been overwhelmed and had also wanted to laugh at how absurd it was. How could *he* be a Mosby? Not that there was a damn thing wrong with being a Tucker. He was proud of his family, and Penn loved Gus and Penny with every fiber of his being. But he was just a simple, gangly goober who loved his skateboard and got excited about tofu. The Mosbys were magic and *everyone* knew them.

And Penn had been even more enchanted when the afternoon transformed into a fantasy with a trip to the co-op. It should have been a chore and they should have been safe, perusing the tofu and inspecting the kale. Yet Penn's heart had raced as Morris teased him for being a nerd about cashews. And he'd humored Penn as he babbled about making soap. The afternoon had turned into Penn's ideal date—and *first date*—and now there were plans to visit Gus in Hoboken.

What more could Penn want? He and Morris fit together so easily and so well and the day had felt like a dream. Morris had had fun too and he was relaxed and in high spirits when they returned to Lenox Hill and parked in front of the house. It was easy to imagine *they* were a family and had just returned from a perfect day with the grandparents as Morris went to get Cadence out of her car seat.

Penn saw Morris's smile dim when he spotted the flowers, signs, cards, and stuffed animals that had gathered on the stoop along the right handrail. The area had become a memorial to Michelle, and Penn did his best to keep it neat and prevent the tributes from taking over the stairs. He was creating a scrapbook and saving as much as he could in tote bins in the garage.

Morris usually hurried past it whenever he left the house or he came around the side and jumped into his car without looking at the front door. But now his eyes lingered and he smiled at a teddy bear holding a picture of Michelle.

"Want to take Cadence over and check it out while I unload the trunk?" Penn offered.

"Yeah," Morris nodded and Penn was so proud of him. Morris still had a hard time talking about Michelle, but he wasn't avoiding her pictures or her things as much as he used to. He was also accepting phone calls and answering the door instead of telling Penn to ignore it or send whoever it was away.

"Take your time. I can handle this."

"Thanks." Morris sniffed hard and whispered a shaky "Here we go" as he kissed Cadence's hair.

Penn kept an eye on them as he carried everything in and then took his time in the kitchen. When he glanced out the opened window, he spotted Morris talking to a gorgeous Black man holding an armful of lilies. He was tall and well-built and dressed in a soft gray suit that coordinated beautifully with the bouquet. They shared a one-armed hug and Morris was cool with letting him hold Cadence. Penn waited until he heard Morris apologize as the other man laughed and passed the baby back before fanning his face.

That was officially his cue so Penn raced down the front steps. "I'll take care of that diaper," he said cheerfully.

The other man gave Penn a quick once over and looked at Morris curiously. Morris didn't seem to notice as he passed Penn the baby. "Thanks. Penn, this is T. Winslow, The Win."

"Oh! Right!" Penn said and offered his hand while cradling the baby against his chest. He felt a little foolish, not recognizing the famous rapper and producer.

"Win, this is my friend and Cadence's nanny, Penn Tucker. He's been holding my life together and helping me get a handle on this," Morris explained as he gestured at the baby.

T. Winslow's eyes brightened and widened as he clasped Penn's hand. "My friends call me T. or Win. It's good to meet you and thanks for taking care of my man. I've been worried about him," he said, but Morris shook his head and waved it off.

"I'm alright. Thanks to Penn."

Penn's face got hot and he felt weirdly giddy as Win went from wary and doubtful to grateful and impressed. "That's great. You let me know if there's anything I can do to help or if you need anything, Penn."

"It's nothing. I'm just doing my job," Penn insisted and held up a thumb, ready to retreat. "Let me get out of your way and get our little princess cleaned up. She was just about to go down and she's due for a nap. It was nice to meet you."

"Same, man," Win said as they slapped hands. "Now, tell me what you're working on," Win said to Morris, allowing Penn to escape.

"I haven't had time," Morris said with a dismissive swat. "Cadence keeps us on our toes and I don't know anything about kids. It's like baby boot camp in there." He pointed at the house and Win laughed. "What have you been up to?" Morris asked, turning the conversation away from himself.

Penn wondered if Morris was lying for professional reasons or because he wasn't emotionally ready to face going back to work. Either way, it wasn't any of his business, and Penn was definitely out of his depth around T. Winslow. A few of Morris's famous friends had stopped by to check on him and offer their condolences and Penn had made himself scarce, hiding in the nursery with the baby.

Penn had a feeling that this was just the beginning, and he didn't want anyone to get the wrong idea or to embarrass Morris. There would be more visitors, and they'd run into more of Morris's peers and fans as he went out more. And word would spread that Morris was transitioning out of deep mourning and possibly making music again.

All of that was wonderful and exactly what Penn was

hoping for, but he could throw a wrench in all of that by drawing the wrong kind of attention to Morris's recovery. Penn might not be all that savvy when it came to social media and he didn't pay much attention to gossip, but he knew what people would think and what kind of things they'd say. Penn wasn't bothered by other people's opinions when it came to *him*, but he didn't want his "weirdness" to be an emotional burden on Morris.

Oddly enough, Morris hadn't seemed all that embarrassed when he introduced Penn as his friend and Cadence's nanny. If anything, he was happier to sing Penn's praises than talk shop with Win. And Morris had flirted in the car and he hadn't acted like Evelyn was being ridiculous about the two of them.

There's no way he's into me like that.

They were good friends and Morris wouldn't jeopardize that with a one-night stand or a cheap fling. That wasn't his style. But Penn could tell that Morris was considering *something*. Not something serious, because that would be ridiculous.

Right?

Penn wasn't as certain as he should have been as he watched from the window with Cadence. Morris said goodbye to Win and hunkered down in front of the memorial. Why hadn't Morris been more impressed by that big bouquet of lilies or lingered with Win? Penn had sensed Win's interest and that he was happy to see that Morris was doing better. But Morris had barely noticed.

Which was strange because T. Winslow was famous enough for Penn to know he was a big deal *and* he was hot and queer. He was also really cool as far as Penn could tell and seemed to have a lot more in common with Morris. Maybe Morris wasn't interested because Win was too connected to the music industry and too high-profile.

"You know what?" Penn asked Cadence and held her up so

he could see her face. "I'm gonna stay out of it. Let's go, Smelly Kelly."

Morris might not be ready to date someone like Win yet, but he would be soon and Penn wasn't going to get in the way. The idea made Penn's stomach sour as he carried the baby up the stairs. In fact, the idea of Morris with someone else stank worse than the mess in Cadence's diaper. But Penn had his own reasons for staying single. Plus, he was all wrong for Morris.

"Between you and me, I really wish we could," he confided.

He was still a little tipsy from the mimosas and their trip to the co-op. Fooling around with Morris while they put away the produce would be the best way to cap off Penn's perfect first dream date. He did his best to keep his thoughts tame while changing Cadence and rocking her to sleep.

Penn was slipping when he laid Cadence in her crib because he imagined jogging down the steps and pulling Morris into his arms. He knew exactly how they'd pass the time while she was napping and that *was not* what Reid was paying Penn to do. And that was not what Morris needed. The sex would probably be hot, but Penn knew they'd be opening Pandora's box. There would be emotional, social, professional, and physical ramifications because Penn could tell by how well they clicked in just about every other way that they'd click in bed too and they wouldn't be able to stop.

Maybe Morris was right. Maybe brunch had been a bad idea.

Chapter Fifteen

as that as pathetic as it seemed?
Morris knew why The Win had shown up with those lilies. He'd already sent a card with his condolences and flowers to Morris's parents' house just after the funeral. Win was picking up where he left off and making good on the hints he'd started dropping just before Cadence was born. The idea had been tempting before, but Morris had sensed that Win's motives weren't purely romantic. He'd shared his suspicions with Michelle and she had agreed that Win would have a lot to gain from a high-profile relationship at this point in his career.

Morris found himself pondering the same questions as he began unpacking bags from the co-op. Would T. Win attempt to capitalize on all the attention and sympathy by inserting himself into Morris's life just as he was making his return to the public eye and possibly writing a big comeback album? Absolutely.

Iffy motives don't automatically make him a terrible person and he sure is nice to look at.

Michelle had told Morris to go for it before and he had a feeling her advice would still be the same. Fake relationships weren't uncommon in music, film, and theater and they could be a good way to use unwanted attention and publicity to an artist's advantage.

Win was smart, funny, sexy, and he was hot in the studio, too. He was on the rise and Morris didn't need a PR team to tell him that the internet would eat it right up, if word got out that T. Win was comforting him in his time of mourning. There was also a chance that Win might actually like Morris, and he was rumored to be a genuinely kind and laid-back person. But Morris had been more interested in discussing Penn and had blown Win off.

What was the point? It wasn't like he could ask Win to collaborate on his new "passion project." And Morris would have to hide what he was working on if they started hanging out and that was no way to start a relationship. Especially if Win truly liked Morris.

Because Morris was falling hard for his nanny.

"She's out like a light," Penn said as he came down the stairs and went to work on the canned goods. He laughed and dodged Morris when they almost crashed in front of the pantry. "Evelyn says Cadie's hair will be long enough to twist in a few months and that we need to get her used to sitting still for us."

Morris hummed in agreement. "I'm surprised it took Mom this long with all the hair that girl has. She'll get tender-headed and be too fidgety if we don't practice and get her used to it while she's little."

"Can you teach me or do we need to take her to a salon?" Penn asked and Morris made a *pffft!* sound.

"I can teach you. Michelle and I got good at braiding each other's hair because Mom didn't have a lot of time with everything going on at the bakery. And Michelle was always seeing something in a magazine or on the street that she wanted so I learned how to do everything," Morris explained.

"I used to braid Penny's hair, but all I know is the basics and I doubt she'd trust me if she was going someplace nice," Penn mused with a snort. "Not that she'd ever go anywhere nice."

"She'd probably break out in hives," Morris agreed, but he'd gotten caught in memories of Michelle's hair. She had straightened it less as she got older and was favoring her natural curls. But every now and then, when they had a slow weekend, she'd put on a series they could binge-watch and Morris would braid her hair. Michelle would sit between his legs on the floor, and now he suddenly ached to feel her head resting on his thigh as he worked and she nodded off.

"Fuck!" Morris held onto the counter because he wasn't ready. He was tired all of a sudden and his legs didn't feel as solid when the urge to scream and sob came on. The wave crashed into him, but Penn gathered Morris in his arms before he was pulled under.

"Hey. I've got you," Penn whispered. He cradled Morris's head in one of his hands as the other spread protectively across his back. "Breathe and hold onto me."

They rocked from side to side for several minutes, and Morris took comfort in the feel of Penn's heart beating against his chest, soothing and lulling until the ache and the wave of grief retreated. The burning anger eased as Morris filled his lungs with Penn's bright, clean scent.

All was still and peaceful and it was just them. Penn's hand splayed and roamed Morris's back and shoulder, kneading away the tension, replacing it with warmth and making him lighter. A thumb stroked Morris's jaw and his ear tenderly while their breaths mingled, the soft huffs punctuating each heartbeat and setting a drowsy rhythm. They synchronized into bliss, their bodies a lazy metronome swaying at thirty beats per minute.

Morris let out a weary, relieved breath. "Thanks. I..." He didn't know what to say because how did you put something like that into words? One moment, Morris was drowning. And the next, he was safe and whole. He laughed softly as he rested his forehead on Penn's, grateful for the warm connection they shared.

"This is why I'm here," Penn said with a chuckle.

"I'd be lost without you." Morris brushed his lips against Penn's, nudging them affectionately. At least, it was meant to be a casual, affectionate kiss. But they both groaned and Penn's tongue swept along Morris's lips, inviting him to take more. Morris leaned into him and slid an arm around Penn's neck and the soft, easy bliss was replaced with heat and hunger.

Their tongues swirled and thrust urgently as Morris's head spun. Penn tasted like sunshine and honey and Morris wanted to taste him everywhere. He was dazed and disoriented when they finally came up for air.

"Wow." Penn looked stunned as well as he blinked back at Morris. "I'm starting to think you might like me," he teased. He pressed a quick kiss to Morris's lips as if he could undo their last kiss and replace it with something more comfortable. He pulled Morris into a tight hug and clapped him on the back before releasing him.

"Okay. I like you," Morris admitted, calling Penn's bluff. He wasn't afraid of what came next but Penn was. His eyes widened and his lips pulled into a too-wide smile as he nodded and hugged his chest. Morris could see the panic and regret written all over Penn's face.

"Well... That's progress!" He said and winked at Morris as he reached for one of the bags on the counter. "I was thinking I might try this new roasted salad recipe Penny sent me. I love kale, but it's a sturdy vegetable and apparently, roasting it takes it to the next level." He was clearly changing the subject so Morris snorted and went back to putting the groceries away.

He knew about Penn's aversion to relationships, thanks to Reid and Gavin. Morris couldn't remember if either had mentioned *why* Penn was only into casual sex and never dated. But Morris wasn't wired like that. He was shy and he wasn't in all that much of a rush, but Morris wanted someone of his own he could write poems and love songs for.

I could write sonnets about those lips and how he's as slow and as sweet as honey...

Morris's brain did what it had often done when he composed poetry. A melody had been stringing itself together in his head for days. Clusters of notes glowed and arranged themselves in his brain and he occasionally ducked downstairs to peck them out on a keyboard or doodle on the dry-erase board. Morris hummed as he and Penn worked in the kitchen, and he was *happy*. He felt more solid and present than he had in weeks.

"That's nice. What is that?" Penn asked, leaning against the counter while Morris put away the shopping bags.

Morris shrugged. "Just something that I've been puttering around with."

"Really?" Penn asked excitedly, and gave Morris's shoulder an encouraging squeeze. "You should keep going and get downstairs before you forget it."

"We'll see." Morris gave his head a dismissive shake. "Melodies come to me all the time." He was lying because they didn't come to him all the time and it felt like...magic, but Morris couldn't release that song if Penn wasn't his.

First of all, Penn would know exactly who Morris was writing those lyrics for. Who else had hair and lips like wild mountain honey and warm skin that had been kissed by the sun? Second, the torture would be excruciating and last for months if Morris fucked around and turned it into a hit. He had songs blow up in the past and bite him in the ass before.

What might be a catchy earworm to most became nails on a chalkboard for Morris after weeks of perfecting a song in the studio, then hearing it clipped, sampled, remixed, and made viral. He would always be grateful for the support and love his music received, but it could be a double-edged sword.

Especially when a song had real significance to Morris. The lyrics and arrangements were more personal and he took it personally when they were tampered with, as if his own feelings and memories had been altered and rearranged. That was the nature of making music in the modern digital age, but it was harder to let go when Morris put his heart on the page. And some secrets weren't meant for the airwaves. Penn would be one more heartbreak Morris wouldn't be able to escape until the song ceased to be a hit and a new viral earworm took its place.

He'd put his first crush in a song and it was one of Morris's earliest hits. Morris had been safe for a few years, then the SoundCloud revolution happened and a hundred baby rappers sampled it and a Europop version blew up. He'd had an out of body moment on the train, hearing his pining for Brian from AP English set to a thumping disco beat. Half a dozen girls in Girl Scout uniforms had danced in their seats while a white guy with dreadlocks rapped along and serenaded the woman across from Morris, completely unaware of his presence.

Brian from AP English was history and he didn't matter. A song about Penn would be a confession and it would bare Morris's soul. Why would he want to hear that sped up and distorted while he was waiting in a check-out line?

No thank you.

He didn't know how Taylor Swift could step foot on the

internet, but Morris wasn't a masochist. He wasn't going to leave boobytraps for himself all over social media and television.

Morris cast the melody aside, mentally dusting off his hands. "Think I'll head to the barbershop and get this cleaned up," he said, pointing at his hair.

"Sounds good..." Penn's eyes tightened as he studied Morris. "Are we cool?"

Morris cocked his head. "Us?" He snorted. "Why wouldn't we be cool?" He asked and held out his hand.

"Good." Penn grabbed it and they hugged and slapped each other on the back. "I'll get started on dinner while you're out."

Morris did need to get his fade cleaned up, but he didn't head straight to his favorite shop. He stopped by Reid and Gavin's first, hoping for some guidance. Or a few clues as to what was going on inside Penn's head, at least.

Reid answered when Morris buzzed the intercom at Briarwood Terrace and let him in. "I was just about to grab a beer. Want one?" Reid asked on his way to the fridge.

"Just one," Morris replied. "I was headed to the barbershop and I have to be home in time for dinner." He thanked Reid when he passed him a beer and they each grabbed a seat at the table.

"You look like you've got something big on your mind." Reid pointed the neck of his bottle at Morris.

"It's nothing big or serious," Morris reassured him, then winced. "It's more of a...tall and lanky...situation. But it's not a problem," he insisted and Reid's brow hitched.

"You ever notice that when someone says something isn't a problem, it usually *is* a problem, and they're just afraid to admit it?"

Morris gave his head a quick shake. "It's not a problem! We just kissed but we both agreed that we're cool," he said and punctuated the statement with a firm nod. But he heard how silly that sounded and winced at Reid. "We're cool, right?"

"I certainly hope so," Reid said with a heavy frown. He sat back in his seat, hugging his beer as he considered Morris.

"What?" Morris looked up warily, then narrowed his eyes when Reid attempted to wave it off. "No, you don't. What does that mean?"

"It's just... You know how Penn is," he said. But Morris didn't.

"Not really. We don't go back like you two do." Which was why Morris had come to Briarwood Terrace. He didn't know if they were actually "cool" or if he should be worried.

"Well..." Reid stalled and squirmed in his chair. "You know I love Penn like a brother and I would trust him with *anything.* But—" He raised his brows at Morris suggestively.

"But what?"

"Hmmm..." Reid stalled a little more before grimacing at Morris. "I love Penn and I'd trust him with my life or Fin's. And I can't think of anyone with a bigger, kinder, gentler heart. But I'd never set Penn up with one of my friends. Definitely not you," he added, and Morris's face and stomach dropped.

"What? Why?"

"Not because of you!" Reid said, reaching across the table and grabbing Morris's hand. "It's Penn," he said, and his expression softened along with his voice. "Someone broke him in college before we met. He was already hurt and bitter about something, but then his mom died and Penn...*changed.*"

"A lot of people change after something like that." Morris hadn't meant to snap at Reid and mouthed an apology. "If anyone can understand, it's me."

"I'm sure he told you, but she died of a stroke," Reid said hoarsely. He was unable to raise his eyes to Morris's as a tear rolled down his cheek. "I was afraid this would be hard for him because of her, but you were in so much pain and I was hurting too. He's the best I had to offer and I knew he was exactly what you needed so I sent him. I don't know why, but I was hoping this might help him heal as well."

"Two birds with one stone?" Morris asked and Reid nodded.

"He said that it was the deepest, most consuming grief he'd ever experienced. And he said it showed him parts of his heart and himself that he'd never seen or explored and allowed him to be more open and understanding. But something broke in Penn or maybe he locked it away because I've never known him to let anyone in. He'll do anything for the people he loves, but he won't let anyone love him. It's the one thing he won't give."

"How could you *not* love Penn, though? He's the easiest man in the world to fall in love with," Morris said, and laughed in disbelief at his own words.

Reid nodded and laughed with him. "Everybody loves Penn. He's got an immaculate soul and he's pure sunshine. But I keep him away from my single friends unless they know better. Or they just wanna get laid. I didn't think I had to worry about the two of you, though. I thought you were immune to Penn."

That earned him a hard look from Morris. "It's not that I didn't like the guy. I just didn't appreciate him stealing my best friend," he explained with a teasing wink.

"Stop it! No one stole me, you just had a lot going on."

"I know and I know that if we go months—or even years—without talking that it'll feel like we're still kids and nothing's changed when I do make time to call you."

"You also know I'm proud of you and that I'm always going to be here, right?" Reid asked, giving Morris a playful kick under the table.

"Yup." There was a catch in Morris's throat and he nodded.

"I was still jealous of Penn and it took a minute for me to get over that."

"I get it. I'm jealous of Penn for all sorts of reasons and I miss you too," Reid said. "But look at all that you and Michelle have done. That took so much time and work. And it was fucking worth it, Morris! The whole world knows you're a genius and your music will outlive us and touch people for decades to come."

"Thanks," Morris said, wrinkling his nose. It was still surreal to have that kind of legacy and he did his best to keep everything in perspective. He was more concerned with the present and what he was walking into when he returned home to Penn. "So...you don't know why Penn's a player and sleeps around," he summarized, earning a hard wince from Reid.

"When you say it like that..." He groaned and scrubbed the back of his neck. "He's always upfront about it because Penn won't risk hurting anyone. He says he likes being free to explore and enjoy sex without the complications and expectations that come with relationships."

"Sounds like a player..."

"Maybe," Reid conceded. "But we do have some mutuals who have hooked up with Penn and it's a life-changing experience from what I've heard."

Morris coughed and choked on his beer. "Really?" He hoped Reid was joking because that wasn't the kind of information he needed in his hard drive.

"Mmmhmm." Reid nodded slowly, staring at the table between them. "Penn's out there slinging dick like John Wick and I'd tell you to go for it, but I don't think you can be as casual about sex as he is."

"Nope," Morris admitted freely and drained his beer. Penn wasn't his and Morris had absolutely no claim on him but the thought made him sick. He didn't want to think about Penn with other men. "We're definitely wired differently. I'm happy for him, though," he said as he got up and went to throw his bottle in the recycling bin under the sink.

Reid rose, sensing that Morris was ready to leave. "You know, I'd tell Penn to get it together before he blows it with you, if I thought he'd listen or change. I'd rather play silly games and help this along, but I don't want to see you get hurt and I don't want to fight Penn for breaking your heart."

"I'm good and I can keep it in my pants."

"Good." Reid nodded, then canted toward Morris and gestured for him to lean in. "I have complete faith in you, but just in case, I do know that he's on PrEP and he's always prepared. He goes to the clinic with me every other month because Gavin hasn't had sex in two years," he whispered.

Morris blinked back at him. "Nothing that you just said was any of my business."

"I'm just letting you know," Reid said, then cleared his throat. "In case you can't keep it in your pants."

"I can keep it in my pants."

Chapter Sixteen

The basement had been sound-proofed, but Penn could hear music faintly if he kept really still and the rest of the house was quiet. He opened the dishwasher, cutting it off, and closed his eyes and listened.

Morris was "tinkering" and rarely spent more than an hour or two downstairs at a time, but Penn was haunted by the bits and pieces he'd heard and wanted so badly to hear the whole song. He'd caught himself humming it while they were in the car, but Morris was cagey when Penn asked if he would get a chance to hear the finished song soon.

"I don't think you'd be all that into it," Morris had said dismissively.

Penn had laughed it off and said it was cool at the time, but the remark had hurt more than he was expecting. He'd been the wrong man before and swore he'd never allow anyone to make him feel like he wasn't good enough. Yet there Penn was, wishing he was the kind of man Morris might date.

Fool me once...

He'd been a fool his freshman year of college and fallen

head over heels for his roommate, knowing the relationship would never leave the confines of their dorm room. Tristan was "totally straight" and was "just trying it out" with Penn on the down low. They pretended they were tolerating each other when they crossed paths on campus because Tristan was a quarterback and had a full-ride scholarship. He was going to be a star by the time he was a senior and Penn was...how had Tristan put it?

First of all, I can't be gay. And even if I could, I wouldn't be with someone like you. No offense, Penn, but you're...not cool.

Up until then, Penn had thought he was cool. To him, cool meant being the kind of person everyone liked and got along with because you were mellow and gave everyone a chance. He'd always been unconventional and thought that was a good thing until Tristan had laughed at Penn for getting carried away. They'd been having sex for months and couldn't keep their hands and lips off each other when they were alone. Penn had mused out loud about taking a weekend trip to someplace like Boston so they could go to dinner and hold hands like dorks.

He should have broken it off then, but it was too late for Penn. He was already in love and he couldn't say no to Tristan. They acted like they were on their honeymoon behind closed doors and Penn fooled himself into believing it was bliss.

And it was fantastic. It was the most sex Penn had ever had in his life and it was *good*. Until they had run into each other at a fraternity party. Tristan was pledging and Penn had talked some friends into crashing with him because he was curious. Everyone was welcome and the party had turned into a rager by the time Penn had arrived. It had taken a while to find Tristan and he had his tongue in Mandy Rudolph's mouth and his hand up her skirt when Penn finally caught up with him.

Come on! She's hot and everyone expects us to go out.

Penn had slammed the door shut after that. He had sex with anyone he wanted, living just for the moment and "the spark" so he could leave his heart free and open without it getting trampled on again. And Penn vowed he'd never allow anyone to make him feel inadequate or ashamed.

But once again, Penn was embarrassed and frankly a little disgusted with himself. Morris was in a whole different stratosphere of cool that mediocre men like Tristan couldn't even fathom. Morris was on the same level as Miles Davis and Tyler, the Creator. He was iconic and he was composing another masterpiece in the basement while Penn rolled out strips of pasta in his thrift shop overalls.

He had bored Morris on purpose, listing the various pasta shapes and fillings on the day's agenda, in hopes that he'd flee to the basement. Penn was glad it had worked, even if he felt a little left out and bummed. He loved rap, R&B, and hip-hop, but Penn had to accept that he'd never fit into that part of Morris's world.

It was difficult enough for Morris, being out and proud in the music industry. Several queer artists had broken barriers. But genres like hip-hop, country, and gospel had taken longer. Morris defied those boundaries, though, and worked with an incredible array of music legends from all genres.

And Morris was "R&B's soulful shy guy." He carried himself with confidence and swagger and he was *always* put together when he left the house. Reid and Gavin had giggled about it for weeks because they couldn't believe Michelle had convinced Morris to do a whole fashion spread. They speculated that she had worked out a deal with the magazine to include his Nikes. The piece had also featured his shoe collection and proclaimed Morris one of New York's most dedicated Sneakerheads. But the article turned out to be a brilliant move, to Michelle's credit. Music fans knew that Morris was prolific and understood that he was a genius. But the article high-lighted all of his accomplishments, revealing a breathtakingly vast and diverse discography. Morris was a household name and one of the city's most eligible bachelors after that.

None of it had gone to Morris's head, and the media and the public had respected his privacy after Michelle's passing, thank goodness. But it would be newsworthy if Morris was dating someone. And Penn had a feeling a lot of people would be disappointed if Morris chose someone like him.

Morris deserved prestige and power. He deserved someone who could sweep him off his feet and spoil him, not a wandering hippie like Penn. People would probably think that Penn was taking advantage of Morris and had recruited him into a cult. There was no way anyone would believe that Morris was genuinely attracted to a thirty-eight-year-old nanny. Especially when they got a look at Penn.

A well-respected and wealthy sports agent or a rapper and producer like The Win would be heartwarming and a relief, signaling that Morris wasn't mourning on his own and was getting back on his feet. A fling with his long-haired, tattooed, middle-aged nanny would look like a man in crisis. Morris didn't need that kind of attention when he was starting to feel normal again.

Penn took it as a sign and acted normal when he heard Morris coming up the stairs. He used his knee to bump the dishwasher shut, starting it again. "How's it going down there?" He asked, smiling cheerfully as Morris closed the basement door.

"Fine." His gaze was distant because he was still working. He hummed softly as he made himself a glass of ice water, hypnotizing Penn.

Penn couldn't help himself. "That's really beautiful. Will I get to hear it soon?"

"Maybe. It's..." Morris's lips pulled tight and his shoulders bounced. "It's not something you'd be into."

"You don't know that!" Penn said loudly, then bit down on his lips. "Sorry," he whispered, glancing at the monitor. He was stunned and mortified at the outburst.

"No... I'm sorry. I shouldn't have—"

Penn shook his head, cutting Morris off. "You *should* set boundaries when it comes to your art. I'm not entitled to anything and I can't fault you for protecting your work."

"It's not that!" Morris said, waving his hands.

"So... You think I'm too much of a hippie or a hillbilly to appreciate it?" Penn guessed.

"What? No." Morris's face twisted. "When have I ever—?"

Penn gave him a loaded look. "Don't tell me you've *never* thought I was weird or a little bit of a flake."

"I *like* weird and I don't think you're a hillbilly. I might have...jokingly thought of you as one a few times, but you're *not*. Maybe you are a little bit of a hippie and maybe *I like it*," Morris said, once again daring Penn to address the elephant in the room.

Penn didn't want to do that because he'd have to admit that he was insecure and then he'd probably have to tell Morris about Tristan. He shuddered inwardly and packed that revelation up and put it away.

"Look. I know I don't fit in your world. I'm not blind, Morris." He gestured at his upcycled overalls and his T-shirt. The design was so faded, he couldn't remember what band, bar, or cartoon was on it. "I know I'm not your target audience because I don't use AppleTunes or Snapify. And it's really cool if you're not comfortable sharing a work in progress." Penn smiled at Morris to reassure him, but received a wry laugh in return.

"How about you chill with the sympathy and stop giving

me passes," he said, his sharp tone startling Penn. "You're saying a lot of things for me and about me, but I can't help but wonder if you're doing that so we don't have to talk about you."

"I talk about myself," Penn argued and turned to the sink to wash his hands so he didn't have to look at Morris.

"No. You talk about your mom a lot when you're high because you know that makes me feel better. You'll talk about your dad, Penny, Reid, Gavin, and your expenses. But we never talk about *you*."

Penn laughed nervously as he floundered. "What's that they say about dating poets and musicians?"

"I don't know. Have you ever dated a poet or a musician?" Morris challenged.

"Um... No," Penn croaked.

"Are you thinking about dating one?"

"I told you, if you weren't Reid's I—"

"I'd like to think I'm yours now too," Morris interrupted and Penn nodded. "And I'm talking about a relationship, not a one-night stand or a fling."

Penn squeezed his eyes shut and prayed he wasn't about to make everything worse. "You're right and I have thought about it a lot lately."

"And?"

"And..." Penn dried his hands as he turned and shrugged. "I don't know. It feels a little wrong because that's not why I'm here and I'm not what you need."

"How do you know?" Morris crossed his arms defiantly. "Because sometimes, it feels like you're *all* I need. But the only thing I have to go on is my own gut. I can't read minds like you so I have no idea what's going on with us. I don't know what you want or what's holding you back."

"That's it, though!" Penn waved at Morris wildly. "You want answers from me, but I don't have them! Everyone expects me to know everything like I'm a wizard or some kind of guru. I love that and it's amazing when I'm solving everyone's problems. But it tears me up when I don't have the answers. Like right now! I *know* I'm letting you down because I am lost, Morris!"

"You're lost?" Morris laughed, sounding surprised.

Penn swept a hand through his hair. It had come loose while he was panicking and ranting so he imagined he looked rather disoriented as well. "I need you too and I don't want to mess this up because I got selfish and couldn't control myself."

"Okay..." Morris nodded slowly. "This is finally...something," he said, wincing awkwardly. "And it's nice to know you are human and that I'm not the only one who's a mess."

"Thanks, but it's my job to fix things and help you get back on your feet, not complicate everything and make a bigger mess."

A heavy sigh rolled from Morris. "You wouldn't be here if life was that simple and went the way we wanted it to. And I wouldn't have trusted you if you were cold and perfect. We are who we are and I like it when you're human and you get messy with me. I don't feel like I'm alone."

But that was the difference between the two of them and Penn didn't know if he could articulate that without sounding arrogant or selfish. He didn't have the luxury of getting complicated and messy because he had so many more people depending on him than Morris did and Penn *wanted* to be the guru and carry the weight of the world on his shoulders.

"I don't know if I have the capacity to be the kind of partner you deserve," he explained. "I think that's what's holding me back. Too many people depend on me to be there when they need me and they look to me for answers, including you and Cadence. How do I find the time and the energy to rearrange all of my priorities so that you're the center of my universe? Because you shouldn't settle for less. I won't let you."

"Easy!" Morris scolded and pointed before snatching Penn's wrist and reeling him in. He pulled Penn's arms around him and they slid together easily. Instead of kissing him and smashing his wits with passion, Morris tapped his forehead against Penn's. "Don't make those kinds of decisions for me. But I can understand how you wouldn't have the emotional bandwidth for a relationship and it makes perfect sense, knowing you. Think about what *you* want and let me worry about what I need in a partner."

"I'll try, but I can't make any promises," Penn said solemnly. He didn't know if he could change his DNA like that. He didn't want to. Morris wasn't asking Penn to change, but change was inevitable and outside of their control.

"As long as you're trying. Baby steps, right?" Morris said, making Penn laugh.

"Baby steps. But it's weird getting the 'baby steps' pep talk. That's my job."

"Deal with it." Morris knocked his forehead against Penn's and released him. "I'm gonna put last night's game on and take a nap on the couch."

"Sounds like a perfect way to spend the day. I'll hang out and watch it with you when I can step away from all of this," Penn said, hitching his thumb at the assembly line he was creating. He'd planned to while away the afternoon making the week's pasta and beating himself up over the kiss. Watching Morris nap and making pasta while the Knicks were on was a much better alternative.

Chapter Seventeen

"Engagement is through the roof and you've been low-key trending for days!" Penny scooted in closer on the sofa so Morris could see her phone. Dash was pressed against Morris's other side, pointing helpfully at emojis and translating them. Thanks to Reid, Penny and Dash were officially on board as Morris's new PR team and were monitoring his social media accounts. His notifications and inboxes had become unmanageable as rumors spread that a "comeback" might be in the works.

"That's the salute emoji! It means she's ready to tell everyone that you're back!" Dash explained. "Everyone is so excited!" He muffled an overjoyed squeal. "Look at all these clapping and crying emojis!"

Things were getting out of hand. Officially.

Morris smiled and pretended he was following along and processing everything Penny and Dash were telling him, but he wasn't the least bit concerned with his social media presence or that he was trending again. He had bigger things to worry about at the moment.

His parents and Penn were convinced that he was back in the studio working on a new album. Thanks to Morris's mom and the auntie network, word was spreading outside of the family and expectations were building. He didn't want to give anyone the impression that he was anywhere close to functional or creating something viable.

He had one song and scraps of two—possibly three—other songs. That wasn't the same as working on an album and so far, everything was about Penn. But that first song... It was *good,* and Morris could feel it in his bones: Michelle would love everything about it. The song was a nostalgic fusion of soul, R&B, and funk. It was smooth and had a romantic retro beat because that was how Morris felt and how he wanted to *be* with Penn.

The song was about Penn, but it was all the things Morris would tell Michelle about him if he could. She'd understand what Morris meant if he said the vibe was silk sheets, scented candles, bubble baths, and gettin' high. And she'd understand why it had to sound old-school and like a "they're playing our song" kind of song because Morris wanted to love Penn the way their father loved their mother.

Morris could write a hundred songs about all the things he'd tell Michelle. Every day he learned something new about Penn that amazed, enchanted, or befuddled Morris. Maybe it would make a good album, but it wasn't the kind of thing he could share with the world without baring too much of his soul.

It was kind of like blowing out the candles and telling everyone what he'd wished for. He didn't want to jinx himself like that. And maybe it made him selfish or petty, but Morris didn't want some jerk in Pennsylvania getting laid or dancing at his wedding to a song about Penn. Not if Morris was still alone and pining over him. He wasn't *that* dedicated to his craft.

"Can I please, please, please remind you all that I am not

back?" Morris asked. He whispered an apology as he unwedged himself and got to his feet. "Everything that the two of you have done has been amazing and you have my complete trust and approval." He swiped at the air in the shape of a cross, blessing them, then pressed his hands together and bowed. "Do whatever you think is best, just don't promise that there will be any new music in the near future. Maybe not ever," he added gingerly.

There was a gasp from the kitchen and Penny and Dash stared up at him in horror.

"What are you talking about?" Penn hurried around the counter, wiping his hands and frowning at Morris. "I've heard enough of at least one song and pieces of a few more to know that you're making something and it's incredible!" He insisted, but Morris shushed him.

"That's just for me and even if I did decide to release it, I'm light-years away from being ready. An album isn't anywhere on the horizon."

Dash blinked up at Morris, then looked at Penny. "Is he making new music or not?" He whispered.

"I think so," she whispered back. "This may be a 'he doth protest too much' situation or it might be a secret," she said and Dash's head tilted.

"That he's making music? Isn't that what he does?"

She scrunched her nose at Morris. "He's got a point. People assume Emeril's cooking something just about every day."

"Oh!" Penn perked up. "I know who that is! He's a chef and sells kitchen stuff."

"Right..." Morris didn't roll his eyes, but he was just about there. "It's almost the same, except I'm not sharing a picture of some gumbo I made for lunch or selling an air fryer."

"It could be the same, though!" Penn said, widening his eyes at Morris. "You don't have to share what you're working on or promise anyone anything. But you can share that you're mixing and cutting and doing what gives you joy, just like Emeril."

Penny clapped. "I love that! We don't have to make it about the end product, we can make it about the joy of making music."

"Fine," Morris conceded. "Make it about the process, not the product. I don't want to get anyone's hopes up, especially my mom's."

"We're on it!" Penny said as she stood and Dash hopped to his feet. "You're in your journey era and it's about learning and growth, not the destination!"

Dash made an excited sound and followed her around the coffee table. "I've got some gorgeous waterfall shots from our last camping trip! We could use those and start a hashtag like #JourneyEra!" He babbled.

Penny pushed him out the front door and blew Penn a kiss, then pointed at Morris. "Are we still on for tomorrow night?"

"Unless I find a way to break a foot between now and then," Morris said. They were going skating in the park. Morris was going to take his headphones and see how the song sounded when he was skating. His parents were into roller skating, and family trips to the park for "skate nights" had been a regular part of Michelle and Morris's childhood. Morris wanted Penn's song to sound like something his parents would have skated to when they were dating.

Penny and Dash left, leaving Morris and Penn laughing and scratching their heads.

"That Dash is..." Morris cleared his throat suggestively.

"Hot but a little too pure for this world?" Penn guessed and Morris raised a hand so he could slap it.

"You read my mind. Again."

Dash had the physique of a quarterback, the good looks of

an anchorman, and the boundless energy and the gentle heart of a golden retriever. He didn't appear to have an ounce of ambition for himself, preferring to use his eye for art and photography and his bubbly charm to help friends and family feel better about themselves on social media. Penny had enlisted him to manage Morris's content and everything appeared to be up to Michelle's standards so far.

"He's a good kid," Penn said, then caught Morris's elbow before he could head back downstairs. "What was that about?"

"What?"

"You said you may never release new music. I told Evie you were making music again to reassure her and give you a little breathing room. I didn't mean for it to blow up like this and I'm sorry if I've made it harder for you to work again."

"I promise, you've made it easier, and Mom was going to find out eventually. It's a foregone conclusion. Everyone knows I'm going to make music the way everyone knows Emeril's going to cook something. She would have heard me working while she was here being her usual bossy self and she was going to tell anyone who would listen because she's always going to brag about what I'm doing."

"That's a relief, but why do you sound like you're retiring?" Penn asked and Morris's shoulders bounced.

"Because I might be? My priorities have changed and I don't need to work. I just want to focus on my family and..." Morris's lips fluttered as he considered the things that mattered most to him. Before babymania had overtaken the Mosby Music machine, all of Michelle and Morris's focus had been on breaking barriers and the next chapter in his musical legacy. Awards and accolades no longer thrilled Morris as much as beach parties in the backyard and secret chocolate cakes. "I don't know..." Morris continued, then smiled. "The journey.

I'm in my journey era and I'm not sure if there's an album in that yet."

"I guess that's fair," Penn said, his brow furrowing as he studied Morris. "Is all of this too much? Penny and Dash can back off and give you more room. And I'll talk to your mom and tell her I misspoke and that we need to give you more time."

"You didn't, though." Morris gripped Penn by the shoulders and gave him a gentle shake. "You told Mom the truth and she jumped to conclusions."

Penn exhaled in relief. "You seem like you're feeling better but I wasn't sure if I was setting you back with this and...the other thing," he said sheepishly.

"The other thing?" Morris chuckled and shook his head. It was all fun and games when he was pinned down on the toilet, but they weren't talking about the kiss or their feelings for each other yet. After two days, this was the closest they had gotten. "I've been in the studio and I'm feeling better. But I'm just writing for myself right now. It's more like dreaming out loud and I'm having fun with it. I'm not worried about what anyone will think or if it will sell and I think that's why I can handle it. And I think it's helping me process...the other thing."

"Ah." Penn made a knowing sound. "It does help to have a distraction and to stay busy. I've been drying pasta and making one of those cube shelves for the nursery."

"I noticed." There was enough pasta drying in the kitchen to feed an Italian platoon. Penn had lines suspended between cabinets and a folding laundry rack was set up in the pantry. Morris had also seen the planks of stained wood and molding in the backyard and assumed Penn had pulled an all-nighter. "Let me know if you make any progress with that," he said and decided he'd escape to his studio and leave Penn to his pasta. A new hook was coming together in Morris's head and it might work for that third song...

Chapter Eighteen

Adding wine to their bedtime joint was probably a bad call. Morris had opened a bottle of Riesling to go with the primavera and then Penn had opened a second bottle while they were doing the dishes. Morris had left music playing in the kitchen and the doors were open, casting the back garden in a soft glow as they smoked, sipped, and hummed along to Etta James and Stevie Wonder.

It was the sort of night Penn might describe as his perfect night. Probably because it was the sort of night he'd witnessed his parents sharing at the family cabin. Every summer, they packed up the van and moved to the Catskills. The Tuckers had spent their days hiking, climbing, fishing, swimming... And the evenings were spent on the back porch, singing songs, playing cards, and telling stories. His mother had loved her porch swing. She'd enjoyed the breeze off the lake as she read and stargazing with Penn's father in the evening.

Penn would sneak down after he'd been sent to bed so he could listen to his dad play the guitar and hear his mother sing. She'd smoke a joint and Gus would drink a few beers and every now and then, Penn would have to scurry away when the music stopped and the clothes came off.

Penn never wanted those perfect nights for himself, though. He'd done his best to avoid them the way his father avoided the back porch and couldn't look at the swing whenever they visited the cabin. It had taken years for Gus to recover from the loss of his wife and Penn could see the holes that had been punched in his father's life. They were in the shape of a porch swing and her seat at the table. Those haunting voids threatened to suck Gus in if he looked too long and thought about her.

What traps were forming around Penn as he watched Morris take a long drag from a joint and nod along to "As." Would it be the song or moonlit nights in May that haunted Penn later, he wondered.

Penn had yet to find any answers and the questions were getting scarier. Would he be disappointing Reid and damaging their friendship? What about Penn's friendship with Morris? That had become just as strong and as vital as his friendship with Reid in just a handful of weeks. Penn didn't want to lose either of them. And Penn wasn't sure if he could give 100% of his heart to Morris and have enough of himself left for all the people who depended on him. What if he couldn't balance it all and he missed out on valuable time with Gus? Time was already slipping through Penn's hands with his father. Could he carve out enough time for Gus if he was caught up in Morris?

Then there was time itself. Penn was the same age as his mother when she died. In the years since her death, Penn watched his father grieve and carry on without her. He'd helped patch the holes for Gus the way he covered the chair in the nursery and was secretly learning to braid hair from Evelyn. Penn was practicing on a mannequin head she had given him, instead of asking Morris to teach him again. He didn't want those holes in his own heart because Penn was afraid he'd have to carry on like Gus and he was also afraid of dying and leaving someone like Morris broken and full of holes.

"Good thing I turned on the music. You're terrible company tonight." Morris elbowed Penn to get his attention and passed him the joint. It was just about spent so Penn took a long hit and put it out on the step between his feet.

"I'm in a quiet mood, I guess."

"Liar, liar, your weed is fire!" Morris sang. "But your game is..." He paused and his lips twisted. "Dire?"

"Definitely. And you don't want to know what kind of mood I'm in," Penn said with a wry chuckle. He'd been all over the place all day and was even moodier once he put Cadence down and it was just him and Morris.

"That's where you're wrong. I'd love to be able to read you as easily as you can read me," Morris murmured into his glass before taking a drink.

"You're getting better." Penn bumped his shoulder against Morris's, then looked at him. "Go ahead. Guess what I'm thinking."

Morris swung around and made a thoughtful sound as his eyes searched Penn's. "Well..." But something happened and Morris's brows pinched as he stared at Penn. His pupils dilated and Penn watched as a joke or a clever comeback faded and Morris realized they'd made a mistake.

Penn knew better and had vowed he wouldn't even think about kissing Morris again, but he couldn't stop himself from leaning in or stop his lips and his hands from reaching for Morris. And he couldn't stop his body as he rose and threw a leg over Morris's hips.

Their tongues swirled and thrust hungrily and a burst of heat and need rushed down Penn's spine when Morris's fingers speared through his hair and twisted possessively. They fused for a moment and Penn was enthralled and euphoric as they kissed, panted, and rocked against each other. Their bodies locked and found the same rhythm and Penn was so *ready* when Morris grabbed a handful of his ass and sucked on his tongue.

"Wait!" Morris wrenched his lips free and gasped for breath. His eyes were seeking, reflecting the lights and stars behind Penn. "What's happening here? I need to know if this is...serious or if you're still lost or chasing a spark or whatever you call it."

"What?" Penn laughed but his voice got higher and it cracked. He grabbed the handrail and pulled himself up and off Morris. There was another strained laugh as Penn yanked the elastic from his hair and hastily ran his fingers through it. "I wasn't thinking and then I was just going with it. Maybe I was hoping it wouldn't be a big deal. It's just sex, right?"

Morris's lips pulled into a hard line as he shook his head. "It's a big deal to me and we both know this is a hell of a lot more than sex," he said, gesturing between them.

Penn nodded. "You're right. I'm sorry." He stepped back, hugging his arms and cringing. "What if we got it out of our systems and—" He started but stopped when Morris laughed.

"I don't want to get it out of my system, Penn!" He explained while keeping his voice down. "I want it all and I want to know what it's like to get lost in you."

"Oh. I—" Penn looked around to see if there was somewhere he could hide or a hole he could bury himself in. He had never felt two more wildly conflicting emotions at once. There was the obvious dread at the thought of needing Morris and then losing him, but Penn also felt giddy and joyful.

"I know. You don't do relationships and you like to keep sex casual," Morris said without a hint of bitterness or judgment.

He looked sad, though, as he shrugged. "I don't want to be casual about you. I want to know if every bit of you tastes as sweet as your lips and what it takes to get you to swear good and loud. But I won't get there by rushing. I have to take my time until I know your body better than I know my own."

Penn's eyes stung and blurred with tears of frustration. He'd never wanted anyone to know or want him like that, yet he suddenly yearned for that with Morris. Then, he remembered that his parents had had that. "What about when it's over? Because that kind of magic doesn't last forever and it wrecks you when you lose it."

A loud breath whooshed from Morris as he pushed off the step and stood. "Don't I know it? You can't stop living, though. At least, that's what everyone keeps telling me."

"You're right," Penn conceded. "But what if I'm not as strong as everyone thinks I am? Everyone depends on me and I live for that, Morris. Loving *everyone* is who I am and I'm scared I can't do that if I start punching holes in my heart."

"I can totally understand that and I don't blame you. And you would put *everyone's* needs before yours."

"I'm mostly scared," Penn said with an apologetic smile. "And I know that I don't have a lot of time left with my dad and that…" His nose began to tingle and leak as he cried in earnest, and he felt true fear. "I can't stop what's coming or run away from it and I can't risk being broken when he needs me. Then, there's everything that comes after that and I don't know what's going to be left, once he's gone."

"That's when you let us take care of you. You won't be alone," Morris promised. Penn believed him and knew Morris would be there no matter what happened between them. And Penn knew that Reid would make sure he and Penny had around-the-clock support when they had to say goodbye to Gus.

"I know. I've never been good at letting people take care of me. It feels backward and wrong and I'm happiest when I'm open and tuned into other people's needs."

"Right..." Morris squinted and craned his neck. "But avoiding commitment and hooking up with random guys has to get old. Don't you want more?"

"More to lose?" Penn countered, holding up his hands. "And I don't have to choose between my boyfriend and my dad or worry about how much time I'm putting into my families. Can you imagine someone trying to date me? I live with my clients and when I'm not with them, I'm with my dad and Penny, or Reid and Gavin."

"I try not to think about that if I'm being honest," Morris said tightly, giving Penn's conscience a hard jab.

"Would it be better if I left? I can talk to Reid and we can find someone else if this has gotten too complicated," he offered gently, but Morris jumped.

"No! We need you and you belong here. You're family now and that's always going to matter more to me than sex."

Penn let out a relieved sigh as he reached for Morris and pulled him into a hug. "Thank goodness because I was totally bluffing. I'd be lost without you and Cadie."

"You don't have to worry about that. I can keep it in my pants and I'm cool with just being friends." Morris held him tight and Penn reveled in the feel of him in his arms. His warmth and his scent seeped into Penn and he wondered if this was as close as he'd ever get. "I don't care how complicated *we* get. We're family and a team now," Morris said as he released Penn.

"Me too. I can totally keep it in my pants and I'll always be here for you," Penn said, then halted when he leaned toward Morris's lips. He laughed and wrinkled his nose. "Better not risk it."

"Seriously. Knock it off," Morris teased and elbowed Penn away. "I can keep it in my pants if you can keep your hands and your lips to yourself."

"Sorry! I can't help myself," Penn admitted as he threw an arm around Morris and led him back into the house. "My lips just want to be pressed against yours all the time." He was joking and trying to lighten the mood, but it was true and Penn didn't want it to stop.

"That sounds like a you problem. Goodnight, Penn." Morris pulled free and didn't look back as he strolled through the kitchen and headed for his room.

Should I go after him? Should I apologize? Should I go for it?

The questions began stacking up in Penn's brain again as he lingered in the kitchen. He was so tired of overthinking and worrying about *everyone*. Penn wondered why his idea of happiness required sacrificing himself and giving up the thing he wanted most.

The door to Morris's room was open and Penn could hear him singing softly under his breath. Penn's feet carried him a little closer and he stopped and asked himself what he'd do if everything went wrong and he lost Morris.

"That's right. I'm a tall, goofy chicken," he said to himself, then turned and ran up the stairs to his sewing machine.

Chapter Nineteen

Self-care.

Morris woke up to the smell of coffee and the sound of Penn working in the kitchen. He was at his wit's end with wanting Penn and would have pulled all his hair out by now if he had any. But somehow, a safe, nurturing life had arranged itself around him, and Morris was feeling particularly grateful as he yawned and rubbed the sleep from his eyes.

Despite his kicking and screaming, the heavy cloud around and inside Morris was lifting and he could *feel* the warmth of his friends' and family's love and support. Instead of feeling pathetic or guilty, Morris wanted to honor the care they had showered upon him by...showering and putting a little extra care into himself.

He didn't know how long the mood would last so Morris sprang out of bed and let it carry him into the shower. Instead of obediently scrubbing himself down from head to toe with a washcloth and body wash, Morris took his time and used a detoxifying and hydrating face wash and sugar-scrubbed his "dry areas." He wallowed under the hot water, stretching out the kinks in his neck and shoulders and let the steam clear out his sinuses.

Morris felt refreshed, and there was a little extra bounce in his step as he patted himself dry and applied his most luxurious body balm. He hummed happily as he brushed his teeth and gave his beard a quick touch-up with the clippers. He'd let it grow out of neglect and because the minimum had been the most he was capable of, but Morris didn't hate what he was seeing, as he stepped back and considered his reflection.

He was wearing a towel tied around his waist and nothing else. While Morris would always be thick—and thick around the middle—he thought he carried it well. The beard made him look like a bear in the really *good* way, and he decided he'd keep it for a while.

Most of Morris's insecurities were tied up in his personality not his appearance, thankfully, and he was pleased enough with himself to contemplate real clothes. It seemed like a shame to put on joggers and a T-shirt when he'd taken so much time and used his very best products this morning. He mentally perused the flyest of his retro tracksuits as he picked his favorite serum and lotion from the tall cabinet.

He was grateful to Michelle for nagging him about his skin-care routine and filling his bathroom with fussy products. He'd done it to humor her in the beginning, but the little moments of pampering were nice. And the clean citrus and herbal scents doubled as aromatherapy, brightening Morris's mood and raising his energy level.

But there was a record scratch and Morris's self-care spa day came to an abrupt end. "What in the...?" He frowned at the serum in his palm. It was clear and runny, instead of thick and pearlescent. And it didn't smell right. "I just opened this!" He grabbed the bottle to confirm that it was practically new. Morris held it up to the light and wasn't thinking when he braced the hand with the "serum" on the edge of the sink.

He attempted to press the nozzle again, but it was stuck. "Oh, no." Morris's eyes dropped to his other hand. He tried to raise it and swore at the tugging and tightness of his palm as it remained sealed to the porcelain. Morris squeezed his eyes shut and clung to his frustration. "I'm checking *everything* in this house as soon as I'm free." Especially the toiletries and foods he hadn't touched since Michelle's death. "Hey, Penn?" He yelled and counted down from ten to ease his temper and lower his blood pressure while he waited.

"Everything okay?" Penn called back.

Morris gave his reflection a hard look. He'd walked right into another one of Michelle's pranks and he didn't relish what was coming. "Could you give me a hand in here?" He glanced at his own hand and rolled his eyes.

There was a quick tap at the door before it opened and Penn leaned in. "Sure. What's up?"

"My hand's super glued to the counter," Morris said, gesturing at his ineptitude.

"What?" Penn asked, then burst into laughter as he hurried into the bathroom. "What did you do?" He demanded as he bent at the waist to get a closer look. For a moment, Morris was too distracted by Penn's naked torso and ratty pajama shorts. They hung low around his hips, revealing a tempting trail of hair beneath his navel and a portion of a very interesting tattoo. Morris could only make out a few of the words that snaked around his hip and dipped beneath the waist of his shorts.

"I didn't do anything," Morris mumbled weakly. He was suddenly thirsty and he had to lick his lips to get them to work. "Looks like another one of Michelle's pranks. I think she thought the pump would glue itself together but the glue didn't dry."

A thoughtful "Hmmm…" floated from Penn and he was all business as he inspected Morris's hand and the bottle. "I think the serum in the mouth of the pump acted like a seal. The other end was submerged inside the bottle and never dried."

Morris let out a loud, relieved breath. "Whew! Thanks for solving that mystery, Mr. Wizard!" He wiped his brow with his free hand, then widened his eyes at Penn impatiently. "Do you have any idea how to fix this?"

"He's always so serious," Penn said, clicking his teeth at Morris. "May I?" He asked as he pointed at the linen cabinet next to the shower.

"Go for it."

Penn gave him a thumbs-up and began snooping. He was whistling as he ducked and hunted amongst the cleaning supplies. "Any first-aid stuff?" He asked Morris.

"I keep all that on the top shelf," he said and Penn straightened and went back to whistling while he poked at bottles and tubes.

"I noticed that you're taking a lot of allergy meds…" Penn said as he glanced over his shoulder at Morris. "Is there anything serious I should watch out for? Do I need to keep an EpiPen on me?"

"Nope. They're mostly seasonal and environmental," Morris said with a dismissive shrug. There was also a bottle of PrEP front and center on the top shelf but he didn't want to talk about that with Penn. "Is there anything in particular you're looking for?" He asked, hoping to move the process along.

"Some rubbing alcohol would probably work…" Penn murmured, not seeming at all interested in Morris's PrEP, to his relief.

"That's with the real first-aid kit in the kitchen."

"Yeah. All you've got in here is some ointment and a few

Band-aids. What about nail polish remover?" He glanced over his shoulder again and Morris shook his head.

"You can try Michelle's bathroom. I know she had some."

"I have a bottle," Penn said, holding out a hand so Morris could admire his new manicure. His nails had been a pale blue the night before but were now painted in different pastel colors.

"Very nice."

"I'll be right back."

Penn dashed from the bathroom, leaving Morris stuck to the counter and stuck thinking about the bottle of PrEP in the cabinet. He went through the motions—getting tested, keeping his prescription up to date, and taking the pills—in hopes that he could somehow manifest a love life without the tediousness of meeting and conversing with men. That would require Morris to leave the house and have a modicum of personality.

He snorted at his reflection. What was the point of pretending and setting up false expectations? For close to two decades, R&B, soul, and hip-hop luminaries had passed through Morris's studio and the world assumed that some of their charisma had rubbed off on him. But he was still just a nerd with a soundboard who loved to write poetry and knew how to play a lot of instruments.

Win had been the first man to show interest in a while and he had practically delivered himself to Morris's doorstep. But Morris didn't want a relationship that began with a lie or ulterior motives like that. He'd feel like a fraud and like he was forcing something to be there that wasn't. And how would he know what was real and what was business? They'd already be off to a questionable start because Morris wasn't sure if Win actually liked him for who he was. Which seemed very unlikely because they barely knew each other and Morris knew he wasn't all that cool without stylists and a PR team.

What if he could fool one person into believing he was cool and had a personality? What if he had someone to write poetry and love songs for? He had one smooth-ass quiet storm slow jam, and four more songs were in bits and pieces in the studio. It had been *years* since an album had spoken to Morris this loudly and clearly. The melodies and lyrics were simply there and in his ear whenever he thought about Penn or heard his voice.

But Morris had to keep all of that to himself. Those songs could never leave his studio. Penn had made his intentions clear and Morris understood why those boundaries had been raised.

"Got it!" Penn announced, brandishing a bottle as he hurried into the bathroom.

A roll of paper towels was tucked under Penn's arm and this time, Morris was too aware of how little they were wearing as their bodies bumped and brushed. Morris kept his breathing calm while Penn soaked wads of paper and made a ring around the half of his hand that was on the sink's ledge.

"We'll let that sit while I see if I can loosen the underside," Penn said and began dabbing at Morris's palm.

"Thanks."

He missed this—the thrill and the heady allure of another naked body. It had been so long since Morris had a naked man in his bed and his bathroom, since he had felt the intoxicating slide of hot, sweating skin against skin. Morris craved the damp huff of a man's breath against his neck and his lips.

I want Penn.

He couldn't have Penn and Morris had to move on before the situation became unhealthy. "I was thinking I might try dating again," he blurted out, then bit down on his lips.

"That's..." Penn kept his head down and squinted at Morris's hand. "I think that's a good idea."

"Do you?" Morris asked, but Penn only nodded as he poured more of the nail polish remover onto the counter. He used another piece of paper towel to guide it around Morris's hand. He hadn't meant to do it, but Morris had trapped Penn in the bathroom with him.

"You're beautiful and brilliant, Morris. And your body..." He whistled softly and attempted a playful wink, but there was heat in Penn's eyes when they flicked to Morris's. "Someone should be worshiping you," he added shakily. His burning, lustful gaze drifted down Morris's body and lingered on the towel.

"Penn!" Morris captured his cheek with his free hand and pulled Penn's eyes to his. He couldn't take Penn looking at him like that. "I'd worship *you*!" He confessed raggedly, sliding his fingers into Penn's hair and drawing him closer.

"We can't—!" Penn's resistance only lasted a heartbeat, though. He groaned as the arm holding the bottle wound around Morris's neck. His other hand pushed down Morris's back and beneath the towel. Penn dug his nails into Morris's ass and they were both hard and starving as they attacked each other's lips.

"I know, but you taste so good." Morris lapped at Penn's tongue, already drunk on his sunny sweetness.

Penn made a sound that was half moan and half whimper. "You have no idea how bad I want to taste you."

That's when Morris's towel fell. Of course.

Penn stepped back and slid Morris a tortured look. "I am so sorry." He swallowed loudly, then widened his eyes at Morris before allowing them to drop.

"I get it," Morris said because he would have looked if their positions had been reversed.

"Oh. Shit."

It was definitely an "Oh, shit." situation when Penn

dragged his stunned gaze back to Morris's. His jaw stretched and his tongue extended as he started to slide down Morris's body.

"Wait!" Morris's fingers twisted tighter in Penn's hair, halting him and pulling it loose from its ponytail holder.

Time stopped and Morris imagined Penn on his knees. He had a fistful of Penn's hair and was guiding his head back and forth as he greedily sucked and slurped. Penn's wide, laughing lips were stretched around his shaft and Morris's toes were curled on the tile.

"We can't!" Morris recalled, returning to the present.

Which was presently pornographic because Morris was still naked and Penn still looked like he was ready to go.

"We can't?" Penn sounded forlorn as he stared at Morris's cock again.

"We can't. Unless you're ready to take this seriously."

"I..." His brow furrowed and Penn nodded. "I... I do think about it, Morris. A lot. But I—" He was saved when a groggy cry came from Morris's phone and the monitor app made it flash on the counter. "You know how she gets if you keep her waiting," Penn said with a pained grimace. "That should start to loosen, just go slow so you don't rip your skin. I'll check on you once I get little miss settled." He ducked his head at Morris, then ran from the bathroom.

Morris was left naked and reeling. And stuck to the sink with a raging hard-on. "Not the kind of self-care I had in mind," he muttered as he hunkered over his hand and began to slowly peel his palm off the lip of the sink. "I'll definitely be needing this hand later," he said under his breath.

He was a bit too frustrated to fully appreciate it at the moment, but Morris would get some mileage out of how willing and eager Penn was to drop to his knees.

Chapter Twenty

W as there a point anymore? Penn suspected he was in denial and playing Sisyphus because he was scared of letting the boulder roll.

But it felt like the boulder was already rolling as Penn's body swayed from side to side with the momentum of the F train. He became hypnotized by the soft rhythm of the subway car on the rails and he was no longer headed downtown on the Coney Island-Stillwell Ave-bound line to make his connection to the PATH train.

Penn was on his knees in Morris's bathroom, licking and sucking to his heart's content. He'd been grateful that it was Saturday and he had an excuse to flee the house, but Penn was still there, mentally.

The kicker of it was, Penn was so *happy* when he fantasized about Morris like that. It was also incredibly hot, but Penn experienced a hit of euphoria when he imagined touching and tasting Morris. He had a hundred heavy reasons to keep his hands off Morris and Penn forgot every single one of them when they kissed.

That's what Penn was running from when he told Morris he was heading to Hoboken to see his dad. He couldn't fight something that good for that much longer. His instincts told him it was inevitable and Penn was losing the will to resist.

What would the boulder destroy and what parts of Penn would be left crushed in its wake? How could he give all of himself to Morris and still have enough left over for his father and his sister and all of his friends? Would there be enough of him left for Morris after Gus was gone? And how would Penn recover and have anything left for anyone if he gave his heart to Morris and lost him?

It was such a selfish risk to take, yet Penn could see the cliff coming and he wanted to jump. He would have happily taken the dive and drowned in Morris earlier in the bathroom. The blowjob would have gone on and on until his knees were raw, and then, Penn would have pulled Morris to the floor and rode him until the room *stank* and the mirrors fogged up.

They could have had all day to play because Evelyn had picked up the baby shortly after breakfast and wasn't bringing her back until Sunday night. It could have been ecstasy, but instead Penn was on his way to Hoboken because he was running out of weekends with Gus.

He scraped all those thoughts aside as he climbed up the front steps of the house he grew up in. He'd spent about a third of his life up at the cabin or scrambling around the Catskills, but Penn had learned his hardest lessons and lived the tenderest parts of his childhood in the modest brick rowhouse on 7th Street. It was years before Gus could go back to the cabin with them and Penn had watched his father fall apart, then slowly pull himself back together.

Gus wasn't the same laughing teddy bear Penn had chased through the woods and napped in hammocks with as a child, though. He kept himself up and running for Penn and Penny, but Gus was more withdrawn, preferring to spend his days alone, watching fishing shows and recorded Knicks games.

They thought he was going to let go when prostate cancer tried to take him. Gus had held on, thank goodness. But he was frail and was having more trouble getting around every time Penn visited him. Penn had brought Cadence the last time he visited and she had cheered Gus up tremendously. He'd ask about bringing her more often, but Penn thought it might be nice if Morris came with them too.

Gus was backing himself into the living room when Penn tapped on the door and let himself in. "Hey, Pops!" Penn pressed a kiss to Gus's cheek before taking the wheelchair's handlebars.

"I wasn't expecting you today."

"What are you talking about? I always come by on Saturdays when I'm off."

"You should be with Morris and that sweet little Cadie Rose."

Penn chuckled and steered them into the living room. Cadence's middle name was Eve, a nod to Evelyn, but Gus had given her a middle nickname of his own. "They don't need me today. She's hanging out at the bakery this morning. Evelyn and Morris Sr. are keeping the baby every other weekend now. Morris has to take a break too," he explained.

Gus threw his hands up and made a disgruntled sound. "That's what I'm saying! It's the perfect time to take him out to dinner or maybe you two could do the Netflix and chill."

"The Netflix and chill?" Penn laughed as he helped Gus out of his chair and into his recliner. "What do you know about that?"

"Morrie told me that one. He said that it's what you young people call going steady but you turn on Netflix and skip right to the good parts."

"I don't know if I want you hanging out with Morris Sr. anymore." Penn set his hands on his hips and frowned down at Gus. "He's putting weird ideas in your head."

"I bet they're in your head too," Gus said and made a knowing sound as he pointed up at Penn. He waved it off and went to the kitchen for their beers.

"We're just friends."

"That's not what Penny says. She said you're like peas in a pod and that you've never been happier," Gus called, his head peeking around the side of his recliner.

"Dad." Penn gave him a hard look before ducking behind the refrigerator door. He used the moment to brace himself and said a quick prayer as he swiped two bottles off the bottom shelf. "I don't *have* the kind of time a man like Morris deserves. And he deserves someone really cool who can put him and Cadence first."

"Where do you fit in?" Gus argued, but Penn made a dismissive sound as he twisted off one of the bottle tops.

"What are you talking about?"

"Let's say Morris finds someone cool. Why do they need you if he's so perfect and puts them first?"

"Oh. Well..." Penn stalled. "I'd be stoked for my friend and Reid would find me a new family," he said, but Penn couldn't look his father in the eye as he handed him a beer and went to sit on the sofa. He had a mental meltdown, his soul kicking and screaming as he sat and attempted to appear outwardly calm and casual.

"I bet you'd be stoked," Gus said and chuckled into his beer.

"I'd be fine." Penn's arm stretched along the back of the sofa and he hummed absently at the game on the television. The volume was turned low and the faint whistles and cheers weren't enough of a buffer. Penn could feel Gus staring at him. "What?" Penn finally asked.

"I sure wouldn't mind if the two of you brought the little one around more. I found some nice scraps in my workshop and thought she might like a doll house," Gus mused, then smiled. "It'll have a recording studio and Penny Lane can make mini-Penn and Morris dolls to go with it."

Penn flashed Gus a wide smile. "That sounds precious. Just leave room for someone else. Morris and I have talked about this and I'm not right for him. And I don't have the kind of time he and Cadence deserve."

"What are you talking about? You practically live with them," Gus argued and Penn pointed.

"That's exactly why we can't date. I'm already giving 100% when I'm with them. I have to maintain a boundary and reserve enough of my time and energy for the other people who need me."

"Says who?" Gus growled as he sat forward.

"Umm... Me?" Penn attempted warily. "I worry enough about how much I've been putting on Penny lately. I'm barely here during the week as it is."

"By God, Penn, if I find out you're blowing it with Morris because of me I'll—"

"Easy!" Penn held up a hand, halting Gus before he got too riled up. "Not just because of you and it's more of a general policy, when it comes to men and dating. Morris is..." He laughed softly and shook his head. "He's perfect and he'd probably be the one, but I decided a long time ago that I didn't want any of that. I don't want to be in that kind of relationship and Morris understands. We're cool just being friends," he said with a nonchalant bounce of his shoulders.

Gus's face twisted and he threw a sneer at Penn. "The only

person you're lying to right now is yourself. When did you decide that?"

That was the last thing Penn wanted to talk about. "Why does it matter? I love you for believing I'm good enough for him. But I'm all wrong for Morris and we're happy with things the way they are."

"You're up to your neck in bullshit, son. When did you decide you didn't want any of that?" Gus demanded and leaned over the arm of his chair so he could pin Penn with a glare.

"Well..." Penn stalled and fiddled with the label on his bottle. "I saw what losing Mom did to you and I don't want to go through that or cause anyone that kind of pain," he admitted quietly.

"Is that all you remember?" His father asked, the gruffness in his voice softening to a rasp. Penn shook his head. He remembered his parents teasing each other at the dinner table and holding hands as they rocked in the swing and sang to each other at night. But those moments seemed more brutal when Penn recalled how long and how hard his father had grieved.

"I know how much you still miss her and that it still hurts like hell," Penn said and reached for his father's hand. Gus gave his a squeeze and they were both quiet for a while, letting the game distract them until they had recovered.

"I wouldn't do a damn thing differently," Gus finally said, then snorted. "I take that back. I would have loved her more and I would have loved more of her." He cleared his throat and raised his brows suggestively.

Penn snorted and raised his bottle in salute. "I wouldn't be here if you and Mom had joined the clergy."

"I didn't need a church when I had a goddess at home." Gus's smile spread as his stare grew distant and stretched over Penn's shoulder. His parents had always been playful and affectionate and he was grateful to have those memories as well. "I'd like to know that you've found something like that before my time is up," Gus said, pulling Penn from his thoughts and hurting his heart.

"Dad!" He started to get up so he could hide in the kitchen. Gus hummed loudly as he sipped, warning Penn to keep his butt in that seat and listen.

"You and your sister are my life, but loving your mother is the greatest joy I've ever known. And every memory she left behind is a gift. There are times when the pain's as bad as the day I lost her. That's just how it goes and there's nothing I can do but ride it out and remember the good times." He needed another moment and Penn needed to hold his dad's hand again. Gus sniffed hard, fighting back tears, but they rode the wave of grief together. "I think about how she'd iron my shirt before bed every night and leave it hanging on the bathroom door. She liked to wear my shirts after I took them off and she'd sleep in them. I can still picture Laurel with her hair all twisted up and held in place by a pencil, wearing my shirt and singing to herself while ironing the next day's shirt."

"I didn't know," Penn said. He could picture her so vividly, though, and it was nice to learn something new about her and add a new memory to his collection.

"You were usually in bed by then and I doubt you'd appreciate how sexy Laurel looked in those shirts."

"Nor do I need to," Penn replied, making Gus laugh.

"No, you don't. But those are the memories she left me with, and I have more than twenty years' worth of them to ease the pain. What are you gonna have and why would you let someone else make those memories with Morris? Your smile gets bigger when you talk about him and you're head over heels in love with that little girl."

"She's everything, Pops," Penn sighed dreamily. He

missed her so damn much and wondered what Evelyn had dressed her in. The two of them and their fashion shows... "I love her and maybe I do wanna Netflix and chill with Morris."

"*Just* Morris," Gus added pointedly.

"What have you heard?" Penn asked and narrowed his eyes at Gus.

He smirked back at Penn. "I know you get around."

"You and Morris Sr. should get a hobby. You listen to too much gossip and you need to stop meddling."

"You're telling me you aren't a ho?"

"Dad."

Gus snickered and sipped his beer. "Penny told me all about that too. It's one thing to sow your oats, son, but you're getting a little old to be carrying on like that."

"I can't believe I came all the way to Hoboken for this. I've never hurt anyone and I'm doing my best not to hurt Morris," he explained slowly and gave Gus a hard look, asking him to back off.

"You're hurting yourself, Penn. Laurel would want you to go for it. She'd want you to be happy."

"I can't—!" Penn popped to his feet.

"What are you scared of?" Gus called after him as Penn stepped around the coffee table and strode back into the kitchen. It felt claustrophobic and he wished the house wasn't so small, just as he had in his twenties during Gus's darkest, bitterest days. Those days had ripped Penn's heart to shreds. But he'd never fought harder than he had to save Gus after his mother died. And nothing seemed unsurvivable after that. Except for losing Gus or Penny.

"I was afraid of letting everyone down, but now I've got to worry about disappointing Mom too," Penn complained, yanking the fridge open and swiping another beer.

"You could never disappoint her. And you've never disappointed me," Gus said softly.

"Dad..." Penn dragged the back of his hand under his nose as he trudged into the living room and sat down.

"All we've ever wanted was for you and your sister to have big adventures and be happy. You're missing out on the greatest adventure of all, hiding like that," Gus scolded as gently as he could. But Penn could hear his father's frustration. "I did wonder why you hadn't found anyone, but I never thought it had anything to do with me and your mother."

Penn flailed a hand at Gus. "How would it be anything else? It killed you to lose Mom and we never got you back. You stayed for us but she took the best parts of you with her," he said, whispering an apology as he scooted closer and took Gus's hand again.

"She did and I am sorry that I wasn't stronger. I regret a lot of things and losing myself like that is one of them. That's why I wasn't a pain in the ass about chemo. I'd already put you through enough."

"What are you talking about? You were still a pain in the ass about chemo," Penn said with a watery laugh. But he knew what Gus meant. Not fighting the cancer had been discussed and Penn and Penny were grateful when Gus agreed to try for them.

"This is what I held on for. You have a chance to have everything. Don't miss out on the adventure, Penn."

Penn used his palm to sweep the tears from his eyes so he could see. "Okay! I'll think about it!"

"You don't know how much time—" Gus started but Penn shushed loudly.

"I promise! Can we please just watch the game?" He pleaded. "The last few months have been...a lot and I was already fed up with myself when I walked through the door."

"Eh!" His father swatted at the television. "I watched it twice yesterday. Want to get my scooter so we can go out to the shed and see about that dollhouse?"

"Best idea all day!" Penn said and went to get the scooter, desperate for the sweet relief of sandpaper and power tools.

Chapter Twenty-One

He couldn't find Michelle.

Morris searched the studio and called for her as he raced up the steps and checked her bedroom. She wasn't in the nursery either. His heart raced with panic and dread as he hurried down the steps, checking the living room and the kitchen again before he threw the basement door open and shouted her name.

He came awake in the dark, his heart thrashing in his chest. His fingers were twisted in the duvet and *he* was clenched like a fist. Morris was caught in the terror of the dream, *needing* to find Michelle, while fighting off the awful, awful truth that came with consciousness.

She's gone.

"No!" Morris curled onto his side and screamed into his pillow. His body shook with his sobs and the pain was brutal. It punched him in the ribs and the gut, knocking the wind out of him.

"I'm here!" Penn called as he rushed into the room. The

bed dipped next to Morris and he was pulled into a tight embrace. "I've got you!" Penn whispered, cradling the back of Morris's head.

"It's not fair!"

"No, it's not," Penn said softly.

He nodded along and cried with Morris, letting him vent and be bitter until the storm had passed. They held each other and Morris became more and more aware of Penn's fingers as they traced soothing swirls across his back.

"Thank you." Morris exhaled slowly as his muscles unclenched and relaxed.

"I couldn't sleep so I came down to smoke again and heard you."

Morris raised his head and narrowed his eyes at Penn. "When was the last time you had a decent night's sleep?"

"I get by on a few hours here and there. I've never been a big sleeper. I'm too restless." Penn shifted on the bed and wiped the tear clinging to Morris's lashes.

"That's not what I asked you," Morris complained. "You can tell me you're having trouble sleeping. I won't think you're less of a miracle worker."

"I'm not a miracle worker. I'm just stayin' busy so I don't climb the walls, and I like helping people."

"Nope." Morris shook his head. He got up on an elbow and captured Penn's cheek. "What are you running from and why won't you let yourself rest?"

"I told you. I don't know if I can be everything you need and still be me. I don't know if I'm good enough."

"This is more than enough, Penn." Morris grew warmer at the feel of Penn's skin sliding against his. He reveled in the smell of Penn's breath and his body as they rolled and writhed and eventually kicked the duvet away. "Do you remember what I told you? Worry about what you want and what you need."

"I want you," Penn breathed against Morris's lips, a soft, shaking confession in the dark.

Morris pulled Penn's hair loose and tangled his fingers in it as he kissed him, desperate for more warmth, for more of Penn. "You have to mean it this time. I can't stop," Morris warned, shoving Penn's ratty flannel shorts down and gripping an asscheek possessively.

"Don't stop!" Penn gasped and arched before rolling them over again and pinning Morris. He rose and Morris's nightmare had been replaced by a dream. Penn's hair fell around Morris's face and shoulders as they kissed and fumbled with their pajama pants until they were both naked. "Don't stop. Take whatever you want," Penn whispered as he settled over Morris.

"I'm taking everything." Morris wrapped his arms tight around Penn, locking them together as he kissed him hungrily. His hands gripped and pulled at Penn's back and ass as Morris's tongue swirled and lapped possessively. Their legs tangled and Morris found himself on top again and groaned in drunken delight as he dove into the corner of Penn's neck.

He licked and sucked on anything he could get his mouth on, gorging himself on the taste of Penn's skin and the sound of his ecstatic cries. They were music to Morris's ears. Each whimper and moan gave him goosebumps and they strung themselves into a beautiful melody as Morris explored Penn's body with his lips and his tongue.

And Penn practically screamed when Morris teased his nipples with playful flicks and nibbles. Morris wound him up and was captivated by the restless, bucking tempo of Penn's hips and the staccato of his breaths.

"Please, please, please don't stop!" Penn's breathless chants became a chorus, drugging Morris and urging him on. He hummed along as his lips dipped into the well of Penn's navel and swept across his pelvis. Penn was soapy, soft, and just a little salty on the inside of his hip and under his sac. His moans grew huskier and his pleas sultrier and even more desperate when Morris held Penn open and lapped at his hole. "I noticed — Christ, Morris! I um...noticed that you're— Morris, Please! You're taking PrEP. Oh, God." Penn rocked his hips and held onto Morris's head, riding his tongue. "I am too!" He squeaked.

"Mmm..." Morris spit and worked a finger into Penn.

"I have condoms upstairs! But...I don't...need one," Penn choked out, setting Morris's whole body alight. He'd never trusted anyone the way he trusted Penn and Morris didn't want any barriers between them.

"I don't need one. I want everything, Penn."

"Yes! I'm ready. Anything you want!" Penn babbled and undulated on the bed as Morris's tongue swept up his shaft and around the head.

There was *a lot* of Penn to get his lips around and Morris was rewarded with a slick burst of pre-cum when he took him deep into his throat and sucked hard. He strummed and stroked, plucking at Penn's strings as Morris feasted and made sweet music with him.

"Morris! Come on!" Penn begged as his heels dug into the mattress and his feet curled.

Morris smirked up at Penn and crawled over him to get to the nightstand. "If you're in a hurry..." He pulled it open and found the lube. Morris sat back on his heels and opened the cap and Penn sat up and got his knees under him.

"Wait! Let me taste you first," he said, flipping his hair over his shoulder and bracing his hands on the bed. His jaw and his tongue stretched as he lowered and Penn groaned in delight as his lips slid down Morris's length.

"Fuck, *Penn.*" Morris gathered a handful of Penn's hair and leaned back so he could watch. "Fuck, fuck, fuck..." His cock was wrapped in sucking heat as Penn's head rose and fell at a decadently slow pace. Morris heard *their* song, the one he'd written for Penn, and it was as if all those hours in the studio had wished *them* into existence.

"Mmmm..." Penn dragged his tongue down Morris's shaft, then angled his head. His tongue lashed at Morris's sac before he sucked and tugged with his lips. "You taste even better than I imagined," he mumbled and licked his way up Morris's cock. His tongue teased the slit as his eyes trapped Morris's and it was hard to breathe, hard to believe any of it was real.

"Come here!" Morris tightened his grip on Penn's hair and pulled him up for a kiss. "You have to mean this," he growled and pushed Penn onto the bed, falling with him. He kissed Penn deeply and possessively, claiming him with his lips, his tongue, and his hands, promising to give him everything back in return. "Tell me you're mine now."

"Yes!" Penn nodded frantically as his arms and legs pulled Morris closer.

Morris raised his head and held onto Penn's hair, trapping his gaze. "You mean it?"

"I mean it. I'm yours."

"Mine." That was all Morris needed. *Mine, mine, mine, mine, mine, mine, mine,* went his heart like a drum and Morris heard chimes as chills spilled down his spine. He could feel that it was real and Morris knew Penn wouldn't have said it if it wasn't true.

There was a little fumbling as Morris hunted for the lube and coated his length with shaking hands. But it was better than he'd dreamed as Morris lined up the head of his cock with Penn's hole and slowly slid all the way home.

They were so close, and so slick, and he was so deep, and Penn was so tight.

Morris rocked his hips and Penn gasped and arched beneath him. "Yes! More! Don't stop!" His strained whimpers became a heady melody that got louder and louder with every thrust.

And Penn stole Morris's breath with his beauty. His hair swirled around him and his lips were swollen from their desperate kisses. His head was pulled back as he arched and chanted Morris's name and urged him on.

Morris rose and leaned back so he could watch. Penn was *so tight*. And Morris was enthralled with the sight as his cock plunged in and out of Penn's slick, gripping heat. He draped one of Penn's long legs over his shoulder, making his strokes deeper, and Morris had never felt such bliss.

He'd never felt closer or known his partner better, and Morris had never felt as much trust. His hands worshiped Penn's thighs, stomach, ass, chest... Every bit of Penn he could touch was wondrous and sacred because he finally could. But Morris also felt like he was home and safe. He wrapped a hand around Penn's cock and Morris heard his gasp, felt him clench with each stroke, and they were one.

They were in perfect harmony and Morris had never heard anything as sweet as their song came to a crescendo.

Gasp, gasp, gasp.

Slap, slap, slap.

"Fuck, fuck, fuck, Penn!"

Slap, slap, slap.

Gasp, slap, gasp, slap.

"Morris! More, Morris! *More!*"

Slap! Slap! Slap! Slap! Slap! Slap! Slap! Slap! Slap!

Gasp.

Penn froze and the music stopped. Morris would spend days in the studio, layering instruments and beats until their song felt just like this. But he would never write a chord or lyrics adequate enough to convey the awe and reverence he felt in that moment.

Penn was stunning with his back bowed off the bed and his hands twisted in the duvet. His knuckles were white and his feet were curled as his eyes rolled in delirious ecstasy. Sweat dampened the hair between his pecs and covered his tattooed limbs in a soft sheen, making him glow.

He was ethereal, his hair was a wild, golden halo. Morris wished he was a better writer so he'd have a way back to this, so he'd never have to let go of Penn.

"Please be mine," he prayed.

"Yes!" Penn nodded drunkenly as he reached for Morris. "Yours."

The music was back and Morris let go. He fell forward, losing himself in Penn's lips and his body. It was like falling into the most beautiful song he'd ever heard and Morris was crying as he pulled Penn's leg around his hip and dove deeper. Morris dug in with his knees and swallowed the moans and sobs that poured from Penn's lips.

"*Penn.*" Morris couldn't see or hear anything. He burst into bright heat, his nerves flaring and pulsing with radiant pleasure as he came deep inside of Penn. Waves of joyful warmth rolled through Morris and he knew it was Penn's soul touching his. "Penn."

He was truly lost and there was nothing but Penn as they held onto each other and waited to catch their breath and for their bodies to cool.

"Jesus, Morris! Were you trying to kill me?" Penn finally wheezed, making Morris grin.

He hummed happily and was smug as he rolled onto his side and gathered Penn in his arms. "I heard you were out there slinging dick like John Wick so I—"

"What?" Penn burst into laughter. Morris laughed with

him and it was magical, combined with the post-coital flickering of his nerves. He had never laughed during or after sex. Morris wasn't sure if he'd laughed all that much before sex with any of his past partners, but he had a feeling he would always laugh with Penn.

"It was just something Reid said when he warned me not to sleep with you," Morris murmured as he swept the hair away from Penn's face and pecked at his lips.

"I...think I know who that is and I'm glad you didn't listen to Reid."

Morris laughed softly. "He said he'd tell me to go for it if you were ready to change and settle down."

"I didn't realize I had such a dark reputation or that those guys gossiped so much. Dad and Morrie could gossip less too, now that I think of it," Penn grumbled.

"They'll find something else to talk about now that you've retired."

"*Pshhh!* You think that's going to stop those chatterboxes?" Penn looked genuinely disgruntled until he winked.

He made Morris laugh again and he didn't want to let go. "Stay here tonight," Morris said, winding his arms around Penn.

"I'm not going anywhere unless you're carrying me," Penn replied with a hard yawn, then rubbed his nose against Morris's. "Or until sunrise. I'll make sure you know I'm leaving, though."

"You could sleep in. Cadie's with my parents," Morris suggested, but Penn snorted.

"I've changed, but I haven't changed that much."

"Good." Morris closed his eyes and burrowed into the corner of Penn's neck and his hair. "I like you and I like us just the way we are."

"Me too," Penn stated. "It would be perfect if everything

went back to the way it was before things got tense and weird, just with lots of sex."

"Nothing has to change," Morris vowed, but everything had changed for him. There was warmth and beauty in his world again and Morris was smiling as he drifted off to sleep with Penn in his arms.

Chapter Twenty-Two

Everything had changed.

Everything within Penn had been rearranged and several of the doors and drawers had been left open. But there wasn't a "What have I done?" moment as Penn stared at the ceiling and listened to Morris sleep. He didn't regret making love to Morris because how could he? For the first time in his life, Penn had *made love.*

It wasn't sex or fucking, even though it involved all the same body parts and the same moves. It tasted like sex and it sounded like sex. And it certainly felt like sex when Penn came with Morris buried deep inside of him. But Penn had used every bit of himself, leaving gaping holes that were now filled with Morris.

Penn couldn't pretend he didn't know what he was doing when he climbed into Morris's bed with his wounds raw and stinging. And he knew that Morris was open and bleeding as they cried and mashed their wounds together. They were bruised, tired, and tear-soaked as their bodies cooled, but they laughed and whispered in the dark. Penn could feel their scars healing and the bond between them growing stronger.

He thought he'd been in love before and it had crushed him. But everything he'd experienced with Tristan was nothing compared to the joy and soul-deep satisfaction Penn felt as he gave himself to Morris. He felt whole and right, then, but as Penn dwelled alone in the dark, he wondered "What do I do without him?"

He'd kept his heart open and free for everyone for so long that Penn felt selfish as their heated cries echoed in the still of the night. What had he taken from his father, Penny, and his friends? What if he couldn't give Cadence all the love and attention she needed because he was obsessed with Morris now?

How could he not be? Penn had never shared anything that deep, that raw, and that *real* with anyone before. He knew what Morris's soul felt and tasted like and he'd left pieces of it stashed inside of Penn. They'd always be there and Penn was already worried he'd taken on too much and was getting overwhelmed.

That didn't stop him from waking Morris up with his lips a little before sunrise. Penn needed to touch and taste everything he'd missed the night before. He'd been too swept up in Morris's need, too happy to give up control and let him take whatever he wanted.

I'm taking everything.

Penn had happily handed it all over and he'd do it again and again. He'd never get enough and Morris's *"Mine."* grew and spread within Penn's psyche, claiming everything it touched. What could matter more or be better than belonging to *him*?

There was also the matter of Penn's reputation. He wasn't getting out of that bed until Morris begged for mercy. Penn had learned his lesson when it came to his friends' lack of discretion and would make sure he left that man wrecked.

"Holy fuck, Penn!"

Morris whimpered and bit into his pillow as Penn held him open and lapped at his hole. It was so easy to pause his existential crisis and sink into the sweet, clean taste of Morris's ass. There was the faint salty tang of sweat and Penn was in heaven as he feasted on Morris and made him beg and swear.

He swore enough for both of them. Especially when Penn slowly worked two, then three fingers into Morris's ass, getting him slick, restless, and ready. Morris leaked as Penn fingered his prostate, coating his tongue in pre-cum.

"Jesus fucking... Shit, Penn!" Morris slurred and pulled a pillow over his face to muffle a scream as he came. And he came, and he came, and he came, and he came. Penn milked every drop from Morris until his legs were shaking, then rode him slow and hard.

"Is that good?" Penn whispered huskily against the back of Morris's neck and bit into his shoulder.

"It's so good!"

"How about this?" Penn asked, pinning Morris's chest to the bed and angling his thrusts so he could drive deeper and harder.

"Yes!" Morris's strangled cry took Penn even higher. He dragged his fingers down Morris's back, collecting his sweat before Penn jammed them into his mouth and sucked. Penn was ascending and could already feel the sun. Pleasure swelled in his groin as Morris moaned his name and swore like a sailor.

"How's that?" Penn asked as he held onto Morris's hips and ground hard.

Morris yelped and planted a hand on the headboard. "So good! Fuck! You're so good!"

"What about this?" The loud slap of Penn's pelvis against

Morris's ass filled the air. He was so close. Penn's rhythm became jerkier and his strokes more desperate as his nerves fizzed and sparked wildly.

"Penn!" Morris screamed and writhed beneath Penn as he came again.

Penn gritted his teeth and held on, giving Morris time to recover before he swung forward and whispered in his ear. "Tell them John Wick was here."

A loud cackle exploded from Morris and Penn grabbed onto it. He shattered with the sound of Morris's laughter ringing in his ears and Penn swore he'd give anything for them to feel that good and that happy again.

There he was, obsessed and so thoroughly and completely Morris's as they kissed and whispered. "I'm gonna get up and do a little yoga before breakfast."

"You have got to be joking. After that?" Morris mumbled and shook his head. He was already retreating, pulling the duvet up to his ears and nestling into his pillow.

"Go back to sleep." Penn kissed his cheek before slipping out of bed.

His body ached and Penn was exhausted, but he rolled out his mat on the back porch just as the sun was coming up. He had hoped that he'd feel balanced and recharged by the sun. He didn't hear his mother's voice or feel her presence in the sun's rays, though, as they warmed him and eased his sore muscles. Instead, he felt Morris's hands and lips on his skin and Penn heard their sultry gasps and moans.

He wasn't troubled because he knew she'd always be there and he'd be able to find her again. But Penn sat on his heels on the mat, scrubbing his face in frustration as he felt himself ripping into two. Half of him craved movement and productivity. Penn was ready to rise and *shine* for Cadence and the rest of the world, while the other half of Penn's being longed to fall back into Morris's bed and get lost again.

Penn was scattered and moody as he prepared Cadence's bottle and a loaf of banana bread for breakfast. He told himself it was normal to get caught up in a new relationship and that he was just panicking because he wasn't used to it. But Penn wanted to be better than that and was disappointed in himself as he stumbled out of the shower and into a pair of shorts before the baby woke up. He was irritated when he hurried back downstairs to get Cadence's bottle only to remember that she was still at Morris's parents'. He realized he could have slept in and had tied himself into knots over nothing.

It was all minor in the grand scheme of things, of course, but this was just the beginning. Things would only get more complicated. Wouldn't they? Penn had accepted that there would be consequences and he would accept responsibility. He just would have appreciated some time to get a grasp on his own feelings before he had to explain himself.

"I really do think I might be in love with him," Penn murmured while watching Morris's door from the kitchen. Morris was still sleeping and Penn could see his foot hanging off the side of the bed.

There was a knock at the front door and Penn didn't need to check the security camera to know it was his sister. "Penny Lane!" He said as he opened it.

She danced by on her tiptoes, kissing his cheek as she passed. "Good morning, brother mine!"

"What are you up to?" He asked.

"I thought I'd stop in and see if you wanted to go to Briarwood Terrace for breakfast, but you probably want to stay in and have sex with Morris again. Dash is meeting me there and afterward, we're going to—"

"Hold on!" Penn ordered, cutting her off. "Why would you say that?"

She stared at him for a moment, then shrugged and opened her oversized denim tote bag. Penn had made it for her from old jeans and overalls. "Do you need any condoms? I grabbed a bunch the last time I was in the clinic in case Dash had a sex emergency."

"No." Penn closed the bag and ducked so he could find her eyes and get her attention. "I'm good."

"Oh! Went right to skinny dipping, I see!" She winked knowingly at him and gasped when Penn pinched her nose between his knuckles.

"What do you know?" He asked slowly.

"Blessedly little when you consider the capacity of the human brain."

"Penny." Penn widened his eyes at her threateningly. There was a chance Morris had texted Reid, but Penn was more concerned that *he'd* already changed in some obvious way. It was also possible that she'd had another one of her premonitions or was picking up on some residual lust in his aura.

"I know that those are not Morris's shorts," she said as she pointed across the living room at Morris's room. Penn spotted his discarded red pajama shorts peeking from under the duvet and hanging off the end of the mattress. "And you've got that rosy post-smashfest glow." She gestured airily and pirouetted. "My little love bug isn't here, is she?" She asked, her eyes scanning around the room.

"She's with her grandparents," he said, and Penny's lips twisted.

"Not much for me to see here, then," she decided and turned to go.

"Wait!" Penn grabbed her by the back of her overalls, then spun her around. "I didn't say I *didn't* want to go with you."

"Why would you? Why are you even talking to me when you could be in there with him?" She asked and cocked her thumb at Morris's room.

Penn's lips pulled tight as he leaned and looked behind her. "I was but I'm letting him sleep in. And I need to get this straight," he said, tapping his temple.

"You're doing it, aren't you?" She narrowed her eyes at Penn. "You're feeling big things and it's freaking you out because you're not supposed to want anything for yourself."

"Just a little," he admitted as he hugged his chest. He glanced back at Morris's room. "I've never had to separate my sex life from my personal life and my work life before and I don't know how to do that. I've never had all three collide like this."

"Do you still consider this work?" She asked him.

Penn laughed wryly. "I'm still earning a paycheck, as far as I know," he countered, earning a snort from Penny.

"A really nice one. Did you know Reid's been paying you overtime and gave you a bonus? We all got them for the agency's anniversary."

"I haven't really looked in a while and I don't feel comfortable taking their money anymore. I'll talk to them later," Penn said. Penny usually paid their bills online so he gave her access to his account so she could take whatever she needed without having to bug him.

"And did you know...?" she continued pointedly. "Dash moved into your room two weeks ago. Fin and Riley helped us move his stuff. We've got all of your stuff packed up, we were just waiting for the signal and for someone with a van."

"I'm sorry," Penn said, and hung his head. "It's been weeks since I've been home and—"

"Don't you apologize to me!" She scolded, wagging a finger at Penn. "I have waited too long for this."

"For what?" He raised a brow at her.

"For my big brother to find his prince and live happily ever after," she said obviously. "You had me worried for a while there, but now I know that you were waiting for him and Cadie." She nodded at Morris's room.

"That's so much responsibility and I already have so many people who depend on me. What if I can't handle it all?" He asked her.

Penny made a thoughtful sound. "I have good news and I have bad news."

"Bad news first."

"You don't have a choice anymore. This is your home now and you belong with them. You'll give them your whole heart whether you want to or not because you've been waiting for this too."

"I don't know, Penny... I have to look after you and Dad still needs me. And then there's Reid and the agency," Penn mused.

Her jaw fell and she planted her hands on her hips. "Who says I need you to look after me? Have you ever considered, string bean, that I've been looking after *you*?"

"You're absolutely right," Penn said as he hooked his arm around her neck and kissed her hair. She wrapped her arms around his middle and hugged him tight.

"It's your turn, Penn. Dad and I are gonna be just fine and you better not let Reid find out that you're sacrificing your own happiness for a nanny agency, of all things."

When she put it like that, it didn't make a lot of sense.

"You said there was good news."

She beamed up at him and Penn could see and feel his mother so clearly. "This is going to work!" She whispered excitedly, her eyes sparkling with joy. "You've been dragging your feet and finding excuses because you're scared of getting hurt, but it's going to be okay. You're the smartest and the bravest person I know. And you've got me! What else could you possibly need?"

"You've got me there," Penn chuckled. They could probably pull off a heist or build a working rocket if they put their minds to it. The two of them had always been a team and she would always have his back. *Nothing* would change that.

"Don't forget that you've got Reid and Gavin and Fin and Riley and Dash," she continued. "And you've got a boyfriend. It's not *that* serious."

"It's a little bit more than that," he argued and pointed at the stairs. "I *live* here now. And I work here. We aren't just dating, we live together and we're raising a baby. *Oh, my God. I'm raising a baby.*" Heat swept up Penn's neck and he felt dizzy. He *loved* Cadence, but fatherhood? That was a lifetime commitment. He didn't hate the idea of having Cadence in his life forever, but what if he couldn't give her everything she needed?

"Newsflash: you were doing that before you became smashmates."

Penn's face pinched. "Ew. I don't like that. It sounds like food might be involved."

She bit down on her lips. "You're still scarred from the time I covered my room in honey."

He hadn't thought about that in years and sucked in a breath as he was hit by a flashback. "It took me weeks to steam the honey out of everything. I still want to strangle you."

"What can I say?" She shrugged innocently. "I really love honey and bees," she said and pointed at the bee and its dotted flight path tattooed along her clavicle. "And les-*bee*-uns!"

"How many times have you used that line in a bar?"

"Just in a bar?" Penny asked and clicked her teeth. "It

works everywhere. I have to go, but you might already have everything you've ever wanted and were too afraid to ask for."

"I know and I'm ready. I just need to catch my breath and see if it's as big of a change as I was afraid of or if it was all in my head."

"Either way, we'll make it work!"

Penn thanked her for her input and sent Penny on her way. He had a feeling he might be catching up with her soon, but he'd wait and talk to Morris before taking off.

"I wouldn't want him to think I panicked and ran."

Chapter Twenty-Three

Morris didn't have any expectations when he finally pried himself out of bed and took a shower, but he was hoping to see more of Penn, sooner. He took his time in the shower, in case Penn wanted to join him. And Morris did several laps past his bedroom door with a towel tied around his waist, in an attempt to lure Penn, but he wasn't in the living room or the kitchen. They eventually crossed paths when Morris was pouring himself a cup of coffee. Penn came downstairs dressed to go out in his overalls and Converse.

"Morning!" Penn pressed a kiss to Morris's cheek on his way to fill a reusable coffee cup.

"Morning," Morris said and raised a brow at Penn.

"What?"

"Everything cool?"

"Everything's great!" Penn said, crossing the kitchen in two big strides and looping an arm around Morris. He captured Morris's lips for a swift but brain-scrambling kiss. "I was thinking I'd run over to Reid and Gavin's for brunch if that's okay."

Morris blinked down at his T-shirt and track pants. "I wasn't really in the mood to get dressed and go out…"

"That's cool! Why don't you enjoy a quiet morning in? It's been a while and I'm sure you could use a little peace before your mom drops Cadie off later," Penn suggested.

"Oh." Morris was more than a little embarrassed. He assumed Penn would want him to go too. "Okay. Cool… I guess."

"Are you sure?" Penn asked warily. "I thought that since I had the day off and it's been a while since I stopped by for brunch and saw everyone…" He winced at Morris, but he waved it off.

"Don't worry about it. I can handle breakfast and entertain myself for a few hours."

"There's a fresh loaf of banana bread and some fruit salad, but I can stay if you want me to."

No. I want you to want *to stay.*

"Go, Penn. I'll be fine. I had something I wanted to work on in the studio and I would have felt guilty spending the morning down there if you were here."

"There you go! I'll be back in a couple of hours and we can hang out for the rest of the day."

"If you feel like it," Morris said casually and went to finish his coffee downstairs, but Penn stopped him.

"I swear, I'm not blowing you off," he said and Morris's head tipped impatiently.

"Do you want me to trust you or not?"

"Okay. You're right. I was a little…scattered and over-whelmed this morning and then Penny came over and it got kind of heavy. But she helped me put some things into perspective and I just want to get out and get some fresh air."

No one ever needed fresh air for a good reason. Morris's heart sank as disappointment began to set in. "You were sure you were ready last night." He'd trusted Penn and everything had been so good before he left Morris to do his superhuman sunrise yoga.

"I am ready and I don't have any regrets," Penn said clearly. "But I'm still scared and I'm still sorting out what exactly it is that scares me the most."

"Is commitment one of the things you're scared of?" Morris asked and Penn immediately shook his head.

"Not even a little. Not getting to be with you forever scares me the most. Living without you isn't an option anymore."

"Why would you—?" Morris started to ask, but the question died on his lips. He knew the answer better than anyone, and Penny had warned him that Penn had deep wounds of his own. And Morris couldn't tell Penn that they were too young to worry about their mortality.

Penn pulled Morris into his arms again and they began to rock from side to side. Morris had noticed that Penn did that when he was holding a bag of groceries or a package. The instinct to calm and soothe was so deeply ingrained in his psyche that he didn't even realize he was doing it.

"I didn't feel like myself this morning so I want to ride my skateboard around the block and swing by Reid's. That's it."

"That's it?" Morris asked. "I don't like that you don't feel like yourself, but I guess it's good that it isn't a commitment issue."

Penn's teeth scraped his lip as he considered. "I think it would be worse if I was exactly the same and if I didn't care about the consequences."

He had a point, but Morris didn't want to think about consequences and "heavy things." It had been years since Morris had experienced the giddy nerves and infatuation of a new relationship, but Penn was ditching him to get some fresh air and hang out with Reid and Gavin and the gang.

"You're right. You should go," he said simply.

"You could come too. Penny and Dash'll be there and Fin and Walker usually drop by. Penny just sent a text and Riley's there with Luna." Penn made an encouraging sound, but Morris could tell the offer wasn't sincere.

"I'm not ready to be around that many people," Morris said and he wasn't saying that just to make Penn feel better. He loved Fin like a little brother and his husband, Walker Cameron, seemed like a hell of a guy, but Morris wasn't in the mood to socialize with people he barely knew. And it would be awkward if Reid asked if they were "a thing" yet or how it was going because Morris didn't know now. He'd fallen asleep a few hours earlier thinking he had a boyfriend and that they were past the will-they-won't-they stage.

"Fair enough!" Penn said briskly. He kissed Morris and melted his brain, then headed out with his skateboard.

"Is it, though?"

Morris felt petty and selfish as he yanked open the door and stomped down the steps to his studio. He passed the over-sized leather sectional in the listening room and dropped into his seat at the soundboard. His fingers usually itched at the sight of all the dials and switches, but Morris was far away and he couldn't hear any music.

Instead, Penn's promises played on a loop and Morris listened for signs of deception. Or had Morris only heard what he wanted to hear? That seemed far more likely because Penn wasn't a liar and his conscience wouldn't allow him to know-ingly hurt someone.

In the end, Morris decided he had to give Penn space and time. Just as he'd given Morris space and time to adjust. That was the mature and reasonable thing to do, but that didn't make for a good love song and Morris was left feeling deflated and frustrated.

"You can't stop living. You gotta move on," he mimicked in a nasally voice and sneered. "I'm trying but what if he's not ready to move on with me?"

Chapter Twenty-Four

Briarwood Terrace was bustling when Penn pulled up on his skateboard. He could feel a warm, buzzing energy as he jogged up the front steps and greeted Norman.

"Full house today! Riley brought the baby!" Norman said, the old man's face shining with delight. "I got to hold her, and boy, is she a stunner!"

"She certainly is!" Penn agreed and rubbed his hands together and went to see if he could steal a whiff of little Luna Ashby and snuggle her for a bit.

One would think that Penn would be immune to the allure of that "new human" smell and their tiny bald heads, but he'd never get enough of babies. They were like crystals, precious and fragile and reflecting light. Babies were pure emotion, unadulterated and undiluted by conscious thought, and free of any motivation other than to be loved and nurtured.

If you were holding a clean, well-fed baby, you were holding the closest thing to pure love on the planet.

He could hear his friends' chatter and laughter and it drew

Penn like a lodestone. But Penn's steps slowed as he reached for the door. His brain was finally doing all the scary math and based on his calculations, it appeared that Penn might have a family of his own. Including a baby.

"That was fast!" He laughed shakily and held onto the door's handle. Penn rested his forehead against the cool wooden panel and took several deep breaths, riding out the racing of his heart and the churning in his stomach.

Having his heart broken and letting the people he loved down was so...minor now, as far as Penn's worst fears went. Losing Morris wasn't even *the worst* thing that could happen to Penn anymore. He had a family that depended on him and a child of his own to cherish and protect for the rest of his life. How would he survive if anything happened to them?

"Holy—"

Penny saved him from cursing out loud. He sensed her and jumped back just before the door was pulled open.

"Are you coming in or not?" She demanded, then frowned as she looked behind Penn.

"He wasn't feeling up to being around a lot of people."

Her eyes narrowed and she huffed up at him. "You ditched him because you're still panicking."

"I didn't ditch him. I told him I needed to get out and clear my head and he was cool with it. He told me to go."

"Ha!" Penny laughed and swatted his arm as if he'd told a dad joke. "You're just full of it this morning. Why are you over-thinking this? You have a boyfriend. Get over it." She said it like a boyfriend was as exciting as a grapefruit. Although, in Penny's case the grapefruit would be the more exciting option.

"It's a pretty big deal. It's huge, actually," he whispered as he peeked around her shoulder. Everyone was in the kitchen and when Reid spotted him and waved, Penn waved back. "My boyfriend has a baby and I live with him. We've skipped right past dating and everything in between and went straight to civil partnership and parenthood."

Penny's head rocked from side to side. "I can see why that would seem like a lot, but let's be real here. Shortcuts are pretty handy once you get to be your age. Imagine starting at square one with dating and going through all the stuff in between. How many *years* would it take you to find a man like Morris and an angel like Cadie?"

He mentally reeled as if she'd clobbered him with a mallet. She was right and his heart told him he'd crawl to Hell and back for something that good if he wasn't so afraid of losing it.

"Alright!" Penn gave one of her pigtails a yank. "Enough of you. I came here to take a break and clear my head." He notched his chin at the kitchen. "You'd better get in there and get your friend. Gavin looks irritated," he warned.

She hissed as she spun around. "He does, doesn't he?"

They both knew Gavin well enough to translate his rigid rearing back and wide, blinking eyes as warning signs. He yanked his cardigan tighter around himself and they gasped in unison. Dash continued to babble as he topped off Gavin's teacup.

"Oh, dear," Penn murmured and clicked his teeth. Gavin was very particular about his tea.

"I'm on it!" She promised as she hurried back to the kitchen.

Penn chuckled to himself and wished Dash luck, then smiled as Walker Cameron intercepted him in the living room.

"Pennsylvania," Walker said with a dignified bow of his head, but Penn pulled him into a hug.

"How's it going, brother?"

"No complaints, aside from the obvious," Walker replied dryly and gave Penn's back a stiff pat. But he was smiling and the corners of his eyes crinkled as they released each other.

"Seriously. How have you been?" Penn asked, but Walker was staring at Fin.

"Never better," he said sincerely. They laughed as Fin slapped at Reid's hands and refused to share Luna before Walker cleared his throat. "How are you doing?" He asked awkwardly and risked another glance at the kitchen.

"Fine... Why?" Penn asked and wondered if Fin had sent him.

Walker cleared his throat again and winced as he stepped closer. "They've been talking about you a lot. And Morris. They're worried," he said quietly.

Penn was surprised and touched that Walker cared enough to ask and warn him. The older man often teased and made jokes about communes and music festivals, but Penn could feel that Walker respected him and enjoyed their conversations.

"I'm not going to hurt Morris," Penn said, and Walker nodded and made a thoughtful sound.

"It never crossed my mind. I'm sure they'll be glad to hear that, though. I don't know Morris all that well, but I've gotten to know you and you look...off."

"Off?" Penn parroted. He certainly was off, but he thought he could hide it from everyone except Penny.

Walker studied Penn closely. "You're a gentle breeze when you walk into the room. One feels less stifled and can breathe a little easier and things don't seem as bad as they did before. But you're heavier now and there's a cloud about you."

"I'm fine," Penn said and stopped Walker before he could argue. "Things between me and Morris are a little more compli-cated, but not in a bad way. I'm just...taking a minute to adjust."

"I can certainly relate to that. It's tricky, making room for someone else in your life once you're set in your ways."

"If anyone would know, it would be you," Penn agreed with

a chuckle. Fin had turned Walker Cameron III's life upside down in the loveliest way. But Walker had suffered a terrible loss and was still grieving when Fin arrived at The Killian House to care for Walker's triplets. "Can I ask you a...personal question?" Penn said quietly as he glanced toward the kitchen. Everyone was so happy and Penn didn't want to ruin anyone's afternoon, but he knew Walker would understand.

"Of course."

Penn pushed out a loud breath and mustered his courage. He wasn't used to sharing his own problems and admitting his insecurities and it felt *odd* turning to someone else for help. "Was it harder the second time, knowing how much it hurt when you lost your husband? Weren't you scared of going back and starting over?"

"No." Walker shook his head. "I wanted to go back. Being in love and being loved is the greatest and *the safest* thing you'll ever experience and I missed that. Constantly. I just didn't want to go back to that place without Connor. That felt wrong in the beginning because certain promises are harder for the heart to let go of."

"That's the part that scares me." Penn thought of his father and how he couldn't let go. And Penn reflected on how afraid *he* was of losing Morris and Cadence. It seemed like such a huge risk to add when he was already struggling, knowing he'd have to let go of Gus soon. "That's not easy for me. I'm already scared of how broken I'll be when I lose my dad," he admitted in a whisper. "I don't know if I'll be of any use to my friends, let alone a boyfriend or a husband. I can't promise Morris I'll be there for him and Cadence when I know this...bomb is about to go off in the middle of my life. It's coming and there's nothing I can do to stop it." He heard the panic in his voice. His heart was racing and his palms were sweating. Penn was used to telling it to his sewing machine. It was his mother's, and Penn felt like he was telling her when he let his thoughts unravel while he worked.

"I'm afraid I can't relate there," Walker said with an apologetic wince. "My parents sold their souls and will outlive me out of sheer spite." He gave his head a weary shake, making Penn laugh. Walker slid an arm around Penn and turned them toward the kitchen. "They won't let you down. And I'll be here, for whatever that's worth," he added and gave Penn's shoulder a reassuring squeeze. "My Jewish friends would share this expression that I've come to appreciate in the years since Connor's death: may his memory be a blessing." Walker paused and Penn nodded.

"I'm familiar with it." He'd always thought it was a lovely way of comforting someone who was grieving.

"It's far more than keeping Connor's memory alive, I've realized. It's also a stage in the grieving process, isn't it? To be able to think of the person you've lost and not feel like you've fallen into a trap or like you're being tortured. You have to pass through terrible pain and anger to get to that place where you feel blessed and comforted by their memory. It's a wish before a difficult journey and a promise that those memories will become blessings when you reach the other side, and I think that's a beautiful sentiment."

"You're right," Penn realized as he watched his friends make fools of themselves over Luna. Reid was making ridiculous faces while Fin sang a silly song about a princess in Manhattan. Gavin wasn't immune either. The dry and stoic grump stuck his tongue out, made animal sounds, and even giggled. "They always come through and I know they'll be there for me and Penny. But how can I pull Morris down with me when he's just getting back on his feet?"

"I can't speak for Morris," Walker began, then shook his head and his lips pulled into a hard frown. "Neither should you, frankly. Let Morris decide what he's ready for a year, or two, or three from now," he said. He gave Penn a pointed look. "The only regret I have is that I didn't have more time with Connor. Even the rough patches are precious when I look back because we were there for each other and we grew stronger together. All you're doing is wasting time and you're selling Morris and yourself short."

"Spoken like a true businessman," Penn said with a strained laugh. Walker had swept Penn's emotional feet out from under him. He was using Morris as an excuse. It was easier to tell himself he was protecting Morris than accept that he'd need him for support one day.

"Loving someone is never a burden. Even when it's hard, it's still a gift."

Penn whistled as he turned to Walker. "Someone's done some hard work with their therapist! Get in here," he said, opening his arms wide.

Walker pulled a face but he hugged Penn and clapped him firmly on the back. "Just trying to help."

"You have," Penn said sincerely. "It's easier for me to love others and I've never been good at letting people love me in return, but that's a pretty selfish way to live."

"Selfish is a harsh way of putting it," Walker said, waving as if he was ready to move on. "Tell me. What do you make of this Dash?" He asked and nodded at the kitchen. Dash had retreated to the other side of the kitchen and was laughing as he watched Fin, Reid, and Gavin entertain the baby while Penny and Riley fussed over what appeared to be a new orchid.

"Dash is a sweet kid," Penn said. "He's been one of Penny's best friends since high school. He just moved into my old room, apparently."

"But is he a good nanny?" Walker asked as he squinted at Dash.

Penn shrugged. "He's kind of new to the gig. He was an elementary school teacher *and* has a nursing degree so I think he'll be great once Reid shows him the ropes. Why?"

A calculating grin spread across Walker's face. "My sister's adopting a child. She's selected an adoption agency and submitted her application. We expect that she'll be approved, but she's insisted on doing everything the proper way so it will take some time."

"That's fabulous!" Penn scooped Walker into another hug and hopped excitedly. "You're going to be an uncle!"

"I am rather excited about that," Walker said and set Penn away from him. "We've done enough hugging for today." He tugged at the front of his coat, but Penn laughed and gave Walker's shoulder a playful punch. Penn enjoyed their banter and still had the same premonition each time they met.

Family.

His instincts told Penn that he and Walker would be family; he just felt a different bond with the famously uptight and aloof financier. It tickled Penn because they were complete opposites, but he'd come to genuinely like and admire Walker and enjoyed the older man's dry sense of humor.

"I take it that means she'll be needing a nanny," Penn speculated as he stroked his beard.

"You've met my sister. She'll eat him alive if he's bisexual. Just look at him," Walker said, gesturing at Dash.

"I'm not sure..."

Agnes Cameron was a stunning woman, but Dash clearly had a thing for lanky accountants who dressed in three-piece suits and took a cup of tea by the fireplace every evening. At least that's what Penn was beginning to suspect. It was pretty obvious as Dash openly swooned over Gavin's Dean Martin impression. Gavin was serenading Luna, but Dash looked dizzy as he watched from across the kitchen.

"It doesn't matter," Penn said, turning back to Walker. "He isn't ready for anything long-term yet. Reid would probably send Penny."

"I was hoping you'd say that," Walker replied silkily and Penn gasped.

"Agnes and Penny Lane?" He asked with a dubious laugh, then paused and considered it as he watched his sister with Riley. "That would be a lot of fun... But can you imagine the chaos?"

"It's what my sister deserves." Walker coughed into his fist discreetly. "And I might have noticed something at our wedding," he said out of the side of his mouth.

"Oh?" Penn's brows jumped and his eyes widened in delight. "I wouldn't put it past my sister. She will always choose chaos."

That made Walker snort. "I just noticed some lingering looks and they did dance together," he noted.

"They did!" Penn had forgotten until just then. He'd drunk a lot of champagne and had danced with Riley before wandering off to smoke. It was close to an hour later by the time Penn returned and half the guests had left or found their way back to their rooms. The Cameron family "cottage" in Sagaponack had nine bedrooms and there were two guest houses on the four-and-a-half-acre property. Penn had crashed with Penny in one of the guest houses along with Reid and Gavin, but he didn't run into his sister after he returned to the party. "I can't believe I forgot to ask her about that. She never said anything about it, though..."

"Neither has Agnes," Walker confided, but he slid Penn a sly grin. "But they definitely noticed each other and I'd like my sister to get a taste of her own medicine."

"She's not that bad!"

Walker humphed and crossed his arms over his chest. "My

sister is my best friend and one of the most charming women you'll ever meet, but she is also a scoundrel and a brat. It's time she mended her ways and settled down."

"I'm not sure if Penny would be a calming influence," Penn warned. His sister was a genuine ray of light and incredibly wholesome, but she had a wild streak of her own and lived for adventure. And Agnes Cameron's idea of adventure was probably very different from Penny's. "Does your sister enjoy camping or mountain climbing?"

"Not even a little," Walker said and stifled a giggle. "But could you imagine if your sister got her to try?"

"That would be something," Penn agreed. Agnes Cameron looked like she was more at home in first class and had her meals prepared by a personal chef. "I'll have a word with Reid and see what he thinks."

"I'd appreciate that," Walker said, then wrinkled his nose. "I feel a little guilty, stealing another one of his nannies."

"Nah." Penn shook his head. "Reid has ten nannies now and all but Dash and Penny have been paired up with their dream families. And he says he's getting more resumes every day. All Reid cares about is what's best for us and the clients."

"He's a lot like you," Walker said with a wag of his finger at Penn. "He spends his day fixing other people's problems but doesn't make any time for himself."

"I told you, I'm working on it. I'll talk to Morris tonight," Penn promised and held out his hand so Walker could slap it. He did so warily and Penn laughed as he pulled Walker into one last hug. "Thanks for helping me work through this."

"I'm glad I could help," Walker said, then returned to the kitchen and Fin's side.

They belonged together; Walker was a content and balanced man when he was with Fin. It warmed Penn's heart to see Fin and Walker so happy and he decided that maybe just about everyone in his life was right. Maybe he deserved a little bit of that for himself. The only question that remained was whether Penn was brave enough to ask the universe for someone like Morris because it felt like asking for too much.

"It's too late to turn back now." Penn accepted this and went to join in the familial chaos in the kitchen.

Chapter Twenty-Five

Penn returned home with lunch and big, bright, vague smiles for Morris. They ate falafel and made pleasant small talk—mostly about future playdates with Luna Ashby and the Knicks last game—but Penn was restless and changed the subject whenever the conversation veered toward anything remotely romantic.

And Morris became irritated and impatient with Penn when his mother came in to drop off the baby. Penn encouraged her to linger, peppering her with questions about Morris Sr. and the bakery. She stayed for over two hours and Penn looked like he wanted to follow her out the door when she left.

He made Morris paranoid, staring and then looking away as soon as their eyes met. Morris couldn't tell if Penn wanted to get off with him or dump him. And Morris marveled at how Penn could be tenderly evasive as they chatted over bowls of pasta and roasted vegetables.

"So... Still feeling scattered or did you figure it out while you were riding your skateboard?" Morris asked cautiously.

Penn had finished his pasta and was feeding Cadence her

bedtime bottle. She emitted a drowsy, sated hum with each gulp. He smiled down at her and chuckled softly as he nodded. "You know what it's like when you're out there and you're just vibing: the rumble of the wheels on the pavement rippling through the trucks and the board and up into your feet. There's all that energy and sound and you're soaking it all up. I can't explain it, but I feel the same way when I'm up at the cabin or deep in the woods. There's so much life and it makes you feel small, but you feel like you're connected to all of it. You can figure out a lot of things but nothing in particular."

"I guess..." Morris couldn't be mad at Penn for dodging the question. He was too hypnotized by his rich, low baritone and lazy drawl. He cast his spell, then hid behind the baby, using her to distract Morris until it was time for Cadence's bath.

"So... That's little miss settled for the evening," Penn said when he finally jogged back down the stairs. He whistled casually as he strolled into the kitchen. "I was wondering..." He rubbed at an invisible spot on the counter. "...if you wanted to smoke and hang out...or something."

Morris raised a brow at Penn. "We've been hanging out since you got back from Reid and Gavin's," he said and Penn laughed nervously.

"I know! I just thought you might want to hang out upstairs in my room. Or in yours again," he added with an apologetic cringe.

"Ah." Morris hugged his chest and made a thoughtful sound. "By hanging out, I assume you mean fucking," he clarified.

"Shhhh!" Penn waved and looked around like there might be witnesses. "Yes, but..." He widened his eyes at Morris. "Not just *that*. You make it sound sleazy."

"Isn't that what you want, though? We could skip the bed

and fooling around and fuck right here," Morris offered, gesturing around them.

"I'm sorry," Penn said quickly, holding up his hands as he closed the distance between them. "Today's been...an intense journey and I've had a lot to process."

"That doesn't sound good..." Morris said. He had to catch Penn's cheek and chase his eyes. "Are you okay?" He asked and Penn nodded quickly.

"I thought I was ready for this to get serious, but Penny reminded me of just how *serious* this is," he whispered and let out another nervous laugh. "Like, I've never felt this serious about anyone before and I realized we're like...a family now."

"Oh." Morris leaned back and everything flipped around: he saw the house, the baby, and the boyfriend and understood why Penn felt overwhelmed. But Morris felt overwhelmed by how vulnerable and helpless *he* felt. There wasn't a lot Morris could do if Penn changed his mind and decided it was too much too soon. "And you're sure you're ready for all of this?"

"I am," Penn stated firmly. "I want you and Cadence. I've just got to figure out how to balance my personal needs with my responsibilities. I've never had to worry about that. I've never been in love like this before and it's...draining," he said and frowned as he chewed on his thumb knuckle.

Morris felt a rush of relief and he was elated, hearing that Penn was in love with him too. But he didn't like seeing Penn troubled and uncertain. "Being in love is supposed to be a good thing."

Penn wound his arms around Morris's neck and tapped their foreheads together. "All I've wanted all day is you. I got up and made our coffee and Cadence's bottle and she wasn't even here! My brain was soup and my dick was running the show. All I wanted was to dive right back in bed and lose myself in you."

"Hmmm…" Morris furrowed his brow seriously despite the butterflies in his stomach. "I don't think I would have minded."

"But I'm supposed to be better than that!"

"Come on, Penn!" Morris groaned as he kissed him. "You're not a robot and it's okay to put yourself first now and then. And you're supposed to be horny and distracted when you're in love."

Penn snorted dubiously. But he was hard and his lips clung to Morris's as Penn steered them out of the kitchen. "How do I keep up with my responsibilities here and to everyone else when I just want to lock the door and get off with you?"

"I'm still not seeing the problem," Morris said, then laughed and caught Penn's hand when he swatted at him.

"I want to get wrapped up in you—and you deserve that— but I don't know if I can be me if I can't take care of everyone the way I always have."

"It's okay. You can admit you like me," Morris teased.

Penn hummed and pecked at Morris's lips as he turned them around. "I do like you. I like you a lot."

"Good. What happened to baby steps?" Morris asked and reached behind him for the door to his room. "We can be serious about each other, but nothing has to change until we're both ready. Let's take it day by day and keep taking care of each other and Cadence. I'm just…here and I'm so in love with you, I can't think straight either. It's scary, but it feels so much better than the alternative." His hands were sweating and his legs were shaking, but Morris held on to the adrenaline and didn't think about the thing he was afraid to think about. He wouldn't let grief ruin the moment. "Being obsessed with you and the sounds you make when I'm deep inside of you is so much better than being sad."

"Go easy on me!" Penn whimpered. He grabbed Morris's

face for a deep, desperate kiss. "It's been an emotional day and I'm already turned on."

"You keep acting like this is a problem." Morris reached for Penn when he pulled away.

"That is a problem. I'm used to scratching that itch and getting on with my life but I haven't stopped thinking about us and what happened last night and this morning." Penn sounded disappointed in himself as he freed his arms from his overalls and pulled his T-shirt over his head. "Sex has always been just...sex. What happened last night was so much more than that, but it wasn't enough and all I want is more of you."

"Sounds like you've got love on the brain," Morris said, clicking his teeth at Penn. But he was relieved to his core. He'd spent the day thinking he'd been the only one afflicted and that Penn was having second thoughts.

"I don't want to change, though," Penn said. He stopped to unlace his Converse and tugged them off while Morris quickly stripped out of his sweatshirt and track pants. "I want to be in love with you *and* I want to be able to take care of people the way I always have," Penn continued as he stepped out of his overalls and boxers and reached for Morris.

"What if I promise I won't let you change?" Morris asked. He pulled Penn with him as he fell back on the bed. Morris rolled them so Penn was on top and slipped the band out of his hair, letting it fall free. "What if I love you just the way you are because you're so selfless and because you love everyone?"

"What if it's too late? I couldn't stop thinking about you before and now I can't stop thinking about this," Penn purred as he ground against Morris, mashing their erections together. His hair was a honey-colored blur when he swung his head around and sucked on Morris's earlobe. "And you don't know how badly I've needed to taste you." Penn's teeth dug into Morris's neck, creating a rush of heat and goosebumps. Penn's words and the hot sweep of his tongue made Morris shiver. Penn's greedy, euphoric moans became a hypnotic lullaby as he licked and sucked his way down Morris's body.

"Trust me, I know," Morris said, sifting his fingers through Penn's hair. It was cool and silky and tickled as it danced over Morris's stomach and thighs. Penn's lips wrapped around Morris's cock, sucking and sliding as his hands pumped and kneaded. "That's so good."

"Mmmm..."

Morris didn't want to interrupt Penn with more questions, and pretty soon all he could do was swear a lot at the ceiling and beg God for mercy. "Jesus Christ!" He held onto the head-board and the edge of the mattress as Penn's tongue curled around his sac and teased his hole. "Just fucking ride me, Penn!"

"I love it when you get bossy!" Penn teased as he licked his way up Morris's cock and stomach, then nipped at a nipple before he straddled Morris. "What if I become obsessed? Who am I if all I can think about or care about is you and this?" He asked with a ragged huff as he reached behind him. He quickly coated Morris's shaft with lube and sat back, taking him deep into his ass.

Morris attempted a sympathetic hum, but it was weak and shaky. "You'll get used to it and you won't get lost. I won't let you," Morris vowed.

The grinding slide of Penn's body synced to the heavy beat of Morris's heart and their strangled chants and curses became a sultry refrain. Their lips and fingers tangled as their bodies fused and Morris understood what Penn was afraid of, but he welcomed the all-consuming obsession. Morris devoured Penn with his lips, his hands, his eyes, and his ears. He lapped up every drop of sweat and spit, and every tear, mentally stashing them away so he could cherish them later.

Every sigh and every goosebump was a new line in a poem or a lyric.

He wanted all the daydreams and the distractions because Penn was so much safer and softer than Morris's world without Michelle. Morris had a reason to smile and sing again and there was no aching emptiness when they kissed and touched.

"That's it. Ride me." Morris's hands cradled Penn's ass and his head, helping him bounce harder and faster and holding him closer.

"You're so deep, Morris. You're so deep and so hard," Penn babbled amidst the loud clap of skin against skin. "You're so good. Come inside of me!" His eyes rolled back and pre-cum leaked from his cock between them.

Morris shushed and captured Penn's lips. His tongue plunged and swirled around Penn's, teasing and claiming and pushing him closer to the edge. "Not yet," Morris warned, locking Penn's ass against his pelvis as he bucked off the bed. He kept his strokes hard and slow, crushing Penn's prostate. Morris snaked a hand between them and gripped Penn's shaft tight. He was already slick and hot with pre-cum and things just got wetter and louder as Morris pumped Penn's cock to the same slow, driving beat.

"Fuck!" Penn yelped as his head snapped back, his hair creating a golden halo around him. His back was arched and he was breathtaking. Morris was enthralled by the goosebumps and the sheen of sweat on his skin. The gentle, smiling tattoos sketched across his chest and abdomen had been transformed into straining muscle and flickering flesh. "Morris! Oh fuck, Morris!"

Morris beheld Penn's release with wide, tear-filled eyes, overwhelmed at the bliss and beauty. He was so far gone, there was nothing but Penn and the exquisite tightness of his body as it clenched around Morris's cock. There wasn't a hint of pain or fear in Morris's existence because every fiber of his being was fixated on Penn. He shut his eyes and listened as Penn came, saving it like a sound file for later. Morris held onto Penn and the slow, grinding pace while he licked the cum from his fingers, wallowing in the pleasure and the crisp, tart taste.

"Like green apples," he murmured to himself. "The rest of him tastes like honey and sunshine."

"Hmmm?" Penn licked his lips and gave his head a woozy shake.

"More. I'm not ready to leave." Morris kissed Penn and rolled them over. He held onto the headboard as he drove harder.

Penn's leg hooked around Morris's hip. "Yes!" He clawed at Morris's back and ass, urging him on and begging for more. "Don't stop!"

"No." Morris shook his head. "I never want to stop." He kissed Penn roughly, desperate to hang onto paradise. But his hips rolled swift and hard, a pounding crescendo that made his nerves flicker and strobe as his body grew hotter.

There was a loud gasp and Penn's jaw stretched and his eyelids fluttered. "Morris!"

"That's it!" Morris held onto Penn's waist, drilling hard and deep and wringing out every drop of his release. Morris scooped the flecks of cum off Penn's skin and sucked on his fingers, high on the sour apple tartness and the seductive harmony of their bodies. He was already swept up and saturated in Penn when Morris fell forward and plunged even deeper. "I want to get lost in you," he breathed against Penn's lips, afraid to break the spell. "And I never want to leave."

"Okay!" Penn nodded jerkily as his arms and legs wound around Morris. "Stay. Stay," he said, his voice a damp, trembling breath in Morris's ear.

He was everything, blotting out the world and flooding

Morris's senses and his soul with light and warmth while heat and pleasure swirled in his groin. Morris touched the sun and for a moment, everything was bright and soft before he shattered. He sobbed into Penn's shoulder, muffling his joyful cries as he came.

"Let me stay here." He whispered the words and kissed them into Penn's skin.

"Stay as long as you need." Penn was still wrapped around Morris and his hands spread possessively as they roamed.

"I mean it, Penn," Morris said, raising his head so he could see Penn's eyes. "We can take it one day at a time until this isn't scary, but I have to know that you're...mine." But he immediately mouthed an apology. He knew how old-fashioned and possessive that sounded. "No more going with the moment or chasing sparks or whatever you call it."

"No. I said this wasn't a commitment thing and I meant it." Penn held Morris's gaze, his voice steady and certain. "This is where I belong and I can't keep using fear as an excuse. I'm done wasting time and I'll find a way to balance all of this."

"Good," Morris said and punctuated it with a kiss. "We'll figure it out together. I'm usually too independent and relationships never worked because I couldn't fit anyone in between work and Michelle. I've never had room or needed anyone the way I need you, but I think I'm going to need my space too." Morris shrugged and rested his chin on Penn's chest. "It's weird, how happy you get when you're helping people. And it's what I love most about you, Penn."

"What if something happened and I couldn't help anyone? What if..." Penn paused and sucked in a breath. Morris felt his chest hitch on a shudder and quickly adjusted them so they were on their sides and he was holding Penn.

"You're only human. You can't help everyone and one of these days, your battery is gonna get low."

"I know, but something's coming and it's going to destroy me. You've already been through hell and I don't want to drag you down with me when you're just getting your life back."

"Ah." Morris knew exactly what Penn was referring to and what he was running away from. "It's too late, though. I'll already be there because I owe you and I'm scared of the same thing. But I know you'll be there for me and Mom."

"Of course," Penn said quickly.

Morris snorted. "See? You'd do it for me, but you're not you if you need help."

"I already admitted I like you and I'm not running from this. It might take a little longer for the rest to sink in."

That was only fair, considering that Morris was still in the reconstruction phase himself. A wide grin spread across his face. "You said fuck. Twice."

"No, I didn't," Penn stated with a hard shake of his head.

Morris clicked his teeth. "You sure did. Want to open a bottle of wine and see if I can make you say it again?"

Chapter Twenty-Six

Fate spent the next three weeks laughing at Penn.

Very little changed as far as his routine, except he and Morris were having a lot of sex. *A lot* of sex.

They snuck away and stripped off their clothes whenever Cadence took a nap and they went at each other like starving animals as soon as she was tucked in for the night. There were long, hot baths and so many bottles of wine and so many joints on the patio.

Cadence's nights weren't all peaceful, though. She cut a tooth and got an ear infection, but they took turns checking her temperature and rocking her back to sleep. Afterward, they'd crash into bed, a drowsy, lustful tangle of limbs and lips.

Morning would sneak up on them, but Penn rolled out of bed refreshed and ready for the sun. He'd do his yoga routine, then prepare their coffee and breakfast and Cadence's bottle. The rest of the morning would take shape around him as Penn got swept up in Morris and the baby's daily routine.

Morris was spending more time in the studio during the week. Cadence had check-ups and Penn took her to baby yoga and swimming lessons. The three of them went to her Music and Movers class on Wednesday and they had lunch with Morris Sr. and Gus on Thursdays in Park Slope.

Their life had become delightfully busy and Morris was even getting out more. He went roller skating in the park with Penny and dropped in at Gavin and Reid's a few times a week. It was just the weekends that left Penn feeling out of sorts.

Especially when Penny and Gus decided to go fishing without him and Morris locked himself in his studio. Evelyn wasn't much help either.

"Are you sure there isn't something that needs fixing at the bakery?" He asked when she came to pick up the baby for the weekend.

"Not that I can think of."

"And you're sure you don't want me to keep Cadie so you and Morrie can have the day to yourselves?"

"No! Enjoy your day off!" She pointed at him threateningly when he moved in to help her with the car seat. "We're having our own beach party at the house. Morris Sr. has the pool set up and the grill's ready to go." She cheered as she booped Cadence on the nose, then grinned at Penn over the top of the seat. "I'd invite you, but no nannies allowed. Go have fun or do something nice for yourself," she said and demanded a kiss from Penn on her way out.

He scrubbed the back of his neck to ease the tightening and frowned at the door to the basement. "I know what I'd like to do and that would be a lot of fun, but Morris is busy," he murmured.

Penn didn't want to go too far in case Morris emerged from his studio and wanted company. He decided a trip around the corner to Briarwood Terrace would be nice and Reid sounded happy when Penn pressed on the buzzer for the intercom.

"Is the baby with you?"

"Not this time," Penn said.

"Oh." Reid was significantly less excited as the lock clicked.

Penn laughed at Reid's disgruntled expression when he came around the corner. "I see how it is now."

"It's rude to show up empty-handed," he said but laughed as they hugged and slapped each other on the back. "How's it going?"

"Great. It's my day off and I had nothing to do so I thought I'd see what you and Gavin were up to."

"He went to the office to hide from Dash, but he and Penny took off right after he left. They're taking pictures around the city for 'journey era' content."

"Sounds cool." Penn followed Reid through to the kitchen. His shirtsleeves were rolled up and he appeared to be repotting an orchid. A pot was waiting on the counter under the window and an orchid was on its side with its roots bare and untangled.

"Penny came up with a plan to expand his social media campaign. People have been clamoring for news. They want to know if Morris is okay and there have been rumors that he's recording again. Penny and Dash are using the pictures to make city-inspired mood boards with deep, inspirational themes. She thinks this will give everyone the feel of a comeback without putting any expectations on Morris. It will create the impression he's meditating and exploring the meaning of life," Reid added dramatically.

"I hope it works." Penn bit into his knuckle. "I don't understand what's going on when it comes to campaigns and engagement and I feel like I've made this worse. I'm the one who told his mom and then she started telling everyone." The only person who knew that Morris was recording again was Penn, but he'd told Evelyn and Penny. And Reid.

Did I tell Walker too?

Penn dragged a hand down his face. "I've been telling

people, but just so they'd stop worrying about him and back off a little."

"Is he recording again?"

"He is," Penn said, nodding slowly. "But he's being kind of secretive. Is that normal?"

"No..." Reid shook his head. "He recorded in the dining room when we had that place on Elmwood, before I moved in here with Gavin and Morris and Michelle moved in together. And I used to sit in whenever I dropped by."

"Maybe it's just me, then..." Penn chewed on his lip and told himself it wasn't a big deal and just Morris's prerogative, being the creative genius.

"While we're talking about Morris..." Reid picked up the spray bottle and glanced at Penn before giving the orchid's wide, waxy leaves a few spritzes. "How are things going with you two?"

"We're fine." Penn laughed and raised a shoulder, attempting to play it cool. "We're just..."

"Having *a lot* of sex." Reid finished, his tone loaded with judgment and disapproval.

Penn flinched and hugged his chest. He could feel Reid's concern rising as the current between them became choppy and crackled like a dial had been turned and the signal was fading. "We're taking it one day at a time," Penn said.

Reid's gaze grew more severe. "Don't play around with this, Penn. Not with Morris."

"Easy!" Penn laughed softly and gestured for him to relax. "Morris is *fine*. Better than fine, actually."

"Because he's *in love*," Reid countered and Penn wondered what he was afraid of.

"I am too." He still got a little restless whenever reality caught up with him and Penn remembered *who* he was in love with. Penn turned and paced away from the window.

"We're going slow because we want to keep this quiet and simple."

"Are you sure? Because whenever I talk to Morris, I get the feeling *he's* taking this pretty seriously and he's all in."

"You get the feeling?" Penn snorted. "You're gossiping again, but we're fine. I wouldn't hold your breath if you're expecting us to go public or for there to be a splashy wedding. This'll probably be something we have to keep quiet."

"How do you know? And what does that mean?" Reid bit out. Penn could hear and feel his disapproval mounting. "I don't like what you're implying about either of my friends."

Penn held up a hand, silently urging Reid to calm down and listen. "I *love* Morris and Cadence with my whole heart and there's nothing I wouldn't do for them." He held Reid's gaze and let him see how much Penn cherished them. "I just don't fit into the rest of Morris's world. I belong with him and Cadence *at home.* You said it yourself: people are clamoring for news. A new relationship would be a huge deal. But they're going to want to see Morris with someone more...exciting and stylish."

"Exciting and stylish?" Reid's head canted and his brow furrowed. "Morris isn't like that and he doesn't give a damn about what anyone thinks. And you're...stylish," he said with an apologetic grimace.

"Stop!" Penn's head snapped back and he hugged his chest as he laughed. "Look me in the eyes and tell me you don't want to cut this bun off." He said and pointed at his head.

Reid's pupils dilated and yearning radiated from him. "No... It's cool," he lied and waved dismissively. "And Morris doesn't care."

"I know," Penn said, becoming serious. "But he'd be better off with someone who understands his world and how it works, like Michelle. She was Morris's forcefield with the press and social media and she had the industry in the palm of her hand. She knew how to juggle all of that so he could live and work in peace. I'd just stick out like a sore thumb and draw the wrong kind of attention."

"You think Morris cares about any of that? And Penny and Dash are on it now. Morris can hire a bodyguard if it's that serious." Reid said and shook his head. "I think you're wrong. It takes half a second to see why Morris would be into you. You aren't conventionally stylish but you're a beautiful man, Penn. Inside and out. And people will get it when they see how happy the two of you are."

"Reid," Penn objected, blocking his face and attempting to tap out.

"But that's it!" Reid pointed as Penn turned to the window. "You're afraid of this. I know it was hard losing your mom—"

"Reid!" Penn begged in a hoarse croak. He cleared his throat and sniffed hard, then opened his mouth to offer up an excuse, but Penn needed this wound to heal. Hiding it and lying about why he was afraid hadn't worked. "It's not just Mom," he admitted. Reid gripped Penn's shoulder and gave it an encouraging knead.

"What happened before junior year? I knew you were getting over something. Or someone," he added gently.

Penn grunted at the kick of bitterness and shame. "I got caught up in this thing with my first roommate and it was...*bad.*" His stomach rolled and soured as he recalled how much he'd hurt himself by allowing Tristan to walk all over him. "He was bi but he wasn't out. He acted like we were just friends and I was saving his ass in history and English because he was popular and got in on a football scholarship."

"Oh no..." Reid slid his arm around Penn, turning and pulling him into a hug.

"I *knew* he was using me for sex, but he was my first and I was in love with him. Just...completely and hopelessly. I looked the other way when he came in late smelling like perfume and pussy because he said he had to fit in or he'd lose everything."

"Penn..." Reid leaned back and cupped his cheek. "Give me his name."

Penn laughed and wiped the tears from his eyes. "Why? You gonna fight him? He's on TV now, calling games on the weekends."

That got a hard sneer from Reid. "You know that's not my style, but I'll make sure that the arc of justice swings his way. He hang out around the city?"

"Let it go!" Penn said, laughing and pulling Reid into a tight embrace. "I want to let this go. I *need* to let this go. He made me believe that it was my fault for being gay and...weird. That it wasn't really about him being in the closet because I wasn't the kind of guy he'd date if he was out. And that's how he got away with it. No one would ever believe he'd be into someone like me."

"Seriously, Penn. I just wanna talk to him."

"It's fine, and I promise, karma did its thing." Penn pushed him away playfully. "I spent a weekend with this hot older guy that year I was teaching ski lessons. He was a divorced surgeon and had moved into the family cabin up in Lake Placid for the holidays. He said he had kids my age, but that didn't seem like any of my business until they caught us making breakfast in our underwear."

"You slept with his dad?" Reid clarified and Penn smirked.

"Not on purpose and I got out of there as fast as I could and never looked back."

Reid's brows pulled together and he made a thoughtful sound as he nodded. "Well done, karma. I suppose."

"I should have let it go then," Penn admitted. "But Mom died right after that and I saw how devastated Dad was. I was afraid I'd lose him too. I thought I could protect myself from that if I didn't fall in love."

"And how's that working out for you?" Reid asked gently.

Penn sighed heavily as he held up his hands. "It was going fine until Morris. But I was already in trouble before we started having sex. I think I was in trouble as soon as I walked through the front door."

"Seems like you're exactly where you're supposed to be," Reid said. He squeezed Penn's shoulder affectionately, then went back to his orchids. "You should ask Morris how he wants to deal with the public and do what's best for the three of you," he urged, but Penn shook his head.

"He's making music and it sounds like an album might be coming together. I don't want a whole bunch of people getting in his face about me every time he leaves the house or answers the phone. That would set him back and I can't let that happen."

Reid swore and aimed the bottle at Penn, misting him in the face. "Does Morris's opinion count? Because I think he'd choose love and you over someone exciting and stylish. Not that you aren't stylish in your own way," he added.

"I love you," Penn laughed as he pulled Reid into a one-armed hug.

Reid sighed as he hugged him back. "I love you too. But could you stop underestimating yourself? I don't pay you six figures because you're just a...handy nanny. You're a brilliant, talented, compassionate, and selfless man. *You're* one of a kind and Morris is wild about you. I've never seen him this happy, and that's saying a hell of a lot."

Penn's heart swelled in his chest and a loopy grin spread across his face. "That's all I need right there." He laughed when Reid sprayed him again. "I know you're itching to plan another wedding, but we're taking it slow."

"I am not," Reid said and shook his head at Penn. "Not that I'd pass up the opportunity to plan a wedding with the legendary Evelyn Mosby..." He raised his brows at Penn.

"Stop!" Penn hugged his chest and laughed. "I love that woman, but I can tell you it would not be a cake walk."

"Nice," Reid said with a roll of his eyes and Penn laughed harder when he realized the joke he'd made.

"Totally an accident. She's a general and she'd plan something so over the top."

"Sounds like fun." Reid smiled, daring him. "Go for the fairytale, Penn. You and Morris deserve it."

"We'll see," he said, forbidding himself from speculating about what kind of cake Evelyn would bake or what her and Cadence's dresses would look like. He certainly wasn't going to think about how handsome Morris would look in his tuxedo. That would only remind Penn of how silly he'd look in a tux as he was saying his vows and standing next to Morris.

Chapter Twenty-Seven

They had been sharing a bed for two glorious months, but Morris was having a hard time making heads or tails of the situation with Penn. They existed in a state of domestic bliss; they were connected and both content spending their days spoiling Cadence. And when she was asleep...

They talked, they touched, they fucked... Their souls bonded and Morris felt like he was understood and protected. But today Penn was distant as they cut through the park on their way home from the library. He'd been miles away when they left the house and while they browsed for books.

Cadence was snuggled up to Penn's chest in the sling and it was hard not to stare. Morris had caught several women and a few men watching Penn with open adoration and some obvious lust and felt vindicated.

"Can I ask you something?" Morris caught Penn's elbow, halting him when they reached a quiet spot in the shade.

"You just did," Penn teased, then shushed softly and used half of his hoodie to shield Cadence from a gust of wind.

"You're different when we're out. Why?"

"What?" It came out as a bemused snort. "I'm not. I'm just...careful."

"Careful?" Morris's eyes slid from side to side and he slowly looked over his shoulder. "Why? Are you in trouble?" He whispered.

"Am I—?" Penn smothered a giggle. "What kind of trouble do you think I could be in?"

"I don't know. Why do you need to be careful?" Morris asked and waved around them.

Penn cleared his throat and widened his eyes at Morris. "Don't wake Cadie. We don't want people to think something's going on," he said quietly.

Morris squinted at Penn. "But something *is* going on."

"Right, but you don't want—" Penn started, then stopped when Morris snorted and squared up to him.

"There you go again," he said and looped his arms around Penn loosely, careful not to disturb Cadence. "You think you know what I want." He clicked his teeth as he stretched his neck, offering his lips.

"Someone's going to recognize you and take a picture of us," Penn protested, but he cradled Morris's face and kissed him.

"I don't care. Do you?" Morris whispered. He angled his head so he could take the kiss deeper until Penn groaned.

"Do you want this in the news? That you're dating your nanny?"

Morris hissed and nibbled on Penn's lips. "Have you seen my nanny?"

"Whatever."

"I mean it. He's hot and he fucks like John Wick," Morris panted against Penn's lips.

"I really hope that's a good thing because I still don't know what that's about." Penn's eyelids were heavy as his head lowered and he stole another kiss.

"It's a good thing. And my nanny's so sweet, he tastes like honey."

"Time to go home!" Penn declared as he snatched Morris's hand. "You just turned this into a sex emergency."

Morris laughed and let Penn lead him down the sidewalk but they didn't hold hands for long. The baby fussed and Penn said it was because Cadence didn't want to be in the sling anymore. She wanted to stretch out in her crib and nap in peace.

"Give me five minutes to get her settled," Penn said when they parted at the front door.

"I'll be waiting and ready," Morris replied and dropped the diaper bag on the table. He took a detour to the wine fridge and selected a prosecco since they were in a light, bubbly mood. Morris grabbed two glasses from the rack on his way to his room. Penn hurried in, shedding his hoodie just as Morris was filling their glasses, naked and ready.

"We have to hurry. I want to get dinner started before Cadie wakes up," Penn warned, but he let Morris pour wine into his mouth as he toed off his Converse and unbuckled his overalls.

"Time for a break and to sit on my co—" Morris laughed when Penn shushed loudly and kissed him.

"Don't make this dirty."

But it was *so dirty*.

Penn planted his feet on the bed outside of Morris's hips and held onto his shoulders. The loud clap of Penn's ass against Morris's pelvis filled the air and it was heaven on a Thursday afternoon. It began to rain and the curtains fluttered, carrying the sounds of the city on the breeze. Morris was drunk on the sweet taste of Penn's lips and the heat swirling in his groin. His skin was slick with sweat, and Morris was captivated by the driving beat of Penn's hips and the blood pounding in his ears.

Their bodies and their breaths became a steady, throbbing blues beat. It swept Morris up and he was euphoric as he came with a soul-deep sob. Penn swallowed it with his lips as his arms wound around Morris's neck.

"Now, we can make it dirty," Penn said, bracing his hand on the bed behind him. He guided Morris's hand to his cock. Their fingers tangled and Penn was captivating as he bucked his hips and whimpered Morris's name. He came with a strangled cry as he pulled Morris fingers to his mouth so he could suck them clean.

Morris flipped Penn onto his back. "Everyone I care about already knows I'm in love with you," he said breathlessly. He fell forward, pinning Penn and diving into his mouth. "I don't want to hide this."

"Neither do I." Penn flung an arm around Morris. "You're back in the studio again and you don't need that kind of outside pressure and distraction."

"It's not that serious," Morris said with a soft laugh, gathering Penn in his arms. It felt serious, though, and the rhythm of their bodies and lyrics swirled in his brain every time they touched and kissed. What had started as two or three songs to "scratch the itch" had blossomed into eight deeply personal and sensually stirring slow jams. It felt amazing, being proud of something he'd created, and Morris was less and less afraid of sharing the wishes he'd made in the solitude of his studio. His relationship with Penn grew stronger every day and Morris wanted the world to know that he was in love.

"It will be once word gets out," Penn predicted and Morris made a dismissive sound.

"I could not care less," he stated clearly. "My new publicist can tell everyone to suck it and then Penny and Dash can post some pictures of us looking happy so they can stay mad."

Penn groaned. "Everyone's going to think I have a cult and I recruited you or that I'm your pot dealer. They're gonna make jokes because no one will believe this. They'll think you're struggling and I'm taking advantage of you or—"

"Stop!" Morris captured Penn's face and found his eyes. "Nobody who knows me—or my mom—would believe that and all anyone has to do is spend five minutes with you and they'll get it."

"You know what?" Penn sighed and rubbed his lips along Morris's.

"Hmmm?"

"I love you."

"Oh?" It came from him in a startled laugh. Morris was on his side, but he felt like he was upside down and all the blood had rushed to his head. "I love you too."

"Everything is so perfect right now. Let's fly under the radar for as long as we can. We can work it out with your publicist when the time comes. What about this new album? That has to be way more exciting for your fans than this."

"I don't think that would help and it's not the right time," Morris said. He kissed Penn and backed off the bed.

"Don't you want *anyone* to hear it?" Penn's eyes were big and hopeful as they darted to Morris's.

"Soon... Sure."

Penn was worried about what people would think of them. There'd be no questioning what was going on and how Morris felt about his incredibly sexy nanny if the album got out. And if Penn had felt any pressure before to commit, it would only get worse once the world learned Morris was writing love songs about him.

"I wouldn't mind. If you want someone you can trust to listen..." Penn traced shapes on the duvet.

"That would be—" Morris's face felt hot and he couldn't look at Penn. He was afraid he'd figure it out with his elf-of-the-Catskills psychic abilities. "Awesome. Maybe," he said, wiping his forehead in case it was getting shiny. "I think I'll take a quick shower."

"Do you want me to join you?" Penn asked, but Morris was saved by the baby monitor. "Ack! I haven't even pressed our tofu for dinner yet!"

Morris let out a relieved gasp as Penn forgot about the album and jumped into his boxers and his T-shirt. "Let's get takeout from that vegan place you like on First Avenue," he called and Penn held up a thumb as he slipped through the door. "This is fine. I can keep this up without any repercussions," Morris said with a hard roll of his eyes and went to start the shower. His best ideas came to him in there and it looked like Morris had to create some fake new songs for Penn to listen to.

Chapter Twenty-Eight

Some men might be alarmed to receive a text message from their boyfriend's father, urging them to come over and to tell no one.

> Penn: Tell no one? Is this an emergency?

Morris Sr. promised it wasn't an emergency but that it was vital that Evelyn be kept in the dark.

"I gotta go. Will you be okay with Cadence for a few hours?" Penn asked Morris.

They were on the sectional and dozing off to a documentary while Cadence napped in her new play yard.

"I think I can manage. Everything alright?" Morris asked drowsily.

Penn smiled and kissed Morris. "Your dad's up to something, but Evie can't know."

Morris humphed. "Don't get arrested."

"You're not the boss of us," Penn said as he bounded off the sofa and jogged into the bedroom to get dressed. He had officially moved into Morris's room a few weeks earlier and Penn was still tickled by the differences in their sections of the walk-in closet. Morris only had to clear one corner and a few shelves for Penn's sneakers and overalls. Meanwhile, there were rows and rows of tracksuits, T-shirts on hangers, a wall of jeans, dozens of coats, *hundreds* of baseball hats, and Morris had a whole separate closet for his sneaker collection.

Then again, no one would ever ask Penn who he was wearing and there would never be a glossy magazine spread declaring him a savant or an icon. Which was just fine with Penn. He didn't know how Morris handled that kind of attention and speculation about his personal life. Penn tried to imagine what it would be like if people knew about them as he got on the train at 72nd Street and rode it all the way to 7th Avenue in Park Slope. All he could envision were sideways glances and curled lips.

He told himself it didn't matter—that they'd cross that bridge with Morris's PR team when they got there—as he jogged up the Mosbys' stoop and rang the buzzer.

"Hey! How's it going?" Penn asked when Morris Sr. answered the door.

Morris Sr. waved him in and put an arm around Penn. "Pretty good. Can't complain. You?"

"Really good. We're watching the game at Morris's place next week. You in?"

"You know it." They slapped hands and Morris Sr. gestured at the kitchen. "It's down here."

Penn was glad to see the older man so full of energy and

steady as Morris Sr. opened a door and led them down a narrow but sturdy set of stairs. It was a typical unfinished basement with a washer, dryer, and water heater at the other end of the long room. There could be more light, but there was plenty of open space with boxes and tote bins stacked on sturdy metal shelves.

"What did you need me to look at?"

"This!" Morris Sr. gestured around them. "Evie said something about a home office, but I want her to have a home *spa*. She deserves someplace to relax and *work less*."

"I love it." Penn nodded as he scanned, imagining where he'd hang drywall to separate the laundry area from Evie's spa. "What did you have in mind for the decor?"

"We used to stay at The Plaza every year for our anniversary. Could you help me make this feel like our favorite suite?" He asked, igniting Penn's imagination.

"I love it," Penn said, rubbing his hands together.

Morris Sr. clapped him on the back. "Hire whoever you need and spend as much as you want. We weren't able to celebrate our anniversary this year because I was in pretty rough shape and then with everything..." His voice had dropped and trailed off and Penn felt Morris Sr.'s mood dip as his joy dimmed.

"Tell me about those anniversaries," Penn urged with a gentle nudge.

"She likes the spa and the afternoon tea," Morris Sr. replied distantly.

Penn gave his shoulder a knead. "Okay. How about one of those fancy chairs that heat up and massage?" He asked and pointed at one corner. It didn't really matter where he pointed at the moment. All that Penn cared about was distracting Morris's Sr. "And a tea/wine bar over there!" He said excitedly as he turned Morris Sr. to a bare spot on the wall.

"Yes! One of those fancy wine fridges and some pretty glasses! She likes those Ticker Toks with the freezers full of fancy ices."

"I'll get some help from Penny Lane with the TikTok part, but I'm on it," Penn said with a jaunty salute. "Morris can help me with the sound system. In case you want to *set the mood*," he added and wiggled his brows at Morris Sr., making him laugh.

"I knew you'd get it!"

"I've met your wife, sir. You don't have to explain it to me."

They chuckled about it as Penn counted out steps to get a rough idea of the size of the space. He'd come back later with a notepad and everything he'd need to sketch out a design and get proper measurements.

"You better get your own house in order while you're at it, young man," Morris Sr. said as he eased himself down and took a seat on the stairs. "Not that you're all that young anymore. Aren't you almost forty?"

Penn threw him a How dare you? glare, making Morris Sr. howl. "I'm thirty-eight. We've got a wine fridge and Morris doesn't have room for a private spa."

"Lordy, not like that!" Morris Sr. wiped his eyes and fought back another wave of laughter. "I have a confession to make," he said, becoming serious.

"You know, I can build just about anything but I can't help if you're in legal trouble," Penn teased as he went to Morris Sr. and hunkered down in front of him.

"It's nothing like that," he said and waved dismissively. "Gus and I had this plan. We thought that if you and Morris got to know each other better..." Morris Sr. gave Penn a loaded look.

"You've got to be kidding me." Penn rose, shaking his head

as he crossed his arms. "That's what I get for turning my back on the two of you."

Morris Sr. laughed softly and nodded. "You should know better by now. I had already talked Evie into hiring one of Reid's nannies to help Michelle with the baby. I was supposed to pull Reid aside after Cadence was born and see if you were available since we already knew you."

They needed a moment and Morris Sr. looked like he needed a hug so Penn took a seat on the step next to him. He put an arm around Morris Sr. and gave his shoulder a squeeze. "I can't tell you how *honored* I am. Your son is..." Penn pushed out a hard breath and shook his head, unable to find the words to describe everything that Morris meant to him.

"You don't have to explain it to me," Morris Sr. said gently. "All we had to do was get you two together. We knew you'd be perfect for each other."

Penn gave his head a shake. "How do you figure? We couldn't be more different."

"Not as far as I can tell. At least, not in the ways that matter. You're both good men and you love your families. You're hardworking, you do what you love, and you take pride in your work. And you're both individuals. You don't let other people tell you what's cool," Morris Sr. boasted, but Penn winced and shifted uncomfortably.

"I'm not so sure about that... Morris is in a whole different league and I'm not the kind of guy people want to see him with," he tried to explain.

Morris Sr. turned and gave Penn a hard look. "Who the hell are these people and why should Morris give a damn about what they think?" He demanded.

"Well, I—" Penn started.

"No. You listen to me," Morris said, pointing a finger at Penn sternly. "They don't get a say in this! You do. And Morris does. They won't be around when Morris isn't writing hits and he's too old to be in magazines."

"True," Penn conceded, earning a pleased humph from Morris Sr.

"Not that there's anything wrong with you, but Morris never cared about fitting in. He always found his own way and let everyone catch up with him. That's why I knew you'd fit so well together."

"I've never fit so well with anyone in my life," Penn said and let Morris Sr. make of that what he will.

"Good. That's all that matters and we know you'll take good care of each other when we're gone."

"What?" Penn asked hoarsely.

This time, Morris Sr. put his arm around Penn and rubbed his back soothingly. "Gus worries about you. He doesn't want you to end up alone."

"Dad had Mom and he ended up alone," Penn pointed out.

"That's different and he's not alone. I bet if you ask him, your dad will tell you that she never left him," Morris Sr. said and Penn nodded, unable to speak. "You think Morris will ever leave you now?" He asked Penn with a gentle nudge.

Penn shook his head. His heart spoke up before he could and told Penn he'd never stop loving Morris. "No, sir. I think I might be stuck with him."

"I thought so."

"There's something I need to do," Penn decided and helped Morris Sr. up the stairs, promising to be back first thing in the morning to get started on the basement remodel. They would fool Evelyn into believing he was building them a home office so Morris Sr. could surprise her for her birthday next month.

"Are you going home to propose to Morris?" The older man asked excitedly and with no care for Penn's nerves.

The Handy Nanny

"No!" He cried in shock, then grabbed hold of Morris Sr. for support because the thought made Penn dizzy and a little queasy. He loved Morris with every fiber of his being, but Penn was in uncharted territory, to say the least. Penn had never been on a date or experienced anything even remotely romantic with another man. Not since college, and that had gone badly enough that Penn had sworn off dating and relationships for nearly twenty years. "Not yet," he said calmly. "I should probably ask Morris out properly and make sure that this is what he wants."

"That's not the grand gesture I had in mind, but if you're sure," Morris Sr. replied, rubbing his chin.

"Don't worry. I'm stopping by Reid's first. He'll help me with the grand gesture," Penn said and promised to report back in the morning.

Penn used the half-hour trip back to Lenox Hill to muster his courage. He was dreading what he was about to do, but Morris was worth it.

"What's going on?" Reid buzzed him into the building and was waiting for Penn when he came around the corner.

"I'm ready to make things official with Morris."

"Really? That's great!" Reid pumped his fist and clasped his hands together. "That's *so great*! What can I do to help?" He asked as he let Penn in and closed the door behind them. Gavin was sitting in one of the armchairs and looked up from his book.

"Hey, Gavin," Penn said and received a wave in return before Gavin went back to reading.

"Hi, Penn!" Dash said as he hurried into the living room with a cup and saucer. "Here's your tea, Gavin." He bowed as he set it on the table next to Gavin and backed away. Gavin coughed and mumbled a thank you before Dash blushed and ducked back into the kitchen.

"What's going on here?" Penn asked out of the side of his mouth.

There was a smothered giggle from Reid. "Dash is making progress," he whispered behind a hand.

"He *is not*," Gavin whispered back severely and cast Reid a furious look.

"Really?" Penn asked quietly, but raised his brows expectantly at Reid. "I'll need all the details," he added and Reid hummed.

"After you tell us why you're here and not at Morris's, making things official."

Penn grimaced and scrubbed at his bun. "I'm ready to take the next step, but I can't expect anyone to take me seriously when I look like this," he said as he gestured at himself.

Gavin's head snapped up and he looked just as concerned as Reid. "What are you talking about?" Reid asked warily.

"In the mood for a makeover montage?" Penn asked. He pulled the elastic out of his hair and let it fall. "I think it's time for all of this to go and for me to get a grownup wardrobe."

"Oh." Reid stared at Penn for several moments. "And by 'all of this' you mean...?"

"The hair and the beard. I was hoping you could give me a haircut and Gavin might let me borrow a few things," he explained.

Gavin dropped the book and slowly rose from his chair. "Are you sure you want to do that, Penn?" He asked, trading alarmed glances with Reid.

"Shouldn't you see what Morris thinks?" Reid chimed in. "What if he likes you just the way you are?"

"Of course, he does!" Penn said, but he pressed his hands together. "But I really want to surprise him and show him that I can be the kind of man he deserves."

Gavin spluttered in protest. "This is nonsense, Penn."

"Is that a no on the clothes, then?" Penn asked Gavin carefully.

"I would never say no to you, but I don't like this." Gavin gestured at Penn as he picked up his book and left them.

"Noted." Penn looked at Reid. "Please? Nobody else is going to take me seriously and I don't want people to laugh at Morris because of me."

"Penn!"

"Please! We both know I won't be able to get into anyplace decent tonight. Do you really want me taking my chances at a barbershop?"

"Jesus," Reid muttered as he pinched the bridge of his nose. "They'll give you a high and tight and have you looking like a drill sergeant." He shivered and waved for Penn to follow him. "Come on. I haven't seen you in a tie since Fin's wedding. We'll get you dressed and then we'll talk about your hair."

Chapter Twenty-Nine

I f anyone was looking for proof of unconditional love, Morris was providing an excellent demonstration as he changed Cadence's diaper. He was wearing an apron, surgical gloves, and a cloth face mask. A chip clip had been added as another layer of protection, pinching his nose shut as Morris quickly wiped the baby clean and bundled the used diaper and wipes into the Diaper Genie.

"I promise, I will buy you a car when you sort this business out and get potty-trained," he told her once their ordeal was complete. He munched on her cheek as they headed downstairs to watch some basketball on their tummies. "You won't be able to reach the pedals on a big car so we'll start you out with a tiny Mercedes or a little Lambo."

The doorbell rang, followed by urgent pounding. Morris checked the security camera and became concerned when he recognized Penny. "Let's see what she needs," he murmured to Cadence as they went to get the door. Morris opened it and Penny was breathless as she staggered past him and into the house.

"Gavin called me. You have to get to his place. *Fast*," she panted and bent forward so she could rest her hands on her knees.

"Did you run here and don't you have a phone?" He asked warily.

She nodded, then reached for the baby as she straightened. "You have to go. Stop Penn," she ordered, pointing at the door.

"Stop Penn?" He laughed nervously. "What's he up to now?"

"Reid's about to cut off all of his hair."

"*What?*" Morris demanded, pushing the baby at her.

Penny nodded but she had practically forgotten about Morris and Penn as she rocked Cadence and cooed at her. "I've missed you, my sweet dumpling!"

"Penny!" Morris begged, snapping his fingers to get her attention. "What the hell is going on?"

"Right!" She scrunched her nose as she forced herself to focus. "Penn doesn't think he's cool enough for you, or whatever, so a whole makeover montage is happening at Briarwood Terrace. Reid's stalling, but you're running out of time."

"Why would he..." Morris blinked at Penny as his brain skipped like a scratched record.

She rolled her eyes and shrugged. "He's afraid of embarrassing you and he doesn't think people will think he's good enough for you because of his hair and his clothes."

"No!" Morris shook his head as he backed toward his room. "I don't want him to change! That's *my hair!*" He said, earning a giggle from Penny. Morris turned and bolted to get a jacket and shoes.

It only took him a moment to pull them on and Penny and Cadence were already in the garden. The baby was in her bouncer in the shade next to Penny as she read from an oversized picture book. Cadence was in good hands so Morris was free to run out of the house and down the sidewalk like a bear was chasing him.

He crashed into the lobby of Briarwood Terrace and was out of breath as he waved at the doorman. "Norman."

"How's it goin', Mr. Mosby?" The elderly man asked cheerfully, making Morris scowl at him.

"What's it been, like, fifteen years that we've known each other? It's just Morris," he scolded and shook his head at Norman.

"Sorry. You're a celebrity and those are the rules!" He said with a teasing wink. Morris gave him an easy fist bump, minding Norman's arthritic knuckles. Gavin was waiting at the door for him when Morris hurried around the corner.

"There you are! Reid's been stalling."

"What the hell has gotten into him?" Morris asked as he rushed past Gavin, then dodged to his right before he crashed into Dash.

"How's it goin', Dash?" He said dismissively and humphed at Gavin. "Don't worry. No one's touching that hair."

He stormed past the sofa and into the hallway, then slowed when he heard Reid in the bathroom. "We could get rid of the beard completely, and try an undercut," he suggested and Morris's face pinched as he shook his head.

"What if I look too much like Gavin? I'm already borrowing his clothes," Penn said.

Morris jumped and recoiled at the thought, then mouthed an apology when Gavin caught him.

"We could go even shorter and do a spiky quiff," Reid suggested.

"Alright, this has gone far enough," Morris said, easing the bathroom door open. He leaned against the jamb and groaned.

Penn was seated on one of the kitchen stools and was wearing a shirt, tie, and trousers. They fit him well enough, but Penn looked miserable as he wiggled and tugged at his collar. It was buttoned all the way up and his hair was slicked back into a tight ponytail.

"What are you doing here?" Penn asked as he whipped around. "This was supposed to be a surprise."

Morris nodded. "I heard, but you can't cut your hair. It's *mine*. And I'd like it if you left the beard alone too."

There was a soft chuckle from Reid, who smirked as he wound the cord around his clippers. "Penn's got this crazy notion. He thinks he'll embarrass you because he's not 'stylish' or cool enough."

"What are you talking about?" Morris demanded, but Penn just held up his hands.

"Look at me and tell me this is going to make sense to anyone," he said and received grunts and hard eye rolls in return.

"Makes sense to me," Reid stated as he placed his hands on his hips.

Gavin was shaking his head at Penn from the door. "I'm generally baffled when it comes to men and romance, but it's perfectly obvious to me," he said, and Penn cocked his head at Gavin.

"I would have thought that *you* of all people would want me to clean this up and learn how to wear a proper suit. I don't understand why you're taking this the worst," Penn mused, but Gavin snorted.

"You wouldn't be you without your hair. You're perfectly fine just the way you are," he said with a firm nod. "Reid was willing to humor you until Morris could get here, but this is wrong, Penn. And you clearly have no business wearing a tie."

Everyone except Penn laughed. He made a frustrated sound as he scrubbed his face. "I love you, Morris, and I'm not scared anymore, but I don't want to make your life more complicated when you're just getting back on your feet."

"Penn... I love you too, but this is..." Morris pressed a hand against his chest. His heart was beating so hard and so fast, he was sure Penn could hear it. "All wrong and totally unnecessary."

"Who's going to believe you'd be into me? They'll say you're brainwashed or you're on drugs."

Morris scratched his head as he stared at Penn. "I'm sorry. What?" He laughed.

Reid sighed heavily. "He's convinced people will think he's the leader of a cult or lives in a van."

"Not with that again!" Morris protested.

"We're going to look weird together. You know it," Penn challenged Morris, pointing at him.

"Stop!" Morris said as he captured Penn's hand. "We're different in some very obvious ways, but I think people will get it. You are *incredibly* hot in your own unique way and the people who matter know you're just as beautiful on the inside."

"It's not just the way I look," Penn argued. "I don't fit into that part of your life and I don't think you want me to."

"What are you talking about?" Morris asked.

Penn's gaze slid to the floor as he slouched, but he held onto Morris's hand. "You blow me off every time I ask about the album and that song. You said it yourself, like a dozen times, it's not my kind of thing."

"The song?" Morris squeezed his eyes shut and swore at himself. "Hold on!" He let go of Penn's hand so he could take out his phone and synced it to the speaker in Reid's room. "Here," he said as he pulled up the file and pressed play. "Just remember that it's not done and I might not even release it."

"Shhh!" Penn waved wildly. He leaned in and tilted his head as he listened.

The slow, bluesy piano and drowsy beat began and even though Morris knew every note by heart, he heard it all for the first time as Penn craned his neck and listened intently. Morris's face grew warm and he braced himself because the lyrics were about to give everything away.

See, I get lost in Pennsylvania.
  Drunk on the taste of his lips and the smell of his hair.

He's sweet like wild mountain honey, makes me dizzy when I stare.

His smile's as bright as sunshine, his soul's as light as air.

See, I get lost in Pennsylvania, but go ahead and leave me there.

There were only a few more verses, thankfully. Morris couldn't breathe while it was playing and he couldn't look away from Penn. When it was over, he tucked his phone into his back pocket, then offered Penn a sheepish grin. "That's why you can't cut your hair."

"Okay! I won't cut it," Penn said, and he was crying as he slid off the stool and reached for Morris.

Morris sighed happily as he pulled Penn into his arms. "Thank you."

"That was the most beautiful thing anyone's ever done for me." He kissed Morris and they were rewarded with claps and whistles.

"I can't believe he wrote him a song." Gavin looked impressed, but Reid was shaking his head at Morris.

"Epic move, but way to make us mortals look bad."

"I have officially given up," Gavin declared. "There's no competing with that," he said and Dash gasped from the hallway. He'd been lurking behind Gavin and peeking over his shoulder.

"But you can't! You're—" He blurted, then covered his mouth. "Sorry. It's none of my business." He ducked and turned so he could flee to the kitchen.

Reid, Penn, and Morris traded knowing looks, but Gavin pretended to be indifferent as he tipped his chin back and sniffed. "If that's all, I think I'll get back to my book and my tea," he declared stiffly, offering them a bow as he left them.

"That should be fun," Penn predicted and the three of them chuckled as they watched Gavin take his usual seat in the living room and Dash rush in with the teapot.

"Possibly," Reid agreed, then sighed contentedly as he put his arms around Penn and Morris. "Go home and work this out like sane, mature adults. And once you've worked it out, let Evelyn know I await her instructions."

"Mom?" Morris asked in confusion as Reid and Penn laughed.

"He's chomping at the bit and wants to plan another wedding," Penn explained with a weary eye roll.

Morris shook his head. "I can't see us getting married," he said, shocking Reid and Penn for a moment. "We'll have a commitment ceremony or Penny can bless us with moon water and crystals."

They still looked shocked and Penn cleared his throat awkwardly. "I know we were joking, but your mom isn't going to settle for that. And you shouldn't either," he said and Morris shrugged.

"It's not her turn, is it?" He countered. "I want to do something that feels like *us* when we're ready. Reid can find someone to propose to if he's that desperate to plan a wedding."

That got a sharp look from Reid. "This is the thanks I get? Out of our house!" He ordered as he got the door, but his eyes sparkled as they touched on Penn and Morris. "I honestly didn't see this one coming. I'm so *happy*, though. You're perfect for each other and I think you fit together beautifully."

"Thanks!" Penn hugged him tight until Reid pushed him away.

"Thank you." That was all Morris could say as he hugged Reid. How could he thank Reid for saving him and sending him the love of his life? He'd given Morris something new to live for and the inspiration for an untold number of love songs.

Melodies, poetry, and choruses spilled from Morris whenever he was with Penn. "I owe you."

"Maybe you could write me a song," Reid teased.

"Maybe I will..." Morris replied, utterly serious. He couldn't tell Reid how grateful he was, but Morris could put it all in a song and dedicate it to his best friend.

Chapter Thirty

They held hands as they walked home, taking their time and cutting through a park so they could make out and truly open up as they watched the sunset. Penn finally explained about how he hadn't been cool enough for Tristan and how inadequate he felt when T. Winslow came to sweep Morris off his feet. Like Reid, Morris wanted to "talk to" Tristan and he explained why he had no interest in a fake relationship with Win.

Along the way, a couple recognized Morris, but he held onto Penn's hand as he thanked them for their kind words and hinted that he *might* have new music for them soon. Penn felt like he was going to explode, he was so proud of Morris for so many reasons—finding his way back, seeing a future for himself, and embracing his passion for music again. And Penn was so proud to be with Morris.

That's my *man!*

Just Penn's! He was going to spend the rest of his life with the sexiest, smartest, and most talented man in Manhattan. Penn was brimming with pride and so overjoyed at how far

Morris had come since losing Michelle. And Penn was proud of himself for finally grieving for his mother. He'd been the tallest chicken in the city and had run from his own pain, but he felt stronger now, like he'd be ready when it was time to say goodbye to Gus.

He would have Morris by his side and it would be easier this time because he wouldn't have to worry as much about Penny. They would comfort each other and Reid and Gavin would make sure that things were taken care of. Most importantly, Penn understood that it would be alright if he broke down. Morris, Penny, and their friends would be there to help Penn mend until he was strong again.

"I'm warming up to the idea of something bigger when we have our commitment ceremony or whatever we end up doing," Penn said as Morris's rowhouse came into view around the corner and his heart swelled. It had truly become home and everything he needed was there. He'd take a hiatus from work until Cadence started school, but Penn thought he might set up a small workshop in the backyard. Gus had been on him to take the bigger tools he could no longer use. Until now, Penn had declined, claiming a lack of space. Now, he had space, and Penn would use it to come to terms with losing Gus and sell some reclaimed furniture and do a little handy work on the side.

"You know, that would go a long way to smoothing things over with Mom," Morris mused. "She can't release doves or fire cannons inside a church," he said with a wink.

"Methodists don't allow that?" Penn replied as they climbed the stoop and they laughed as Morris opened the door.

"Hey, you two!" Penny said, waving excitedly as she popped up and hurried around the sofa. "You both look happy and Penn still has all of his hair so my work is done here." She stretched on her toes and yanked on Penn's shoulders so she could kiss his cheek, then reached for Morris. "I knew I could count on you." She kissed Morris on the lips loudly and got her tote bag off the hook by the door. "Her little ladyship had a blast in the bath and just went down," she informed them before giving Morris a salute and slipping out.

"She's pretty awesome," Morris said as he locked the door behind her.

"She is pretty awesome," Penn agreed. His eyes were heavy and he smirked dreamily at Morris. "I want to hear my song again," he said and pulled Morris close.

"You want to hear your song?" Morris chuckled as he held up his phone. He showed Penn how to find the file and synced it to the stereo, keeping the music low and in the living room. The song began to play and Penn cheered as he unbuttoned and unzipped the fly of Morris's jeans and pushed him onto the sofa. Morris reclined and tucked an arm behind his head, enjoying the view as Penn stripped and lowered to his knees. "He's sweet like wild mountain honey, makes me dizzy when I stare," Morris sang softly, sinking into Penn's eyes.

"You don't play fair, do you?" Penn asked and sighed dramatically as he spread Morris's thighs.

Morris shook his head and it fell to the side when Penn eased his cock free. "I had to work hard for this. But you were so worth it, Penn."

"Mmmm... Hard," Penn panted against the head. He purred and licked, glorying in the taste and feel of Morris's shaft as he worshiped it with his lips and tongue. Morris groaned and chanted Penn's name as his fingers sifted through his hair. Penn felt beautiful and loved as he swallowed as much of Morris's length as he could. He sucked slow and hard until he was pulled to his feet.

"Mine." Morris's hands cradled Penn's ass. He whispered tender words against Penn's navel and his cock. They were the kind of words that Penn spent years avoiding. Now, he felt cherished and stronger as Morris loved him with his lips and his poetry. Penn's song brought tears to his eyes and gave him chills while Morris made him *burn*.

The slow, sensual beat hypnotized Penn as he lowered and straddled Morris. *His man* proved to be a master of romance when he passed Penn a packet of lube. Penn coated Morris's cock, then slowly eased down, taking him deep. The song set the rhythm as they kissed and writhed against each other, but Penn had come to know that rhythm like the beating of his own heart. It was the same captivating beat that always enthralled Penn when they came together.

They refused to be rushed, grinding and swaying to the music and *their* beat. Penn lived for the slick, steady slide of Morris's cock, hot and hard in his core. Their tongues swirled while their hands gripped and stroked.

"I'm close but I need to taste you," Morris whispered, striking Penn's nerves like a match. His wicked, clever hands were around Penn's ass again, lifting him onto his feet.

"Oh, fuck!" Penn cried as Morris opened wide and lapped at the head of his erection.

"There you go again," Morris chuckled, then wrapped his lips around Penn and sucked hard. His fingers teased Penn's hole before they pushed deep, causing him to ignite into bright heat as he shattered. Morris fingered Penn until he was shaking and completely spent, and greedily claimed every drop of his release.

Then, Morris turned Penn and pulled him down onto his cock. He bounced Penn on his lap, filling him to the hilt with each fall of his ass until Morris came with a strangled sob. Penn felt as slow as honey, draped over Morris's chest. His head lolled drunkenly on Morris's shoulder as he strummed Penn's chest, thighs, and arms.

"This is the most beautiful song I've ever heard," Penn said and sighed dreamily.

Morris laughed softly, tickling Penn's neck with soft puffs of steam as he nibbled. "I had a beautiful muse and all I had to do was listen. We sound like sweet music when we fuck."

"Shhh!" Penn slapped Morris's hand, but he *loved it.*

There was a silky hum in Penn's ear, drugging him as Morris sang and cast his spell. "See, I get lost in Pennsylvania, but go ahead and leave me there," he crooned as his fingers trailed into the cleft of Penn's ass.

The whole world would know that Penn belonged to Morris and that Morris was his. And not just for ten years or fifty. Their love would last for as long as Penn's song was added to playlists and played on hot dates. It would outlive them and be the soundtrack of future love stories for decades to come.

If Morris chose to release it. Penn finally understood why he'd kept it a secret for so long and why Morris might want to save it for their personal playlist. That felt sacred in a different kind of way and would be an honor too. It would be a Mosby masterpiece that Penn didn't have to share.

"Tell your mom and Reid to do their worst. I don't care if the whole world knows I'm yours and that my man loves every lanky inch of me just the way I am."

Morris's arms wound around Penn's chest. "Good. I want to enjoy every moment with you and Cadence because that's what Michelle would want. She would celebrate this and she wouldn't hold back, she'd make sure the whole world knew how much she loved us. That's how we were raised and how she would have raised Cadence, so I have to honor that and love my family with 100% of my heart. I won't let anyone stop me from doing that," he stated firmly.

"Cannons over the Hudson it is," Penn said, turning in Morris's arms.

Morris bit back a laugh and shook his head. "New Jersey might not appreciate that."

"Probably not."

"Why don't we wait and see what my mom and Reid come up with?" Morris suggested.

"Good idea," Penn murmured as he pecked at Morris's lips. "I came here hoping I could fix your problems and mend your wounds, but you helped me heal and I'm so much stronger now."

"You've always been strong and beautiful and you'll always be mine."

"For as long as this song lasts," Penn said, standing and towing Morris to his feet. "Let's see what it sounds like in the bedroom and the shower."

Epilogue

T *he following summer...*

"Lost in Pennsylvania" was released to announce Morris and Penn's engagement and It. Blew. Up. The song was every-where, hit the top ten in several countries, and was three times platinum by the time they picked the date for their ceremony. Penn was offered his own reality television show after the media learned that he had been a *handy* nanny.

Morris wasn't surprised when Penn declined, but he was in the works with a production company on a limited series. He was going to share his philosophy on upcycling and restoration of thrift and salvage finds while skateboarding around the city and puttering in his workshop. The major streaming services were negotiating with his new agent and Penn was planning to give the proceeds to his mother's favorite environmental charities.

Which was the most perfectly Penn way to repurpose all the attention and interest in their relationship into something good and useful. The response wasn't nearly as critical as Penn had expected. In fact, they were proclaimed "couple goals" and "dream daddies." People were cool when they were out with Cadence, keeping a respectful distance. Morris would sign the occasional autograph and Penn was getting requests as well, even when they weren't together.

He handled it with his usual grace and was proclaimed a "DILF" and a "thirst trap" when Penny posted pictures of Penn in the lily pad pool. His wholesomeness and radiant personality shone through every time carefully shot pictures of him and the baby were posted. Penn was fine with being photographed to help promote Morris's new album as long as Cadence's face wasn't in the photos. They both felt strongly that no pictures of her face be released until she was old enough to consent and decide how those images would be used.

Morris had a feeling Cadence would take the world by storm. She already had her mother's infectious laugh and loved to make Morris smile. Cadence looked more and more like Michelle every day. Morris felt like he was getting a new moment with his sister whenever he laughed with the baby or saw her cast her spell on anyone who beheld her. She had so much of Michelle's vivacious energy and was already too smart for her age.

Their family had so much to celebrate and Penn wasn't the only one who could feel the joy as Morris arrived at the Merchant's House Museum's Secret Garden with his parents. The mild summer evening was perfect for a very intimate ceremony. They'd chosen the venue for its small size and privacy, and Evelyn and Reid had turned it into an enchanted midsummer night's dream. String lights wound around the trees and were draped overhead along with what had to be miles of flower garland.

Morris and Penn had married earlier in the day at City Hall with their parents and Penny as witnesses. The "ceremony" part of the evening would be minimal with a focus on the celebration. The guest list was kept extremely short with only their mutual friends and family in attendance. They'd selected the garden for its fairytale charm and because it was just big enough to accommodate Morris's aunts, uncles, cousins, and closest family friends. Instead of a band, a mixer, turntables, and speakers were set up and Morris was charged with being the DJ in addition to his duties as a groom, playing R&B, soul, and Motown classics. The evening was also a surprise private release party. Morris would finally be sharing the entirety of the new album with their guests before it went live online at midnight.

Of course, their parents and their closest friends had already heard the album and Morris Sr. had predicted it would be the biggest success of Morris's career. It was dedicated to Michelle and Penn and was a tribute to the beautiful highs of being in love and the lonely lows of letting go. Morris had told himself he couldn't release those songs until he was sure they wouldn't jinx any of the wishes he'd made, but he had to be sure it was safe for him as well. He couldn't booby trap the world with songs that reminded him of Michelle until he'd found peace in a life without her.

He had that now and was overjoyed as he and Cadence met Penn in the Garden. It took them a little bit longer to get there as Cadence was still getting the hang of walking, but not a single person minded as she held onto Morris's finger and toddled up to Penn. She looked like an angel in her pale blue gown. Morris's mother had even dressed her in little wings, making everyone groan in adoration.

But it was Penn who nearly broke Morris. He looked so handsome and comfortable with Gus at his side as he waited in pale blue trousers, a blue vest, and a blue bowtie. His sleeves were rolled up, showing off his tattooed forearms, and his hair was down. It bounced around his shoulders as he laughed and danced with the breeze, stealing Morris's breath when their eyes touched.

Morris had opted to wear pale blue as well, but had skipped a tie, keeping with the elegant yet casual mood of the evening. He was ready to tear it all off, though, and steal Penn away when they took each other's hands to share their vows.

"Dearly beloved," Penn began with a warm smile at Evelyn. She had taken their decision to have an informal ceremony instead of a church wedding surprisingly well. Her only stipulation was that the evening had to be fit for princes because her son and Penn deserved nothing less. Penn's eyes sparkled as they swept around, taking in all the smiling, teary-eyed faces around them. "And you are all so dearly beloved. The only thing that could have kept me from Morris was all of you. I was afraid that my heart would be so full of Morris, that I'd be so completely his, that I wouldn't have enough left over for all the people I loved and depended upon to love and need me." He turned to Morris and cradled his cheek as he stepped closer. Penn kissed Morris slowly and thoroughly and they were alone in the garden as their lips clung and they stared into each other's eyes. "But loving you made me stronger and I feel braver. My life and my heart are so much fuller now and I'm not afraid of the future anymore. I'm ready for whatever's waiting for us. And I promise that I will love you and Cadence with every bit of my heart until I take my last breath."

"I know," Morris stated confidently and everyone laughed. But his bravado faded and he was shaking as he smiled up at Penn, scrambling for the first sentence of the vows he'd prepared. "You were right. We were a weird match and I didn't think we'd work at first," he said, causing Penn's brow to cock in confusion. "You walked through my door and I thought 'Not this guy!' But I didn't want you to understand me and I would have rejected anyone who wasn't Michelle. And it was a shock, having this gangly, half-dressed hippie in my house when all I wanted to do was hide. It turns out we were both wrong. You were exactly what I needed and I feel safe and understood when I'm with you. I thought I'd lost that and that I'd lost myself, but you showed me the way back. There's so much warmth and laughter in my heart again and I feel truly blessed to spend the rest of my life with you."

Penn threw his arms around Morris and they cried as they kissed. Once they had recovered, Penny helped Cadence put the rings on their fingers. Which was a good thing, because both Morris and Penn had shaky hands and blurry eyes.

And talk about a cake! It was massive for a venue that only allowed up to thirty people. It was a stunning six-tier honey butter cake wrapped in a swirl of golden spun sugar. Evelyn had created the cake just for them, inspired by Penn's song.

"Don't you dare," Morris said as he wagged his fork at Penn. "This is too good to waste and I don't want to wear it."

Penn snorted and walked away with his plate. "I got what I came for," he said, causing everyone to giggle and snicker before he jogged back over and kissed Morris on the cheek. "You look too good tonight and this cake tastes like heaven."

They traded heated looks, once again feeling as though it was just the two of them in the garden. "You taste like heaven." Morris handed his plate to his mother and reached for Penn. "Hold this for me, Mom. I want to dance with my husband. They're playing our song."

"Lost in Pennsylvania" began and Penn was blushing as he slid into Morris's arms. Morris turned them and guided Penn into an open spot so they had more room and they began to sway from side to side.

"I'm glad we went for the fairytale wedding. This feels like magic," Penn said with a dreamy sigh. His cheeks were pink from the champagne too. Evelyn and Reid had ordered an irrational amount. Buckets of chilled bottles were stationed around the garden and one of the bakery's employees had been hired to mingle and keep everyone's glasses filled.

"He's sweet like wild mountain honey, makes me dizzy when I stare," Morris sang softly against Penn's ear. He shushed and shook his head at Morris.

"Don't start that unless you're ready to leave."

A limo was waiting to take them to The Plaza. Limos were also waiting for their guests because Reid and Evelyn wanted everyone to celebrate safely and without a care.

"I'll behave," Morris said but his fingers were crossed behind Penn's back. "I wouldn't want to miss the fireworks," he whispered and nodded over Penn's shoulder. There was no plan for actual fireworks, but Gavin was dancing with Dash. Dash looked totally smitten and Gavin looked extremely bothered. "I have a feeling my mom and Penny are behind that," Morris guessed.

Penn chuckled as he looked around. "Speaking of Penny Lane... Where'd she get off to?"

"I don't know, now that you mention it." Morris frowned as he searched the small garden.

"Don't see Agnes Cameron either," Penn pointed out and Morris gasped.

"No!" He laughed as he tried to imagine Penny with the older woman Penn had introduced him to earlier. She was elegant and brimming with confidence, but she was obviously a cougar and had a reputation for being whatever the female equivalent of a playboy was. Agnes Cameron was worth a fortune and Morris was surprised when Penn requested she be added to the guest list. "I was wondering why you invited her."

"Hey. Walker Cameron's like family," Penn said with a shrug. "Penny did get a little twitchy about it, though."

"Really?"

"Really." Penn gave Morris a loaded look. "They might have disappeared together after Fin and Walker's wedding so we thought we'd see what would happen if we got them together again."

"We?" Morris asked and a wicked grin stretched across Penn's lips.

"Walker's got a score to settle."

Morris whistled and shook his head. "Agnes is lucky she doesn't have any kids because once Reid finds out..."

"She's adopting!" Penn whispered excitedly.

"Oh, that's..." Morris imagined all the possibilities and his eyes began to water. "That's going to be so messy!" He laughed and Penn nodded.

"We're counting on it, and I have a feeling Reid will be all in once he realizes the potential."

"Let the matchmaking begin," Morris murmured. His mind was on a different kind of potential as he watched his parents dance. He always thought of his parents dancing, whenever they came to mind, because that was one of the constants from his childhood. "That'll be us thirty, forty years from now," he promised Penn and swung his head in their direction.

"That's what I was thinking." Penn rested his temple against Morris's and he was light and loose as he hummed along with his song. He'd done so much hard work with his therapist and was coming to terms with his mother's death and his fear of losing Gus. Penn and Morris were both seeing therapists and Morris was ready for the Mosby Music machine to dominate the charts once more. He'd found the magic again and he had the perfect muse.

Morris pulled Penn closer and hummed in his ear as the song reached its end. "See, I get lost in Pennsylvania, but go ahead and leave me there."

"Alright. That's it. Time for us to leave."

The End

One more prank for old times' sake...

Chapter 1

The following spring...

"Do you want your white Chucks or your pink Chucks?" Penn bit back a smile as Cadence tapped her chin and debated. She had nearly as many shoes as Morris in her little walk-in closet, but her Converse were her favorite because they were Penn's sneaker of choice.

"Pink!" She delivered them to Penn in her pudgy arms, making his heart melt a little more. That happened every time he looked at Cadence and he didn't know how he hadn't turned into a big puddle of goo by now. She looked particularly adorable this afternoon. Morris had parted her hair and styled it into two pom poms with bright pink bows. She was wearing her tiny overalls with her favorite Sesame Street T-shirt and Penn couldn't take it anymore: he picked her up and kissed her cheek loudly so he could hear her giggle.

"Perfection!" Penn declared as he set her on the dresser. He grabbed her foot and gave it a chomp before sliding her sneaker on like a glass slipper. "You're just about ready, my princess."

Chapter 1

"Bubbles!" She clapped and Penn nodded.

"That's right! Do you want to play with the bubbles when Luna and Riley get here?"

"Luna!" Cadence was such a good helper, handing Penn each shoelace and holding his hair away from his face as he worked.

"They're here!" Morris called from downstairs.

"You hear that, Cadie?" Penn cheered as he gave the bows on each sneaker a tug to secure them, but they'd still untie themselves as soon as his back was turned. "They're here!"

"Luna!" She took off as soon as Penn set her on her feet, but he caught her hand before she could get through the nursery door. He swept her up and onto his hip and they skipped down the stairs just as Morris was greeting Riley and Luna.

The girls had become best friends. Riley brought Luna over a few times a week and Morris and Penn would often stop by the Olympia and visit the Ashbys whenever they were on that side of Central Park. This afternoon, Riley was hugging a box as he held onto Luna's hand. She was hopping excitedly and waving at Cadence.

"Who wants to blow some bubbles with me?" Morris asked, reaching for Cadence.

"Bubbles!" Cadence went to Morris and Luna clapped as she followed them out to the garden.

"How's it going, brother?" Penn put an arm around Riley and they gave each other a squeeze.

"Never better! I brought you all some applesauce!"

"Thanks!" Penn took the box and went to put the jars away in the pantry. "Cadence loves your applesauce and eats it with everything."

"I'll let my production team know and we'll increase output. I'll have *two* boxes for Lady Mosby next time we drop by," Riley said with a proper salute.

Chapter 1

"And how's the production team doing over at the Olympia?" Penn asked and a radiant smile spread across Riley's face. He always glowed when anyone mentioned his husband and stepson.

"Great! Milo and Giles are programming a robot they built for a class project."

"That sounds rad!"

"So rad!" Riley confirmed. "And totally over my head, so Luna and I decided to spend the afternoon with you guys. We got stuck in the elevator with that awful Muriel Hormsby on the way out." Riley shuddered, making Penn laugh.

"I've never had the pleasure, but I've heard she's a pistol."

"Ha! She still blames me and Fin for the fact that her nephew Jonathon can't find a husband."

"Is he even trying?" Penn wondered. He hadn't had the pleasure of making Jonathon's acquaintance yet either, but from what Penn had heard, the young "influencer" wasn't all that motivated to settle down.

"Not that I've seen. Muriel won't stop, though. She waylaid Will Kirkland in the lobby when he came to see Giles last week," Riley said and Penn just shrugged. He had no idea who that was. "He's a *big* computer scientist and CEO. Giles is helping him design a new social media platform. Mostly just consulting if Muriel hasn't scared Will away from the Olympia."

"Good thing Giles has you to protect him."

Riley humped. "He still runs the other way if he sees her coming and I don't think we've heard the last of her. She asked about Gavin today."

That got a laugh out of Penn. "Muriel Hormsby might be a force of nature, but she'll be wasting her time. Gavin's impervious. He swears he'll be a bachelor until the day he dies."

Chapter 1

"We'll see. Dash hasn't given up hope and Penny says he's as loyal as a golden retriever."

"Now *that* would be a whole different can of worms," Penn speculated and rubbed his hands together. "What's there *not* to like about Dash?"

"Well..." Riley's lips twisted. "He can be a little...naive and too sweet and wholesome if that's possible. But he's really hot," he noted and Penn hummed.

"The thing is..." He began slowly. "Dash sees things in Gavin that most people miss, except us. I think it behooves us to help Dash out because I don't know when Gavin will get a better chance than this."

"I agree and I'll let Fin know that we've got a new group project. What about you? What do you think about married life? Is it as bad as you were expecting?" Riley teased as he helped himself to a muffin from the basket and perched on a stool.

"Not at all. It's amazing," Penn stated, crossing his arms over his chest as he propped his hip against the counter and watched Morris and the girls.

Chapter 1

He was seated on the porch steps with Cadence on his lap. She was "helping" Morris blow on the wand as Luna chased bubbles on the grass. "I thought I'd have to give something up to make room in here for him." Penn touched his chest and laughed. "But Morris made me stronger and my heart grew even larger. My world is so much bigger and better and I have so much more love to give."

"That's how I feel about Giles. I'm so much bigger than myself now and sometimes, I think I know him better than I know myself," Riley said and Penn nodded.

"It's almost like there's two of me. We have our own identities and things we're passionate about that don't involve each other. But his happiness is my happiness, and Morris carries my heart with him wherever he goes. And I do *know him* in ways I've never known anyone else before. Even Penny, and I raised that wild child."

"Isn't it strange how that works? Especially when it's the last person you'd expect," Riley said with a wry snort.

Penn chuckled in agreement as he watched Morris dip the bubble wand in the bottle and blow on it. "Maybe that's why I know him so well. Everything he does fascinates me and I'm always looking for ways to make him laugh."

"That's really beautiful."

"Thanks. I think I'm getting the hang of it." He smirked and pointed at Morris. "For example, I know he didn't use his Flonase this morning because I 'forgot' to remind him," Penn said, curling his fingers. "And I knew he wouldn't be able to resist a bottle of bubbles if I left it on the counter, right before you got here."

They heard Morris sneeze and Riley's eyes lit up as he glanced at the open back doors. "What did you do?" He whispered.

"You'll see," Penn whispered back.

Morris sneezed again and told the girls to follow him back inside. A full-blown sneezing fit had ensued by the time he herded the girls into the kitchen. Morris's eyes were red and

Chapter 1

glassy and he used the back of his hand to block another sneeze. "Here. One of you hold onto this while I go blow my nose," he said, passing the bottle of bubbles to Riley on his way to the bedroom.

"How about some graham crackers and applesauce?" Penn said, and the girls began to hop and cheer. Everyone froze when they heard a shriek from the bathroom.

"Damn it, Penn!"

"Damn it, Penn!" Cadence mimicked.

A laugh burst from Riley and he covered his mouth as Penn scooped Cadence up. "Shhh! That's something that grownups say when their brain goes *pffft!* and they don't know what else to say. But we don't need to repeat that, okay?"

"Pffft!" She replied.

"Exactly. Let's find those graham crackers," Penn said as he carried her to the pantry.

Morris appeared a moment later holding a strip of toilet paper and glared at Penn. "What are we, twelve?" He asked, waving it at him. Penn had used a fine-tipped Sharpie to draw a spider on the roll before he took Cadence up to get dressed for Riley and Luna. "You know I hate spiders."

"I did know that," Penn confirmed and slid Riley a sly wink.

Chapter 2

He'd finally figured it out and Morris felt rather foolish. It had taken him almost two-and-a-half years to catch on and realize that Michelle had been getting some help from Penn.

Morris should have noticed or at least guessed that Penn had to be behind some of the pranks he had walked into since Michelle's death. The fake pack of gum he'd found in the car's glove compartment and the plastic cockroach inside his Christopher Wallace 13s could have been Michelle's handi-work, but she couldn't have drawn a spider on a roll of toilet paper that had only been in the house for a few days.

He had begun to wonder about the clear school glue in the hand sanitizer and who had mixed M&Ms into his secret stash of Skittles. It had been several months ago and at the time, Morris hadn't touched the plastic tub in the pantry in ages. He couldn't figure out how Penn would have known to even look for it. Morris's stash had been hidden at the back of the top shelf behind the coffee urn they never used.

The little doodle spider had caused Morris to jump and scream because he was a baby when it came to bugs and spiders, but Morris had laughed to himself throughout the rest of Riley and Luna's visit and into the evening. Instead of feeling irritated or truly foolish, Morris was grateful the more he thought about the spider and what Penn had done.

For just a handful of moments, Morris had his sister back. He immediately assumed that she had been the culprit and even opened his mouth to yell at her. His brain boggled at how she could have done it and Morris laughed at the thought of her haunting him with rolls of toilet paper. Then, a more rational voice piped up and pointed out that it was most likely Penn.

The doodle spider and *every* single prank Michelle and Penn had ever played, spanning all the way back to Morris's childhood, became gifts. There had to have been hundreds and individually, they were like gems. But all together, they were a treasure and Morris was grateful as he sat in bed, staring at the section of toilet paper with the little ink spider and waited for Penn.

He'd stepped out back to smoke another joint before bed and was whistling softly when he returned. He was already in his ratty pajama shorts and his hair was loose and damp from the shower. Morris found himself staring as Penn moved around the room, tidying and chatting about the next day's adventures.

"What have you got there?" Penn asked as he set a knee on the bed and stretched toward Morris to kiss him. He recognized the spider and chuckled. "Can you forgive me?"

"How long have you been doing this and how did you know?" Morris searched his eyes, once again wondering if Penn could truly hear his thoughts.

"Hold on. I have something I've been waiting to give you." Penn backed off the bed and went to the closet. Morris leaned so he could see Penn slide something from under one of his

Chapter 2

stacks of T-shirts before returning. He held the slim book out to Morris. "I found this when I was moving into the guest room."

Morris knew it was one of Michelle's many journals without reading the front or looking inside. He began to shake and his vision blurred as he read her handwriting.

He laughed because he could hear her and he knew that inside the journal he'd find her classic fuckery. Morris opened it and tears spilled from his eyes as he read through various diabolical schemes. He didn't recognize any of the dates, but he remembered the incidents well. Morris grabbed Penn's hand because he couldn't speak and find the words to thank him.

Penn scooted around so he was behind Morris and holding him. "I found it in a box with some fake gum and unrippable toilet paper."

"Was that you too?" Morris accused.

Penn chuckled in his ear before kissing Morris's neck. "No,

Chapter 2

but I assumed there were more rolls in play around the house so I was ready."

"What about the super glue in my serum?" He asked and Penn shook his head and clicked his teeth.

"That wasn't me because super glue pranks can get dangerous if you're not careful, but I'm not going to ruin the mystery. They were all her ideas. She's the prank master, I just picked up the baton and kept running with it."

Morris turned and shook his head at Penn, awed by his big, brilliant, generous heart. "You are the most beautiful, magical man I have ever met." Morris kissed him deeply, sliding his body around and easing Penn back onto the bed. "I love you." He cradled Penn's face and kissed him again. "I love you." He sucked on Penn's tongue and rocked against him. "I love you," Morris whispered. "I'll never be able to say it enough or write enough songs to express how much I love you, but I'll never stop trying."

"I can feel it, Morris. I can always feel it." Penn's hands spread possessively across Morris's back and around his head, pulling him under.

He was as sweet as ever, intoxicating Morris with the taste of his lips and his low, lazy moans. Morris sank into Penn, losing himself once again. They paused long enough to tuck the spider inside the journal and move it to the bedside table. Penn stroked lube onto Morris's shaft and it was heaven as he slid all the way home. He set a slow, grinding pace, finding the same seductive rhythm that always guided them when they joined.

They were playing *his* song, a melody that only they knew. It was a song that no one would ever hear because the lyrics were their passionate pleas over the driving beat of their hearts. It was the hot gasps that burst from their lips set to the pounding of their hips and the tapping of the headboard. Their

Chapter 2

lovemaking was a sensual syncopation, created just for their ears and to stir their souls.

There was warmth and sweet peace in Pennsylvania. Morris found a little more of himself, every time he got lost there. He got drunk and high on the taste and the sound of sex with Penn. Morris reveled in the wild beauty of Penn's release, drinking the lustful swears from his lips and glorying in the slick heat of his body as it wrapped tight around him. He gathered up Penn's cum and licked it from his fingers, greedily savoring every last drop.

Morris came with Penn's name on his lips. He was so far gone, Morris could feel the gentle warmth of Penn's soul. It was soft like a nap in the sun and Morris had tears in his eyes as he spilled himself deep in Penn's core. Ecstasy rolled through him and into Penn, a swelling, sparkling tide of pleasure and joy that licked at their nerves and had them twitching and giggling as they clung to each other.

"I take it you've forgiven me," Penn murmured once their bodies had cooled. His head rested on Morris's shoulder and he traced lazy swirls on his chest.

There was absolutely nothing to forgive because Morris would feel blessed every time he looked at a roll of toilet paper and picked up a bottle of serum. And he'd been given a treasure, brimming with his sister's vibrant humor and her love for him. He believed that fate or Michelle had intended for Penn to find that box. Morris would have cried over the journal and packed the box away if he had found it, too afraid to take a closer look. It would have stayed hidden with her books and her sorority sweatshirts until Cadence was ready to meet her.

"You're forgiven, but we're not even yet."

The End

A letter from K. Sterling

Dear Reader,

Thank you so much for your time and for reading *The Handy Nanny*. I hope you had fun falling in love with Penn and Morris! Before you go, I'd appreciate it if you'd consider leaving a review. Your review would really help me and help other readers find their way to us. And I promise, I read and appreciate every single one of them. Even the negative reviews. I want your honest feedback so I know how to steal your heart.

Please help me out by leaving a review!

Once again, thank you from the very bottom of my heart. I love you for sharing your time with us and hope we'll see you again soon.

Love and happy reading,
K.

About the Author

K. Sterling writes like a demon and is mother to Alex, Zoe, Stella, and numerous gay superheroes. She's also a history nerd, a *Lord of the Rings* fan, and a former counterintelligence agent. She has self-published dozens of M/M romance novels including the popular *Boys of Lake Cliff* series and *Beautiful Animal*. K. Sterling is known for fast-paced romantic thrillers and touching gay romcoms. There might be goosebumps and some gore but there's always true love and lots of laughter.

Coming Soon: The Enchanting Nanny

Despite being born into one of the wealthiest families in Manhattan, Agnes Cameron hasn't had that many *good* things in her life. At fifty-two, she's ready to change that. She's adopting a child and putting her playgirl days behind her. And ever the doting brother, Walker Cameron III has decided to send one of Reid Marshall's nannies to help with the transition.

Enter Penny Lane Tucker: thirty, vegan, and a wild child who occasionally sleeps in trees. Like her older brother, Penn, she's a nanny extraordinaire. There isn't a problem Penny can't fix with a little elbow grease and creativity. And while she believes in soulmates and the power of love, Penny suspects fate is playing tricks when she meets her new clients.

Their brothers *might* not be aware, but Agnes and Penny have…history. Of course, neither wants to be the one to explain *why* Reid should send a different nanny. Instead, both decide to play it cool for the sake of Agnes's newly adopted daughter, eight-year-old June.

That proves to be a challenge when the trio decamps to the Tucker family cabin in the Catskills for the summer. Sparks fly around the campfire and love blossoms as they bond and heal. Penny realizes that Agnes and June just might be her soulmates. But can she trust wayward Agnes with her heart? And can Agnes prove she's ready to put her wild ways behind her and tame her enchanting nanny?

Get The Enchanting Nanny NOW!

Milton Keynes UK
Ingram Content Group UK Ltd.
UKHW022028190824
1311UKWH00074B/1769